Merry Christmas Ruthie
1970
from Bonnie

# AN EGYPTIAN BONDAGE

and other stories

Harper & Row, Publishers

New York, Evanston, and London

# AN EGYPTIAN BONDAGE

## and other stories

## JASCHA KESSLER

The author gratefully acknowledges permission from the following magazines to reprint the stories in this volume: *Partisan Review, The Olympia Reader, Audit, Accent, The New Leader, Nugget, Trace, Midstream.*

FIRST EDITION

Library of Congress Catalog Card Number: 67-22133
Designed by The Etheredges

H-R

For my friends in thralldom:

---

*I wanted to find that book.*
*You never heard of that book?*
*He could not finish that book.*
*She wished she had read that book.*
*Had they always known that book?*
*We will need to have that book.*
*Was it after all that book?*
—FROM "THE CONFUSIONS," J.K.

# CONTENTS

# THE DETECTIVE

Thirty years in hotels, and never had Mr. Acker had to put up with what he had to put up with this season! Dizzy, and half blind with righteousness, this pale, soft man slipped through the gray door swinging back on the heel of the head busboy . . . for a change this was a nice boy who could keep order among that squad of the usual rabble of boys: what was his name again? David, of course! They called him Davie—so many came and went, all alike in their black silk tuxedo pants and starched bolero jackets . . . and stopped abruptly, and flapped his arms: Vexation! His glasses had fogged over from the climate of the kitchen, a steamroom's. He tore them off and stood his ground, abstractedly polishing the rimless bifocal lenses with a fresh table napkin he had pulled from his hip pocket, his tired, puffy, redrimmed, weak gray eyes crossed blank but fierce an inch beyond the end of his sharp nose. That he, so scrupulous, methodical, precise, that he, Acker, merely for the sake of a rotten, miserable, yet nevertheless after all breakable contract, should have to take such an abuse! All right, in this business a manager can be a pain in the neck, but you have to have a manager; an owner on the premises day and night is worse; but an owner-manager—*tschuk!* And that it should be even worse than last year, slaving for those cheap Hungarian refugees with the blue numbers tattooed on their left arms; husband and wife, doubly an owner-manager plague! and on top of that, grasping and grim Hungarians whom the world owed a twenty percent return on the bad investment of their reparations money—that it should be this fat four hundred pounds of fake, this ignoramus who could only have stolen the cash, on the black market probably, to buy himself a payment down on a hotel, this American Legion fascist bully who had the gall to make people call him Major! Why Major? How Major? Major what? Try to think of it: Julius Gruber, Major, the United States Army. What kind of monster U.S. Army it must have been! And then his own shriveled-up, nervous stick of a wife—poor thing, so skinny now there was hardly a place to stick the needle—takes to asking him what *the* Major said today, what *the* Major did today . . . how could Acker ever have let himself be talked into such a stewardship? It must have been the long, fat green cigar that Gruber spieled him with, the golden ruby ring on the curled white left pinky and the diamond with six sapphires clustered on the thick right pinky, and the way that hairless gorilla with the jewelry of a pasha on his hands hypnotized him into signing on. Really! He just didn't have to stand for it, Acker decided as he stood there stuck on the thought of making a stand for once on the principle of his individual self-respect, even if it

meant a scandal. What a spot to be in! He began hooking his
glasses on, and halted in the niche on his right where he had
ducked to avoid the trayful of dishes wobbling by him, and surveyed the kitchen.

What a decrepit joint this Metropole was. The *New* Metropole, it said on the stationery. Really! In kitchens you can see all
kinds, mostly the worst crumb-bums, but whose idea of a crew
was this? Even if it was a busy year, there had to be better speci-
mens for hire. There had to! Was there never a bottom to the
barrel? He was looking at the salad man, whose hairy arms shook
with a furtive and anxious ineptitude as he stooped over the ice-
filled counter and laid out single sheets of that tough lettuce,
covering them disgracefully with hacked-up slices of tomato—
and the tomatoes Acker was able to afford this past week certainly
needed more skillful cutting than this. *Mac*—did salad men anywhere ever need another name?—trembled and said nothing because it was his first job in fifteen years: a convict, hunched and
scared and stupid. Fortunately not a drunk: the two drunks, real
old dirty fairy bums, slouched on their stools by the dishwasher,
letting the busboys tilt their full trays over and make a hideous
racket instead of calling for quiet, and smoked one guinea-stinker
between them, suck and puff, suck and puff, turn and turn about.
And down at the far end, quarreling with Chef, those two waitresses long past sixty who thought they bossed the show: what a
collection of hennaed heads and varicosed legs and clackety teeth.
One was whining "Where's my *spec*ials?" and the other echoed
"Where's *my* specials?" Tilly and Riva, terrorizers of the dining-
room floor. But not here, not Chef: "Look, girls, I don't give no
specials today. Just what's on the bill a fare, you hear? I tell you
before, and once is all I tell you."

Mr. Acker watched Hermann. He knew well why he wasn't
giving out specials tonight. But the question was, would his face
tell him anything? Pooh! If it *was* Hermann, he'd been a head

chef too many years to get caught so easy. A lot that nazi cared for the spot Acker was in. A crazy man, always banging his chopper down an inch from you. All he had to do was let Hermann think he thought it was him, and bam! a collection of fingers, a hand even lost; you know—by accident? Accident! Up and down Schulze was known as a maniac, a no-good nazi butcher. And only Gruber was such a bad manager as to hire him at top chef's pay, busy season or no. So it might be Hermann. Very simply it might.

The headwaiter came in and hurried past him, followed by the angry Tilly who had run out to fetch him to the kitchen. It could be this nasty, rotten, skinny, chainsmoking horseplayer, very easily it could be Israel—*Mister* Israel, if you please!—with his bookie, and all his new suits, even for a headwaiter much too many suits and shoes, and, moreover, mind you, not one but *two* apartments in Long Beach, each with a tomato in it. So, you might be a sure winner if you bet Israel could use a little extra, like, for example, a couple or three tons of beef a week? Somebody should feed *him* the nags that ate up his lettuce. He watched him go to complain to Schulze in his soft suave voice about not getting those specials for his best-tipping guests: it meant trouble with the waitresses, and tedious explaining to his customers, who would give so much less a chair in retaliation. Well, if it *was* Israel, he couldn't have it both ways. He, Acker, provided enough specials *and* extras enough. If it was missing it was missing. He couldn't procure twice. And would not. But would Israel be so stupid as to give his girls slips for extras and specials if he himself knew there was nothing in the box tonight? No. Yet he might! Yes, he might! Would it not make Mister Israel appear innocent? Therefore, *you, too,* Israel!

Finally, there was that Gruber himself. He could (and he was the type), he could very easily be stealing out of his own pockets. It was possible, it had been done before, Acker had heard once somewhere. Next thing you knew the Hotel Metropole burns down, say after Labor Day just after the guests go, but before the expense of cleaning up the dump for the holidays. And just who do you suppose would be in a position to collect? Who else? Acker, he adjured himself, Acker, you be sure and get yourself and the books out a couple of days before the end comes! So if it was Gruber, he had his some nerve to yell at him right in the dining room while guests were still eating. And in that animal voice, he had to make a big speech, looking around to see does everybody hear him, "Acker! you're steward here, not me! Acker, you keep track of the pantry, not me! If you can't check off when everything comes in and keep the record straight, what the hell kind of lousy steward did I hire anyway, eh? You get in there, you get busy and make sure there's enough for the party tomorrow too. And if there isn't, you better make goddam well sure there is. You tell me—I'm listening—what in hell is so hard about your lousy little job anyway, Acker? You take in, and you give out. Consequently, you got to have what to give out if—*if*, I say, you hear me? it's a big if—*if* you took it in. Eh? Get me? And if *not*, Acker, why not? And if so, Acker, where is it? You're my steward, you got to be the one who knows. If this happened in the army, Acker, know what I could do to you? Do you know? Court-martial, Mr. Steward: court . . . mar . . . shul! Ten years hard labor, Acker, and I mean hard! Twenty! So get your wheels off the ground, see?"

"But you saw the shop, you saw the box. Cleaned out." And he'd protested: "Mr. Gruber, it's Saturday night. On Saturday night the jobbers don't exactly sit by the phone in their office." But in vain.

"Your business, not mine, Mr. Steward Acker. Get busy. Find out. Get food. When that gala wedding reception for the daughter of Mr. and Mrs. Sydney Smith begins tomorrow afternoon, I want to see full service for three hundred guests, as per ordered.

How long do you think the baker has to wait for his fruits tonight, and when can Schulze start in preparing without his meat? Acker, I'm telling you, it's all paid for on the line: so they better get their good time *with* food."

"Yes, sir, I see."

"Yessir what?"

"Yes sir, Mr. Gruber."

What did he think it was still, the army? Acker felt again the pang of humiliation low in his belly that he had answered like some punk busboy draftee. What right did Gruber have to make him grovel just because he had employed him out of all the others, what right? Acker leaned back against the wall to support himself in this thought of his misfortune and sorrow, and got a jolt of surprise. The wall rattled: it was hollow. He stooped and peered into the obscurity of the angle in which he had been hiding. There was a snaplock there. He pulled, and a door opened. It was a dumbwaiter. What the hell! They must have given room service here once, even in this lousy building. Room service! In Long Beach! Hey hey! He stuck his head inside and peered up into the dark for an instant, until he realized that the ropes were quivering and moving, slowly and quietly and quite as if well-greased. He pulled back, startled, and waited. Sure enough, the next minute the dumbwaiter came on down, empty, and slid past him like an apparition. His jaw fell open; but why he was so amazed he could not at that instant have thought. He looked in again. It had stopped just below. Nothing happened. *What . . . is . . . this?* he murmured, and immediately resolved to find out. Straightening his back, drawing a sharp breath, he stepped out and walked resolutely through the kitchen, looking neither to right nor to left, and marched out the screen door at the back and down the dirty wood steps where one of the colored elevator boys leaned jacketless in the quiet, smoking a cigarette and contemplating half a bottle of beer. Acker went along the sandy alley

until he came to the basement entrance, where he glanced about
to see if he had been noticed by anyone. So far, so good.

As he proceeded down the low-ceilinged, mildewish basement
he struggled to compose himself. Remember, he warned himself,
you don't know what you're looking for, and besides there may
be nothing to find; but if you do, be calm, be logical, be sane.
Now, to think a little, for instance, where would that dumbwaiter
come down? He walked more slowly, and attempted to visualize
the layout of the floor above. He turned left, following the corridor beneath the lobby now—yes, there were the rickety stairs that
continued down from the "Grand Staircase"—and left again,
past the furnace room, of course unused now, in August. It did
not occur to him to poke into the furnace room: for thirty years
he'd kept his nose clean, and he was too used to his decent way
of life. This corridor, now, went to the rooms of the kitchen men
and elevator boys, an area of unpleasant sights and stinks; hence
he went left again, back to the section beneath the kitchen. Here
he found his path blocked by heaps of dirty linens—towels, pil-
lowslips, spreads, blankets, napkins, tablecloths, workclothes, uniforms—all bundled up in sheets tied by four corners. He realized
he was headed for the linen room, the domain of that witch, Mrs.
Jewett. All right, then why was he here? he asked himself as he
clambered over and around the heaped bundles. The question
remained unanswered as he turned the corner and emerged into
a bright and dry zone of the cellar, rather toward the front of the
building under the airy lobby, he should have thought, but as it
turned out in a little while he was quite wrong. He had been
drawn on by the sound of women's laughter. A half dozen of the
maids, three white, three colored, were standing in line, smoking
and chattering, waiting while the housekeeper counted linens out
to them. And there was Mrs. Jewett behind her chicken-wire
grille, her gray head bent, her liverspotted hands skimming piles
of towels and from long custom picking up batches of exactly ten.

The girls fell silent as he burst on them, and the housekeeper looked up, sharp-eyed and testy and shrewd.

"Well, Mr. Acker, how d'ye do this evening!"

"Fine, fine, Mrs. Jewett. If you'll excuse me . . ."

"Well, well, what is it I can do for you? You look as if you wanted something. It is a surprise to see you still here on a Saturday night; shouldn't you be home to supper? Is there something wrong?"

"I'm sorry to be bothering you, Mrs. Jewett. I know how you must be busy, Saturday night and everything, finishing up here, and it's late enough—"

"Late indeed, sir, and you *are* bothering me! Don't beat about the bushes. Come on, speak up."

"Frankly, I don't know exactly, I was just walking around here and . . ."

"What! Mister Solomon Acker! Just speak up, man! My girls can't wait here all night while you stroll about through this miserable damp and dreary hole in the cursed sand to pay social calls on my working hours."

But Mr. Acker felt himself strangely possessed, and paid her no attention. Though he too was surprised at his boldness, he managed to look over her frowning face, trying not to seem to notice her perfect gray wig with its forty-year-old ironed hairdo that never changed a strand. Beyond her he found what he had been searching for: a small whitewashed door: the door to his dumbwaiter. With rude glee he pointed at it, "And what is that, if you please, Mrs. Jewett?"

"What is what, Acker?" she answered with another question, a suspicious note of brass in her voice.

"That door there. Does anyone use it?"

Unwillingly she looked where he pointed. "What do you mean by that question, sir, if I may ask?"

"I mean—" he tried to sound disingenuous, though firm
"—does anyone use it, for anything at all?"

"*I* am *not* anyone, Mr. Acker, and I do not *do anything*."

He found himself almost violently impatient to stop this in-
direct cross-questioning of her and get to the bottom of the lead
he thought he had found. He brushed past the girls, pushed open
the mesh door to her sanctum, and pressed himself in, knocking
over a stack of new sheets. From the side of his eye he noticed
that the housekeeper's mouth was open: probably no one had
forced himself into her private cubicle in forty years. He was indeed risking her bitter enmity. But if there was a first time for him
there could even be a first time for her! *No one had the right not
to be questioned!* Anyhow, his job and his repute were at stake,
he reflected; and so set his teeth together and went on. Inadvertently he upset more linen; worse yet, stepped on them, again
inadvertently, as he reached for the catch on that door. Yanking
it open, he saw what he had suspected: halfway down in the
opening was his dumbwaiter.

"Mrs. Jewett! What is this?" he hissed.

"The dumbwaiter, Mr. Acker. What else?"

"I mean, what is it for? I mean, I just saw it moving. I was
upstairs, in the kitchen."

"It is a very lucky convenience providence designed for me, sir.
If you must know, I give my girls fresh linen and they can send
back the soiled without having to drag it publicly up and down
and around five or six flights of stairs. And what do you find
wrong with that?"

"Oh, I see." So *she* used it. But another idea jumped up in his
brain then, and he looked at his feet, suddenly mortified: was he
suspecting *her*, too? Why not, she was tough enough. But if she
was in on it, a ring member, then she must know his predica-
ment; and if she was spiriting the meat away, he could hardly

expect her help. He saw a bundle of used sheets in the corner. The outside one had a rather large, irregular, rusty stain on it. Obviously, it occurred to him, and without thinking any further, here, *here* was his clue to the missing meat, the five tons of beef gone in less than two weeks. He kicked at it, placed his foot triumphantly on the bundle, and heard himself shouting, "Aha! And what is *this*, Mrs. Jewett? Where does *this* come from?"

"Mr. Acker! I *am* surprised to hear you speaking in this way. This is a hotel, my dear sir, it is open to the public—as well you ought to know after thirty years. All sorts of your people come here. And we who are but servants don't look; neither do we ask. If you must, shame yourself by dirtying your nose with what's none of your affairs, but don't expect *me* to follow where you lead!"

Acker was beginning to say that it was very, very much his affair, when he understood that he was not thinking of the same thing that she was. Not in the least. "Oh, I beg your pardon, Mrs. Jewett. Excuse me, please."

"What is it, for goodness' sake? What can it be, Mr. Acker?"

He smiled deprecatingly, shrugged with his wrists, and then, as the inspiration hit him like a bolt, said out very loud in a completely irrelevant and prophetically rapt voice, "Of course! My God, of course! *What comes down must go up!*" He turned and waddled off, flopping his elbows in haste, and paid no heed to the coughing and the smothered giggles, uncontrollably female, that rose behind him into a stupid fit.

At last, having stopped to look to it that his storerooms and his office were secured, he gained the alley where he paused for a breather. His face glowed with the sweat of anticipation, his heart thumped in embarrassed excitement again because he felt he was going to get somewhere now, he was on the right path, though still he hadn't any notion where it led, and had not given proper thought to his immediate, his real task: procuring a delivery of meat and specialties, and getting it in by morning. In fact, he'd already forgotten that tomorrow was Sunday, that he should have been home long ago, relaxing, and having eaten, and showered, and that he should have been by now all spruced for his wife's evening promenade on the boardwalk where they contemplated the callow princes and princesses playing out their twelve weeks, their brief summer's glory.

Outside, it was not as bad as such a fulminating day might have warranted. Down the alley the sun was about to sink behind the privet which screened the new patio-and-saltwater-swimming-pool of the Miramar, once the Avalon, before that the Empire Royale. He looked at his watch: eight-ten. Overhead the sky was yet light: a pale, weak, Florida blue where striplets of cloud swam, iridescent, much like an idle school of pickled herrings. Luckily, a suggestion of air, perhaps the onset of the seawind that could usually be counted on, except for a day as hot as this had been, stirred off the water. Acker listened, but heard no sound of surf; the Atlantic must have been still and sweet as a pond. Swallows darted chirping through this narrow alley between the back of the Metropole and the old Egyptian Nights hotel. More people used to prefer sitting in lukewarm brackish Turkish baths than swimming in the ocean. He remembered the last time he had been into this place—more than twenty years ago, surely. It was with poor Paulie, his best friend, who'd emigrated to California ten years before and then come home from the desert rich, come home to Brooklyn to die on him, as it turned out. They had had a drink or few, too many it could be, and then gone to these baths to straighten themselves out; it was here the dirty crooks stole his wallet right from the safe, and then had the absolute nerve to accuse *him,* Acker, of lying, only because his bad luck was compounded: somehow he had mislaid his valuables ticket! That was on a Saturday night, he remembered, and it cost him his week's wages. Since then he had never gone home to his wife on Saturday later than nine, and never polluted. When would they tear down this empty, nailed-up hulk already, with its disgracefully weatherbeaten and shredding shingling and its sagging walls and the glamorous name on the front fading away to nothing, and build something decent here? This year, he had often noticed shadows sneaking in and out the busted cellar door there, even in daytime. Couples, he supposed. Why not? The house was empty: what else was it good for, especially because there was no privacy for anybody in laying out on the damp cold sand under the boardwalk, even late at night, but to make the alley such tight work for his delivery trucks. Musing, he looked up at the sky again and saw the crooked flights of the Metropole's corroded fire-escape, which zigged at the landings, each marked by a tin, red-painted door, red the color of stale blood, locked open to catch whatever air. Then he saw a figure, at this hour probably a busboy, come out of the top exit and stand there on the grating —Acker shaded his eyes the better to squeeze him into focus— what would that be, five? six? no, seventh floor, it was. Whoever it was looked around and leaned over; did he think somebody was watching him? Acker waited. Curious—wouldn't that be the attic floor? Then he recalled that the Metropole was unusual in Long Beach in this respect, that whereas in other places the dining-room crew had to live, live! in the basement in cold, wet, cramped and rank-smelling rooms, here they had the whole roof to themselves: busboys, children's waiters, waitresses and maids all scattered together. Not damp, but also not exactly cool today! The lazy band, and the time-wasting office girls, *they* got regular rooms, crummy, yes, but still hotel rooms, and the people who were supposed to look fresh like daisies when they handled the food Acker brought in with such a skillful care for the details— they were treated like the scum of the earth, almost as bad as the kitchen men, who were. Well, what could you do? Now he perceived that the kid up there was eating out of what looked

like a pot held in the crook of his arm, and that every two bites
he swigged from a bottle, milk probably. But if the help finished
eating at five-thirty, why should he be packing it in all over again
so soon? But suppose . . . suppose what? Acker came back to
himself with a start. Food! He wheeled and rushed back to his
office where it was always cold night, picked up the phone and
started methodically working down his list of suppliers, first local,
then Brooklyn, finally all the way over to New York. By nine-
twenty he was through, with fair assurances that his goods would
begin arriving by twelve o'clock, for a price. He sighed, deeply,
as he locked up once more, and headed upstairs to find Gruber
and to vindicate his efficiency as the steward, even under such an
unexpected, crowding and pushing, unkind, almost unfair tide of
fate.

Now the lobby was crowded with those random groups of
every age, standing around after a too-full dinner to recover
breath. In their colorful Saturday night summer-sports and semi-
formal-playclothes and flushed by the sun, they were like proud
and besotted kine of Bashan, and Acker felt ashamed for his
white face shadowed with black beard, his bald brow streaked
with poor strands of hair unthickened by salty water, and his gray
working clothes, crumpled and creased and sweatpatched in their
service. With his eyes cast meekly down, he sidled along the back
wall to the desk, hunting Gruber by ear. The man was apparently
not anywhere in the lobby, where he certainly ought to have
stationed himself, as any proper manager would have done, seeing to it his guests could see him and talk to him in case they
might want something—which the type of nuisances who frequent houses like the Metropole usually did: give them pinkest
salmon steak, and why not swordfish? give jellied cold pike, and
why not poached whitefish? Give, give, give; still there is no end
to their want! Neither was Gruber on the blued concrete veranda
—call this the *grande piazza du Metropole?*—where he saw only

a number of the incompetent young and the childishly senescent rocking every which ways in the last dusky light. Surely the globes could have been switched on by now so that people shouldn't have to congregate in that arid, airless, dead lobby? Acker went round the side of the building toward the pallid rocky garden they called a patio. No one was there, if you didn't count Seymour that loutish children's waiter; and Seymour, Acker noticed, was, as usual, sitting and eating, on either knee a full napkin spread out and the slit-eyed buffoon transferring bones—chickenbones, chopbones, fishbones—from the one to the other as he stripped them. Also, there was a gallon can by his foot, from which Acker saw him extract half a dripping peach with his fingers. What a greedy thing! It occurred to him that that sort of gallon can was an item Seymour rightfully should have no access to, but then, it was customary for the children's waiters to eat as their perquisite whatever remained, and likely the cook had given that pesky, pimply boob the last can in order to drive him away. Without speaking or glancing at him further, Acker went by avoiding. Had he the stomach to look more closely, he would have seen such a picnic laid out that he might have been disturbed in quite a different way from that caused him by the merely obnoxious sight of this young glutton at work. But Acker's virtue was also his failing: he had room in his mind for only one thought at a time. So he kept on to the side entrance, where he quickened his climb up the shaky stairs because he heard even over the loud and painful clatter of the rented Saturday night *cha-cha-cha* band with its absurd cowbells and maracas and woodblocks and bongo-bongos, the grunting voice of Gruber, and apprehended him vaguely as a kind of obscene boar whom he had had to track to his lair.

Parting the bead curtains of the portal to the Cubana Casbah Cabaret, as it was now named, he paused. The "younger people," the "fast set," a gang of long-married couples, were already, and so soon after dinner, flinging about the tiny floor in what they termed dancing, or else sitting around soaking up the sauce. All week these skinny women laid like mummies on the beach, cigarettes stuck in their greasy faces and oily white cotton swabs over their eyes, ignoring their children and waiting for the tired husbands who came out on the weekend to visit with them. Also there were the singles, old maids of both sexes, these balding and those graying, these sedentary and those shapeless, busy hunting each other up and down and all over the bar. Well, it was a hotel. Through this hoopdydo and frenzy, Acker could see him down at the far end of the bar, where he sat fat-assed in fancy white linen pants on a chromium stool. A sport shirt printed with orchids and flamingoes loosely covered the vast, boiled pulp of his upper body, from which stuck two short borschtpink woolly arms: in one mush mitt the big cigar, in the other the familiar tumbler of scotch. Dark aviator's sunglasses obscured the terrible eyes of that buttered, smoldering visage. Acker waited until Gruber saw him and snapped his fingers summoning him; then he came forward through this milling and jangling foretaste of hell which already sufficed to jar his satisfaction over his recent feat of stewardship to incomprehensibly scattered bits.

"Sit down, Mr. Steward. Take the load off!" Gruber dropped his arm across Mr. Acker's shoulders, and he stiffened. "Sit down, sit down, I said." Acker sat. "You got your envelope today, didn't you? How come I never see you spend some of that stuffed cabbage in my little joint here? What's the matter, they got better booze somewhere else, or Momma says no?"

Not exactly the most tactful, was it? First of all, it was none of his business one way or the other what he did or did not do, and second place . . . but was it a hint or maybe an order? If so, he couldn't be told where to go after working hours and how to spend his hard-earned money. Well, but what was this, a company town? Moreover, what did Gruber think he could do to him if he chose *not* to come in here? He had his season contract; so he couldn't be canned without showing cause, which *not drinking* definitely wasn't. Acker answered with what he thought quiet, candid self-respect: "Mr. Gruber, you know very well I have an apartment and wife I can go home to when I finish my time here."

"Yeah, yeah, Acker. Dump it somewhere else. Me too. But that means you can't socialize at the bar once in a while? All my employees are permitted to take a drink here. I even like them to. Maybe not for each and every on Saturday night, but you're on the executive staff here. I want you to feel free, because you're welcome to. So, what do you like?"

"Thank you, but nothing just now."

"Don't talk like a child, please."

"Well, let's say a glass of ginger ale is all."

"Hey Salvatore. Bring Mr. Acker some ginger ale. Make it with the Haig & Haig—Pinch Bottle!"

"Mr. Gruber, thank you, but I don't think I want—"

"Salvatore, make it a double, eh? Say, Sal, I want you to meet the man who has been my steward here, believe it or not, seven weeks already. I bet you don't even know him. Sal, meet Sol; Solly, Sally." Gruber coughed up a dirty chuckle.

"Pleased," Mr. Acker said. "But it's Solomon. Nobody *ever* calls me Solly." And not considering what he might be bringing on himself, he took a long swallow from his glass.

"That's better, Solly," Gruber said, and clapped his back. "Now, what's the story: are you in or are you out?"

Acker smiled a little for the first time today. "We're all set. Don't worry. I have trucks on the way already." He glanced sideways at Gruber to see was he pleased. Gruber seemed not to have heard; or not to care very much. He merely grunted in his throat and held his glass out to the bartender. Ingrate! Some manager—he takes a miracle for granted! What was the use: the

man was a bully, period. Acker drained his glass. All right, he had
to take the chance and drop a hint. "Besides, I have done a little
investigating around here tonight. And . . . I think . . . I have
found . . . something. . . ."

Gruber swiveled from the bar to face him, hauled up a golden
lighter and puffed his green cigar to life. The barman took
Acker's glass from him, poured it half full of whiskey, added a
dollop of soda, replaced it just as unobtrusively into his hands.
Gruber snapped his lighter shut, rapped on the bar a few times
in a gesture reminiscent of the split-second meditation of the
higher military, and stuffed it back into a pants pocket too full
of thigh; then he glared, wearily it might have been, perhaps only
savagely bored, through his sunglasses. "Okay, Acker. Don't
waste my time with guessing games. Spill. What *is* going on
around here?"

"What's going on? What isn't? And furthermore, Mr. Julius
Gruber, it's possible you could know as much as I do, if not more,
eh?" Acker was surprised to hear his own voice delivering this
bold and cool suggestion. He knew he would live to regret it, and
began immediately.

"I know *more* than you think, Acker. Morale around here is
shot. Service is going to pieces. I can feel it in my bones: that's
why I am who I am. From where I sit, the whole works is right
under my nose, see? And let me tell you, mister, I don't like it
one bit. If you want to know, the entire staff stinks like bad meat
to me. There's five more full weeks to this season. I should be
going strong in the black. The place is booked up till Labor Day.
They never had it so hot in the city. But the way things are falling, I can't see to make it, because I take a look at the books and
it's pouring out through a hole as big as the Lincoln Tunnel. How
the *hell* is that possible? Because, Acker, *from your department
alone I stand to lose everything!* Rivers, oceans of food! Last
week, the meat almost two tons short. Canned goods, sardines and

herrings and tunas and salmons that run two arms and a leg, fruits, apricots, peaches, pears, maraschinos even, and oranges and pineapple and melons that cost a small fortune just to look at the crates. Even dairy, juice and milk and cream! Where *is* that tapeworm? Am I running a *mad*house here? I say it has got to stop this very night, or else I am going to see to it personally!" He smashed his clenched fist down on the bartop so hard that Acker's breath jumped down his throat with fright. What was the matter with Gruber? Didn't he know the help steals you blind, no matter what? even right under the unwinking eyes of a zealot like Mrs. Jewett? All right, it was bad; but not so bad as he made it. Consequently, Acker tried to return a soft answer to the anger he had roused. "Well, Mr. Gruber, not so much as that, I would say."

"Oh, *you* would say? A thousand dollars of inventory a week is not so bad?"

Acker smiled forgivingly, emboldened by his drinks, and said in a liquorish murmur that he was again instantaneously sorry for, "Let's not exaggerate, Gruber. It's not a thousand. Even five hundred would be good, too."

"What? Your five hundred, Acker, or mine? A fiver not enough! Why, man, in the army I could prosecute you, even if you were a fellow officer, for a knife, a fork, a spoon—let alone a helmet or a pair of pants! And I could make you, *you,* Acker, personally responsible to see to it that even the top of the mayonnaise jar is screwed on just so and according to the book. Understand? Just so, or else!"

Acker didn't reply. Which set the man off even worse. "I tell you what, Acker. I will give you till tomorrow morning to find out the story. Okay? Then I get Pinkerton. You know what it means if he comes down? All right! If I was you, I'd poke in and out and spot who's in charge of this racket, and drop me the word. And if I was you, Acker, I wouldn't tear up no contracts tonight. Because if you turn around next thing and tell me you don't want this job, I'll know who to look for. Exactly! You wouldn't be feeling so freshmouth and talky. That's all."

Under the sheer force of such a threat, Acker shrank into himself. It was as though he sat paralyzed at a table and watched some stupid busboy's overstacked tray of dirty dishes begin tipping over right above him. Here he had been sweating bitter lemons to pull this gross man out of a tight spot, and he as good as promised to make him into a criminal. Such injustice! When it could be anybody here, even Gruber: anybody, but not Acker, *that* he knew, and he knew Gruber knew it too. So what could he say to the man after this?

"I see you get my point, Acker. Okay, finish that glass and start your manhunt."

"But why should I be—?"

Gruber bashed his fist down again, and looking away into the deep, smoky, blue mirror, but not at him in it, sliced his hand across his bag of chins and growled more hoarsely: "No more, you hear! I'm up to here, Acker! So don't even think of what you might want to say. This is the end of this particular conversation: the interview is closed. My Cabaret is open till three. I want to see you in here again only when you come and say you're finished with your assignment. Otherwise . . . *phhtt!* Go on, get the hell out!"

As best he could, Acker got.

There was no one in the lobby. The air from the sea had actually come into palpable existence: it flowed, sluggish and warm, inflating slightly the heavy blue draperies that even at midday created a byzantinish gloom in the Metropole's entrance, and it seemed to have washed away the mass of congested guests on its slow current. Beyond the unattended desk, Acker stopped in the murky corridor under the main staircase. He tried to collect and contain the fright that was giving him shivers, as if his skin were hiccoughing. Then he could not tell what it was, whether he was suddenly hungry or nauseated. He half-leaned, half-fell back against the knobbly and carved black oak chair with the broken-springed, embroidered seat that guarded the foot of the stair, and seated in which could always be seen either the corrupt bell-captain deciphering his racing form or the elevator boy dozing between rush hours to and from the beach. His palms pressed themselves together hard in his lap. All right, Acker: think, think, think! Now what is to be done? So, he had to resume his search? The idea of what he wanted nagged at him like a ringing tone in the ears through the gradually swelling drone of the waves of fatigue and strain and confusion that had begun to buffet his spirit. But he found he could not think. At first he saw before him a whirling lion-rampant; his lion, Leo, which his wife repeatedly assured him was the sign of protection in July, but then it dwindled, as though sucked down a drain, and its place was immediately possessed by Gruber's terrific sweating head, the sunglasses obscuring those bleary, fuming eyes, that enormous mouth with its stained teeth and the purple swollen tongue that lapped the wet cigar protruding from it permanently. This image remained floating on the turbulent black water of his mind, filling up the narrow space behind his eyelids. Acker groaned low and put his hands to his poor skull, pushing the soft heels of his palms against his empty, wretched temples. What to do, what to do? Unable to stir foot or arm or head, Mr. Acker, slumped on the thronelike chair, looked like a man asleep, though actually he was awake, praying wordlessly, his disordered and feverish brain helpless in the rigor of the situation, like a trussed pullet flung into a corner and waiting bright-eyed for the slaughterer's ritual knife so sharp and swift it is never even felt.

In the blackness to his left, the door to the basement steps opened and shut again with a tiny click. Someone flitted by and went up the stairs behind him. The air in the wake of this shadow

seemed tinged with ammonia, like the memory of the odor of a
moist-muzzled calf he had hugged once as a child in a green
country, long long ago. He did not move. In a little while, the
door opened again and shut. He lifted his lids just a crack and
discerned white lowheeled shoes that appeared to glimmer against
the blotchy maroon ground of this moldy-smelling Mohawk Imperial Persian carpeting: in the shoes, sharpboned and taut-
tendoned ankles, blackskinned, stepped springily by: he heard
the lightness of their passing, listened to their muffled pattering
up the stairs: he sniffed, and thought he apprehended the scent
of newbaked rye bread, weakly sour yet sweet, and what he could
have believed easily to be the breath of strong red wine. Still he
did not move. But when shortly afterward the same door opened
and closed with what was surely unusually mysterious delibera-
tion, and he saw two pairs of shoes go by him on tiptoe, again
one white with darkskinned female legs in them, the other a pair
of scuffed black men's shoes, and listened to them skipping secretly
up the staircase, and got a bitter whiff of stale smoke as of wet
ashes, Mr. Acker awoke, feeling as if he had been lightly struck,
and knew himself resurrected back into himself. For who knows
how long, he had utterly lost track of time. His brain was working
now, and he thought, Yes, the manner in which all those feet had
moved was suspicious. Yes, very much so! On the other hand,
to be absolutely just, it also occurred to him that he could simply
interpret their stealth as natural, because although the help well
knew they should never use the main stairs, at the Metropole
they usually did in the off-hours; yet especially they shouldn't
when a member of the top staff like himself was there, although,
again, strictly speaking, Saturday evening he did not belong in
the lobby in his workclothes either. So, where was he now, with
all this anxious guessing and unguessing to and fro? Nevertheless,
Acker began to climb the stairs, as softly as he was able, feeling
and peering, like an ecstatic diver gone far beyond his limit, up,

up, up into what seemed chiaroscuro depths and deeps—and commenting bitterly to himself that what would have been a flagrant violation of safety in another place, was in the Metropole atmosphere, character, quality even!

The second floor was empty, forward and back. So was the third. Breathing hard in his absorption, and from the attitude of caution he had assumed, Acker continued more slowly to the fourth. He had heard whispering. He stuck his weak chin, level with the top step, around the landing. Down the hall, the linen closet's door was ajar, and the lightbulb in it shed a soft zone over two forms which were close together and appeared to him at first to be scuffling. Concentrating, breathless, Acker watched. It was one of the Negro girls, the maid, Marie, whom they called Bright Eyes because of her enormous, longlashed black eyes, emphasized by prominent, slanted cheekbones, and because her eyes always seemed to be satirically laughing, and one of the busboys. Acker suddenly realized that they were embracing, rocking back and forth into and out of the closet, as if they were dancing. The girl's arms stood out black against the boy's white jacket: Acker watched with fascination as one of the hands slipped down his back, walking like a crab, and bit the boy in the seat of his pants. Acker heard them laughing together: the boy let go to seize her hand, and she pushed him away. Then he shoved her back into the closet again, and in a few moments they came tumbling out, clean towels raining with them. The girl muttered, and dropped to her knees. The boy bent too, butted her in her rear so that she sprawled, and fled down the corridor. Acker had to wait while she retrieved her goods, folded and put them back, buttoned up the white uniform and disappeared after the boy in her shambling girl's run. Monkeybusiness, he said to himself, *some* monkeybusiness!

When he judged they should have settled down wherever it was they had gone, he resumed more painfully crouched. The

fifth floor was empty, except when the elevator rattled open and
ejected two crones in their flowered silk, who helped each other
to their rooms, where they fussed, interminably, with the locks.
All right, he promised, we will now see precisely what is doing
here, heh? On hands and knees, he ascended to the sixth floor;
at the top he moved to the landing with what seemed even
to him infinitely wearying and ridiculously unnecessary effort,
though he made it for the sake of the form, and sat there on the
floor in the angle, leaning over just enough to get a view of the
hallway.

The elevator opened and two waitresses came out and walked
right toward him. He drew back. They went up the stairs to the
attic, their feet tramping hollow and measured, exhausted, on
the bare wooden steps that climbed to the seventh floor. In a
minute the elevator returned. Two busboys came out. Acker said
to himself with heavy irony, Such innocents! Such angels! We
will see what we will see! Acker watched, and saw something that
opened his eyes indeed. They had gone stealthily into the linen
closet for a moment; now they came out, each with gallon cans
under their arms—Acker's cans! Unmistakably! They slithered
down the hall at him and bounded thundering up over his head.
He had a hunch and held himself back, waiting and saying over
and over, Well well well! and Aha! and Oho! In a few minutes,
the pantomime was repeated when another pair of busboys were
brought up, and they darted into the linen closet and also came
out loaded down with canned goods: one had even taken off his
uniform jacket, put the sleeves into the pockets and stuffed them
with No. 2 cans: the other carried his white coat like a sack, and
it was filled full with oranges and grapefruits and whatnot! My
God in heaven, Acker moaned to himself, what have they got in
there? In the next ten minutes, four more boys came up from the
diningroom and visited that depot; moreover, they all made trips
down to reload. Acker stayed where he was, stupefied, and tried

to estimate his loss if such a quantity of provisions was heisted every day. But the question, the paramount inquiry, was: *Where* did it come from? *When* did it? And *how?* He looked at his watch; it read eleven.

Suddenly he was aware of a faint, far-off sound of revelry in the night. It came to him not from any place below, and not exactly from the stairway above—the firedoor had been banged shut up there—but out of the air, as it were, floating down from the blurred multitudes of stars he could distinguish high in the dark universe out of the fire-escape door open behind him: a kind of muzzy singing over bursts of loud talk, and hoots and howls and yelps of laughter mixed up with the intermittent strains of music that you heard when a radio abandoned in some room or other played aimlessly shrill and unheeded by itself. He listened for a minute, confounded by the noise of this unplaceable party: it was like the mockery of a dream that you were in heaven, among the luminous, milky hosts of the skies, and hearing the happiness all about you, and being unable to see anything at all. Recovering his attention, he decided he had delayed much too long, and attempted to rise to an officially important position. But his legs failed him, and he dropped; the left one was entirely numb, the right tingled like an alarm clock. He sat there stretching them and cursing them under his thoughts and massaging them until they grew quiet, meanwhile feeling a peculiarly acrid and constricted desperation of mood welling up in him out of his stomach, or his chest—he wasn't sure which.

When he could get up, he marched directly to the linen closet. It was not even locked: already a sign of fundamental disorder. Mrs. Jewett would have bitten her bloodless lip to come on this! He walked in and pulled the cord. The light revealed nothing unusual: the shelves held clean linen, all quite neatly stacked and ticketed; the floor was swept; the empty water pitchers and glasses, and things like the hotel's thin cakes of Ivory and the girls' mops and brooms and dustcloths and so forth—everything tidy. His questing eyes flickered, then found his desire; almost hidden in a recess in the back corner, the unpainted little door to the dumbwaiter. He reached out and tore at it in an excess of passion. The shaft was empty, the ropes still. Well, after all, what else should he have expected? He had to admit frankly he didn't know, but he could guess. Tugging at the pull rope, Acker brought this too-handy means of conveyance up—and found that, for him, the dumbwaiter had no story to tell: he saw nothing but the bare old box. Despite this disappointment, Acker was convinced that at some time very recently it had contained all his troubles. And would again, tomorrow night perhaps, though it would be of no use to him to be able to demonstrate that fact to anyone, for by then Mr. Pinkerton would have tied him to it, with the goods together. What he badly needed, right now, more than a glass of something to quench his thirst, more even than a couple of his Anacins and a cold shower, was proof—proof, proof, *proof!* And he knew just where to get what he needed. Closing the dumbwaiter up carefully, as if it could make any difference, Acker pulled the light cord and backed out of the closet and started right for the attic—without even pausing to prepare his imagination to cope with what he thought he was sure to find.

He gained the topmost floor with a celerity he had not believed himself anymore capable of tonight. Throwing open the firedoor, Acker walked into an atmosphere so very hot and dry that it smote his face like the blast from a furnace, and confronted a scene he could not believe quite real. Not in all his experience, not in thirty years in hotels, he said to himself out loud, had he ever seen, let alone heard of, such a thing! He stood at the head of the attic hall, which ran the whole length of the Metropole's seventh floor. It was an uncomfortably high-ceilinged, sharp-pitched passage that might have been a nave designed in a superfluous moment of fancy, for it never could have been intended for any serious architectural use. Here and there the ancient plaster had dropped off the walls, where great patches of broken lathing were left bare. Nothing but rats' nests in there. Who knew how long ago it had last been whitewashed? Down its wretchedly illuminated length were the help's low little rooms, on both aisles, looking much like cells because they had no doors. And ranged along both sides of this fake basilica, as far as he could see clearly, which was not more than halfway down, were dozens and dozens of gallon tin cans—the very cans which had once contained his vegetables and his fruits, and if not his, the steward's before him. Now they were empty, but filled with old refuse and rubbish; beer, wine, whiskey bottles, uncountable cigarette butts and so much ash, cosmetic bottles and soiled crumpled tissues and broken curlers and hair nets, rags of clothing and silk stockings and torn underthings like corsets, garters, braces and bands of elastic, cotton, pads, straps, supports, broken shoes, wrinkled old toothpaste tubes, newspapers . . . just everything that comes out of bedrooms, and the worst of everything. Acker shut his eyes, shook his head in grief, and opened them again. The illusion, preposterous as it was, persisted: in and out of the tiny rooms up and down this attic way people were scuttling, dancing, leaping, cavorting back and forth in their underwear, or even, it seemed, less: busboys, chambermaids, waitresses—young and older, white and colored, Gentile and Jew. It might have been the entire diningroom staff and all the maids, as far as he knew. He flung his arms up, as if to command silence, and the weighted ironclad door clanged shut behind him. No one paid any attention: the orgy went on uninterrupted. Acker leaned back against the door, and considered. He had not anticipated anything like this; this was something else! Had everything turned upside down and inside out? This was like the end of the world!

But Acker girded himself and went forward into chaos. Besides, having come so far so late, and by a way so much against his will and bias—creeping and peeping, spying and chasing—from that silent still office of his in the cool cellar down there in the earth, there was no way back for him. Most especially, he told himself to proceed because he believed he had sufficiently witnessed already the evidence of misdemeanor and misappropriation and malfeasance for which he had been seeking. Now he wanted the source. Dark, the first room to the left: a portable radio, fluorescent on the sill of the uncurtained window, blared at him, *Ma-ha-hambo, Corazon! Ma-ha-hambo, Cha-cha-cha!* and as he passed he saw two cigarette coals pulse red and flare near the floor. The next room on his right was lit up like day. He halted outside it. Tilly, wearing nothing more than an old, tattered, cotton housecoat, her bloody hair down in braids, one of her long Russian cigarettes in the corner of her mouth, stood at an ironing board, pressing her uniform; her crooked, gnarled, blueveined feet seemed marmoreal against the bare wood floor; Riva, her roommate, slackbreasted, yellowskinned, lay comatose in a halfslip on her pallet—staring blankly at the cracked ceiling —how Acker hated that gray-striped ticking and broken-springed cot. He waited; when Tilly looked up at him he gestured at the noise of the hall, as if to say, *What's this?* and she glared back at him, her tired face falling easily into a grimace of cynical disgust, and shrugged as if to reply, *What do you think?* Acker went on.

He did not know how he ever managed to reach the end of the corridor; to these people who had made it a gantlet for his undone sensibility, it was as if he were a transient, fluttering shadow passing among them, a schlemiel who had somehow, somewhere lost his body. They jeered at him, bumped into him on purpose, and gave him fierce, uninviting stares which said all too clearly, *Who asked you?* or else, worse, ignored him altogether when he stopped at a room and stared into it like a tourist wandering by mistake through a gallery of lewd exhibitions. Lights went off and on during his long progress, bottles were opened, ice cubes rattled into glasses; four or five other radios played on different stations, and people behaved as they would at the end of a party, rather, a dozen parties. Acker was relieved to discover that he was in no worse condition at the end of his journey than before. But wasn't *that*, he heard his voice inside him imploring, about as bad as one can possibly stand?

The end of the hall was dim, lit by an ocherous, flyspecked bulb, perhaps an old ten-watts. Acker put his hand out gingerly, and stroked the rough boards nailed over what had been the windows of a recessed Moorish arch. Shaggy, splintery, the reality of this cursed wood, that he could touch at least, steadied him. The last room there was dark as a tomb; he heard a girl's spluttering, and then her giggles, and also a warm female laugh come from it. Too strong a light flicked on. A male voice called, "Say, Mr. Acker, is that you?" He turned himself around and went unwillingly to the painful light. He was much too upset to put this movement into words, but he knew obscurely and with no reason that here was the approach to the facts, truth, goal, call it what you want, toward which he had been striving through this tumultuous night.

He blinked at his watch. Already practically twelve. Three people were in this miserable little room. To one side of it, Davie the head busboy reclined in a swaybottomed narrow bed; behind him and against the wall lay that girl, Bright Eyes. They were naked, yes, but at least they had covered themselves up to their bellies with the grimy sheet. Her satinblack breasts, Acker saw at once, were very long and thin, and tipped by granular pink nipples; her teeth shone so white at him, and her eyes were so impudently wide with laughter—why, why was that? Next to her the boy was bony and much too pale. A mess of clothes and shoes were flung beside the bed. Acker saw also a pail of ice with three

wine bottles in it, and a newly opened gallon can of his superior
Bartlett pears. The other bed was occupied by a very stout tan
woman in a transparent nightgown; Acker recognized in her the
children's matron, Nurse they called her; and how much younger
she seemed in the flesh; that is, Acker amended his observation,
out of uniform. The woman lay propped on her side in a luxuri-
ant attitude, sipping from a glass of wine and smoking.

"What's going on here?" Acker said, as if he had just awakened.

"Come in, come in, Mr. Acker," the young man said.

"Davie, I'm asking a question. I want an answer." His voice
bobbled with the effort to sound peremptory. But he had not the
strength.

"Aah, come in and sit down. What's the big hurry? It's been
a hard week. How about it, eh?" Davie leaned down toward the
floor for a cigarette, and lit up while still draped three quarters
out of the bed.

"Well, I'm waiting!"

"That's all right, Mr. Acker, sir, you just come on in now,
and sit yourself down easy. You look, well—not so good," the
big tan lady said in a mellow voice. And she patted the small
space left on the edge of her mattress, just in front of her smooth,
weighted belly, with its deep navel. "Come on now, you hear
me?"

"Davie," he said once more, his will slackening, "Davie, I did
not come up here for a good time. I'm on business, you hear me?
I demand an answer from you. Better talk and explain a few
things. Because it's up to you. Because you're the head busboy.
So let's get it over with."

"See, you crazy thing?" Davie said over his shoulder to the
girl, "I told you once, and I told you again: *I* give the orders!
Because I'm head busboy, see! That's one *you* owe." He laughed
and slid his arm under the sheet. The girl reacted by fastening her

teeth in his shoulder. He jabbed his elbow into her breast, and she subsided. He leered at Acker, confidentially, and said, "How about that, eh?" Acker stamped his foot, and Davie changed his expression, "Okay, have it your way. Whatever you want, Mr. Acker. I'm listening. But first sit down, huh? Please? You make me nervous the way you look. Like a dead man."

If Acker had thought that he did not quite know what he wanted to say when he first laid eyes on this trio, he was worse off as soon as he gave in and sat down, in the only place he could. Immediately, he felt the woman's strong, somnolent stomach pressed warm against the small of his back: the misery which had stiffened his spine and sustained him thus far became as water, as nothing. The boy dragged at his cigarette and said, surely, Acker thought, laughing in his heart at him, "Better? Now, sir, you just have a little to drink, you just take it a little easy for a minute, you'll be all right."

Reassuringly, Nurse patted his knee, then she poured and reached him a full chill glass from her bottle of purplish-black wine and he—fool, fool that he knew he was—drank it. So, what difference could it make? he answered himself. He had finally found what he wanted. She said, "Mr. Acker, you know something? I an immigrant too. I come across water to these States here."

"Really?" he said. "I don't follow."

"I'm not like these lowdown, no-class Americans here, like that girl across the way there—all right, you black thing, you can laugh, you don't know any better!" she scolded the girl. "You see, I was born in Jamaica. And I been educated too; trained for a nurse. My first husband, poor man, he was a lawyer, 'fore God, and he was West Indian man, Trinidad. You know?"

"Really?" he said. "That's nice."

"So you don't have to be afraid with me, Mr. Acker," she con-

cluded soothingly, with a logic that baffled him as to its purpose,
"and it will be all right, because we understand better than those
poor things, the ignorant way they been brought up over here."
She put that square, strong hand on his knee again.

Mr. Acker tried to concentrate, tried to make himself clear. He
felt he knew all he needed to know, and need but speak to be
understood. "Davie, this is it, now. Important. I want you to
listen to me. You're a nice boy, I like you, the way you handle
yourself downstairs; no mess, no bossiness. I don't want you to
go in over your head. It's a hard world, I tell you. I know, it
doesn't forgive. You start off the wrong way, they'll never let you
forget it. So stay out of trouble."

"Wait a minute, Mr. Acker, wait just a minute. Why the
speech? It's too hot, and we're all tired out around here. Now
what's the matter—can't we have a party? Who's bothered?"

"Party? What's the party got to do with it? Who knows what
you kids are up to nowadays, anyway, and who cares? If I had a
kid, I wouldn't be able to look him in the face: after these go-
ings-on tonight I have seen enough to make me ashamed forever.
Awful. But I'm not your father and you're not my son and it's not
my business. I just don't want trouble here. What's more, there's
going to be plenty, you'll see!" He felt tears of certainty and sorrow filling him. The nurse's hand was between his shoulders,
smoothing his back: he wanted her to stop, it was making him
groggy; but he did nothing. "Furthermore, guilty or not guilty,
someone always has to be blamed for it. And the man in charge
is the best choice to get it: it can't be helped. That's the way the
world gets run. So, as head busboy, you will have to bear the
responsibility, let me warn you, for what others may have done."

"Say, what's the matter with you, Mr. Acker? I'm just having
a good time like everybody else. What do you pick on me for?
Why me, out of all the crowds of fellas you seen all your life?"

"You want to know, eh? You really want to know? All right, you will!" Acker pointed to the can of pears. "What do you call this? Where, may I ask you, does this come from?"

"Oh, hell, so we picked up a can of fruit for the night. What's the big deal? Once in a while you take something. So what?"

"One can? Only one can, you say? Once in a while? What's about that collection, that carload of stuff up and down this hall? Am I a blind man? Do you take me for a blind man, *and* a fool?"

"How should I know, for God's sake! Anna, Marie, tell him how long that stuff's been there, for God's sake! This crew came in this goddamned dump a month and a half ago, and he thinks we did all that. Pops, that's one hell of a clever idea!"

"Try and tell me you didn't. Say I'm the judge. You just try telling it to me you didn't!" Acker sneered with worldly sarcasm. "Well? You think anyone old enough to be your father must be deaf, dumb and blind, don't you? Well, some might be. I wouldn't know about that. But here I'm the steward, and it's my business to know what goes on in the food department. So don't you think I don't. All right, I told myself, a little lifting up here and there, you can't blame the kids; it's natural, considering the way they feed them. A piece of fruit, a loaf of bread, a glass of milk—you're entitled to it, *if* the headwaiter don't catch you, and *if* the cooks don't catch you, and *if* I don't. But—God in heaven should only be my witness—twenty, thirty *cases* of gallon cans! Besides everything else in the house! Some nerve you and your gang has got."

"Say, Mr. Acker . . ."

"Now don't make me angry, Davie. Because I've had it, I'm full up to here—and you better believe it!"

"But listen . . ."

"I thought you were a nice boy, Davie. At least *you*, I could count on *you*, the head busboy, to be responsible, mature, to maintain a little order, to keep the boys from running wild. But this!"

"Listen, Mr. Acker . . ."

"No! You listen to me!" Acker screamed, and he would have jumped up, but the woman pulled him back against her, and wrapped her great comfortable arms about his waist. Nevertheless, he continued on a shrill rising pitch, "You listen to me. I hereby give you the last warning, you hear? It has got to stop! I wanted to protect you, Davie, because you're a poor boy. And a better boy, I thought. And poor boys don't have a chance, and the law don't care for better boys either. If I was to speak what I saw going on up here tonight—who knows what they would do to you? The entire godforsaken boom would fall on you!"

"But . . ."

"But me no buts, but shut up I say! You—liar! thief! lecher! Who can tell how bad you are! If you're like this now, God knows what you'll be ten years from today. So answer me what you know: *what happened to the meat?* That's what I want to know. Because you can't eat raw meat. Tonight it's not too late to speak. But tomorrow you will be sorry, believe you me! Well?"

Davie looked at him blankly. Some cool cucumber that boy was! Pickled in vinegar! And then the girl, Marie, burst into a steady jag of laughing, that silly giggling of hers that seemed to have no relevance to the world of this particular instance, as proved by the way she stopped the minute the boy jogged her.

"Will you just wait one second, Mr. Acker? I heard you out long enough. So let's not kid around. You come in here where you don't belong, where people are having a good time. You start in yelling at me for picking up a can of your rotten pears. What is this crazy story about meat now?"

"Davie, your last chance. I don't know how many hundred pounds of fresh beef we lost around here in seven weeks, but this

I *can* tell you: tomorrow the detective comes down! Once he's here on the premises, it will be too late—for everybody."

The boy stubbed his cigarette out on the dresser top next to his head, and looking right at him, said, cold and level, with a voice like a smack in the face, "All right, Mr. Solomon Acker, that's enough crap from you. You think you know so much! A couple cans of fruit, a pineapple, an orange, maybe a bottle of milk—okay? If you're such a goddam cheap little punky steward for your lord and master that son of a bitch Gruber that you have to sit and count over a mountain of stock every night, you just try proving it. Right, girls? Look at this little bastard, he comes sneaking around after his five dollars' worth of goods any decent place would *give* the help once in a while. Then he says he'll call in a detective, a detective yet, for God's sake! because everybody's having fun Saturday night. That's really the best, that's holy! Go on, call the detective down, see what you get!"

Acker reiterated, feeling as if he was being gagged by a slimy dishcloth, feeling as if the earth were falling away, "The meat! The meat! What about the meat! What happened to all my choice meat! I want to know how you did it!"

"What meat? Who knows where your meat is? Don't be crazy, Acker. Meat, he says!"

Acker sought again to rise. He would have throttled the boy lying there at ease with that derisive naked black female. He would have throttled her too. He tried to speak out but could not. The nurse's bulky arms caught him, held him to her, enveloped him, pulled him down. He gave up the useless struggle to force the truth: he turned and wept upon her good and welcome breasts. "That's all right, honey," he heard her say, "that's all right. You just going to stay here with Anna for a while, and it will be all right, you know? I understand, I do, so you just hold onto me good like this. No use fighting them stones."

And then, and then he thought he heard her whispering, but

to whom? And she seemed to be supporting him. They were
going somewhere and she was saying, "The man isn't used to the
heat, you see. Like my second husband, poor man. And then he
took a little wine, too, you see. And . . ." And then he heard a
door bang; and another. Then the soft voice of the elevator boy
singing. "There, there . . ." It was very dark and cool all of a
sudden. A hand had been shaking him violently. He opened his
eyes. And then he discovered that he was sitting; he felt an awful
cramp in his neck. He was back in the chair in the lobby of the
Metropole. He could smell rain, and the salt wind from the sea,
much harder now, blowing into the deserted lobby . . . and he
smelled the special cigar, too. It was Gruber who stood over him.
Gruber. "So, Acker. This is how you do your detective work?"

From the desk he heard sniggering. "All right," Gruber said
over him condescendingly, "I'll take care of everything. Why
don't you go home to the old lady, Acker? She must be up waiting
for you, eh? You don't smell so good to me; but it could be
worse. Stanley, this is my steward, Acker. You know him? Acker,
Stanley, my nightman." Stanley the nightclerk sniggered again:
the very same idiot-sounding laugh as before.

Without looking about, and to no one in particular, Acker
said, "My name is *not* Solly." Then he got up, swaying on his
queered legs. He started for the cool wet air and the thrashing
darkness that he heard waiting for him outside the Metropole,
renewed always, from one year to the next, like time. He lifted
his wrist: his watch read half-past three. It was too late. It was
already tomorrow. The detective had surely been called down to
find out. And he would come. And he would surely settle matters
here, though not for him.

# SECOND
# HONEYMOON

I'm a big girl. I know what to eat and how much not to drink and how to turn off the light by myself. I can even tuck myself in. Anywhere. Hotels are the same all over. When I'm awake Room Service provides for me. If I can get to sleep I don't give a damn. When I think about it, I have to admit I'm a good thirty-nine.

Considering this, it's always a mistake telling them anything. Especially it's a mistake telling you're divorced. Gives them ideas. You say you're married, you say even you're an old maid, you can get through a job without real trouble. Say you're divorced though, and there is a flurry in futures. Their eyes open for a long second. They see you, and I don't mean only they look at you straight. Because they've been looking whether they know it or not. But they see you really for the first time, with the clothes off. It's sad. Until this, they squinted through a dull yellow film of waste products, a fatty film of scotch and nicotine and long hours on the phone. Now something registers. A spurt of blood washes by and somehow that tired brain collects the scattered parts of itself, the pupils sparkle and stretch and you see yourself held inside there in the blank blackness, held, wavering, in focus. They're thinking, something's here. Something to do. You know what. They're sad. So sad.

"Oh," Harry said.

"Oh, what?" I said.

The duel was on. I'm a rotten fencer, but I was going to try to drag it out, make it as boring as I could. I knew it wouldn't help much because his type of shlep, when it feels winded, which doesn't take long, picks up a two by four and—that's all, sister.

"Oh," he said, "I didn't know. So Chamberlain's your married name?"

"I don't follow," I said.

Don't worry, I followed. There wasn't any need to look up my horoscope in the paper at breakfast tomorrow. I foresaw it: a dank, dreary week was coming up. I admit now I couldn't guess the ending, which was the first bellylaugh I've had in two long years. Laughs haven't been coming this girl's way often these days. The plane was still above the clouds in the blinding January sunlight. The pale blue sky seemed frozen way over to the North Pole and then beyond as far as you could imagine, like a lake that has become one block of ice down to the slimy bottom, where the shadows of a few black old fish are drifting. A real winter day. It seemed impossible to believe that under those clouds so white on top, so gray beneath, there were winds full of hail and snow

whirling down the valleys. That in a few minutes we'd be dropping into them and landing in, in oh this time it was Buffalo.
Gray old Buffalo. Not exactly: it was mostly red brick and grand
mansions that I remembered. From long, long ago. And elm
trees. But that had been in June then, under a warm rain. Now
the elms would be glistening black, and swaying their long drooping naked arms in the wind that tore in off the lakes. If they
hadn't been cut down by now with the blight. We would collect
our stuff, bundle up good and shuffle out into that cold wind, that
wind too clean and clear to endure even for the few minutes'
dash to the terminal. Then a week of slaving and noise and exasperation trying to keep the schedule from collapsing. It was all
ready and waiting for us, on paper. But despite a month's preparation, nothing and nobody ever worked out in this charity business, except on paper. That you could take for granted. First, to
the office: a couple of hours on the phone rounding up the models and trying to locate the wardrobes supposedly shipped on
ahead; starting the fittings, how many sessions of that! Meetings
with local chapter workers from the nearby counties, and the
heads and the backers; the talk, the drinks, the more talk;
straightening out reservations, printers, big and little and fake
donors, ladies, husbands, rabbis, and on the average half the
staff of course screwing up here and screwing up there, forgetting
things and losing things and misplacing what was left so that
yours truly had to be designer, organizer, speaker, and finder of
missing persons and assorted objects of supposedly irreplaceable
value (for this week anyway), all in one. And for what? For
three luncheons, a press preview, a preview showing, and the
awful, the godawful forty-eight hours from Friday to Sunday
night. That weekend! Just getting through the big show, the
banquet and the speeches, the auction from the models, the inter-
views, the pledges, the money, the arguments, the frantic packing

up and paying off, confusion on top of confusions, and racing the clock so as to get to bed with a pot of tea and milk and the *Times,* so as to wake up strong enough to get the final hell out Monday morning and back to the office in New York with the loot and the fake reports. And during it all having to do everything five times to get anything done at all. And on top of all that, here is Harry Cohen going to make himself one big fat pest every time he thought he could squeeze it in. Oh I followed him, I followed him all right.

"What kind of name's that?"

"My husband's."

"Yeah, yeah. So what was it before?"

"Smith."

"Smith? Smith?"

"Smith. Jones. Cook. Reilly. What's the difference?"

"I see how we're going to get along."

"Why get along?"

"Why get along, she says. Start off like that. I ask you."

"You have your work. I have mine. It's enough. Ought to be. It was too damned much to begin with. Buffalo has to come through with a million and a half. That's a lot of Bonds for you to handle."

"I'll bring in two million. More. What's two million? But . . ."

He looked so sour I had to smile. To myself, of course. This is also a man? Another shlep. The thing must be set for rejects. They have been stamping out shleps for years now. Tell him to lay off and he's already crying. I felt cramps coming on too today. Oh God, a week of dexies and phenobarb for this girl. And this shlep too. Oh God.

"But what?" I said.

"But—but it's rough without you making up a funeral atmosphere from it too."

"You want interpersonal relations, Mr. Cohen. I bet that's what you want. Right?"

"It's the thing, they say. Going round. Can't hurt, Mrs. Chamberlain. Can't hurt."

"Can't hurt who?"

"Look, I've had a hard year. Worn to bits. We're starting another one. Maybe we never worked together, but let's cut out the Mrs. Chamberlain, Mr. Cohen stuff right here and now. People will laugh. They expect a team. Give them a team. If not for Israel's sake, for my sake. As of now. All right? Call me Harry, as of now."

"I never heard of you until this morning. Where'd you come from, South Africa?"

"Very funny. If I was from South Africa, I'd be giving, not running my ass off collecting. I've been in the Louisiana office with the sourmash Jews. My wife wanted to come home, so she's got her hot soup from Momma and *I'm* on the road, if you please. With you. So call me Harry."

"Do we *look* like a team?"

"Harry."

"Harry. Do we look like a team? I ask you."

"Don't look. Act. I like to have a bonus."

"Depends what you mean, bonus."

"Bonus, bonus. Whatever it is, that's what I mean."

"So I thought."

"Anyway. So. Here we go, Sarah."

"Sally."

"Sarah, they told me in the office. Are you *all* goy? That I don't believe."

"I went into Wellesley Sally. Sally I came out."

"Well, I thought you looked it, but who knows these days?"

"Looked what?"

"Oh shit, woman. Just cut it out."

"Wash your mouth, Mr. Cohen. My husband was Jewish. Also."

"Chamberlain?"

"Jewish is not the issue. Looked what?"

"Like a Sally. Put out the cigarette. We're going down."

He wasn't the least attractive, not as a man or as a person, Harry Cohen. That was bad enough to begin with. It got worse as it went on. Though he wasn't stupid: he knew how to handle them: that I could see as soon as we hit the office. He was organizing the hell out of them in an hour, and if you have ever tried that in this business, even where you may know the personnel, you know it's impossible. He obviously had a lifetime of experience behind him, maybe ten years' worth. The important thing was, he had been born with the talent in him. The fundraising talent. That's a gift from heaven, and not many have that luck, if you want to look at things from this angle. Me he couldn't organize; after a year on the road I was case-hardened. Besides, (a) I had my own job to do, and (b) I don't like the breath that comes from a nervous stomach. Yet I have to hand it to him, with his blue suit, rumpled from the minute he took it off the rack in the store, and with the greasy shadow under his skin an hour after shaving, and the yellowed white-on-white shirt—he could deliver the goods. I didn't have the strength really to wonder how I would get through this week; I suppose I was exhausted after almost a year of this fashion show in which I'd done twenty cities. Harry was on my track, however; he smelled what he smelled, and there was no stopping him. Energy! Where'd he get it from, that energy? After yelling and screaming and crying and dashing here and there through slushy frozen Buffalo all day, he still had enough energy to keep on after me too. He was in an awful rush; he ran a cold sweat, like a dying man with an erection. No talk, no fun and games, no dinner, no drinks, no flowers, not from his type. He was going to get it plain. Or he'd try. And I was afraid he would get at me. I didn't want him. Who needed him? Who needed anyone? What was it, did I look so sexy? It was impossible anyway, the way I knew I was going to be all week. Not for him. On the way up in the hotel, he was already against me in the corner of the elevator. Luckily, the phone was ringing as soon as the boy opened his door for him. I went into my room next door and called down and got it changed to way down the hall, and with a view of the river, toward the Falls. In the mirror, the shadows under my eyes were purple. I had no time to be worried, because my phone started ringing too.

I don't know how it happened, but he managed to get in the same cab with me three times that day. And then they gave us a car for the week. No doubt his idea. It wasn't enough he would come in and feel the girls as I was trying to get the suits on them right; no, he got the hand going on my leg as soon as the cab rolled off the first afternoon. Thirty-nine, I thought, thirty-nine and do I have to start slapping? God. Close the door, say Sheraton Brock to the driver, and his face bleaches out and the hand comes along, plump, stubby, blackhaired on the fingers. I was so miserable I could hardly light my cigarette, and I had to be slapping that face. It was too much. No discussion, no argument even. Just the hand. The first time I hit him he looked so silly, I thought, now he'll start in reviewing the day's schedule. Which he did, all the way back to the hotel and through the lobby. Only at the elevators was he stopped, my good luck, by Schwartz, the Rochester head, who'd flown in for the week's first work-conference. What was it with these guys? They seemed so automatic, they didn't even say Please or anything. The signal is divorcée.

As soon as you say divorced, they just bore right on in. And if you ask them why, they don't know what you're talking about. Unconscious is what they are.

I got through the week, how I don't remember. Curse and all I got through it. They said the blizzard was due in from Saskatchewan Friday night. About noon the thermometer went up, way up in the thirties, the snow softened and sank dirtily in on itself in the old gardens and on the eaves of the big old mansions. Inside our building it was suffocating work because they never turned down the heat; and it was worse in the hotel where I was setting the things up. Then after lunch the sun disappeared, the sky showed twenty colors of gray and started moving eastward overhead with a rush; I couldn't judge a suite of colors from one minute to the next. We hoped and prayed it wouldn't hit so soon, we had enough to worry us getting the show rehearsed and ready for late afternoon . . . that's all we needed was to get snowed in without having the stars on hand. Two guests of honor were supposed to grace this splasheroo, one from the East and one from the West. From Hollywood a jokester, an old lechering lush everyone in the organization laughed about; from the East an Israeli hero from the high command. A meeting of minds, which is typical Jewish, yes. But if they weren't landed on time, we were busted, and bad. I had to throw Harry out of our dressingroom twice after he was off the phone. Oh he had an excuse to crowd in with us; everything was too hectic by then to play games sending him to the back of the ballroom for the other phone. Anyway the girls were too rushed to cover up for him, even though he bothered the pants off all of us just being there in the way. I know a dressingroom's far too messy and too professional to excite even the amateur slob, but that man was even more than models could tolerate. That gives you an idea. Finally there was a long-distance, and I had to let him back in. Where the hell did he get the time even to be pestering around here, in spite of all

he had to be taking care of that afternoon in Buffalo? This
turned out to be a personal call, and I couldn't help listening to it
all as it dragged on. The room was very small, full of people, me
on my knees basting up a hemline, and there he was pacing with
the phone, arguing and laying on the hand now and then as he
went back and forth behind me.

"What? Today? Come on, you're kidding. Why today? You
can't. Because you can't, that's why. No I don't care. Of course
you're welcome, what do you mean? Sure, sure. No what I'm
saying is the weather. Well it's not here yet. Look, it's five hundred miles, not just around the corner. I know they're fast. But
it's going to be a blizzard. That's why you can't. They'll make it,
sure, they're en route, they're already in probably. So you want
to, so all right. Allrightallrightallright! I'll be tied up, you take
a cab in. It'll be the middle of the show, so don't look for me.
Allright. I hope you don't get diverted to hell and gone account
of the storm. Allrightallright. I'm here, yes. Call the office otherwise. Allright. But don't blame me if you end up—yeahyeahyeah,
you said so, I heard you, what more do you want? Yeah."

When he hung up on that one he was in a wet slump. He
didn't have to say it was Mrs. Cohen: who else can kick a hole
in the middle of the stomach of a shlep like him? Just by being
on the line like that. Just by being.

"You heard?"

"What?" I asked through a mouthful of pins.

"She wants to come up."

"For this show?"

"Show, hell. Niagara Falls! It's freezing, that blizzard is about
to wipe the city, the airlines, the whole goddam state off the map,
and she wants to see Niagara Falls. Honeymoon, she says. You
can't even tell where the sidewalks end, I said, the friggin Falls
are frozen solid, and she wants to come up. A honeymoon! At
her age."

"Where did you take her when you were married?" I said. Not out of curiosity, because who cares?

"Are you kidding? They shipped me out of Fort Ord before I could even take a blood test. Put her on the bus back to Brooklyn and went off to have my honeymoon on Okinawa, with a skin fungus. Yeah, she had her honeymoon: six days on a Greyhound. She got off easy too, let me tell you. It was me that—"

"—You were never romantic, were you?" I said.

"Come on, come on, Sally. Don't give me a headache, will you. I got enough trouble for one lifetime. Romance yet."

He lowered his voice, right there, in the little room with six or seven girls listening, and he whispered, "The truth is—"

"I know," I said, "don't tell me. You're not compatible."

"Compatible? What's that, compatible? Compatible! Who cares, compatible. We don't even like each other enough to know. Twenty years, kids graduating high school already, and we don't even know that much to begin with. That's a good Jewish marriage for you. But allright, if she would rather sleep with Momma, so let her."

"So then," I said, pretending to be involved with that hemline and all, and putting him on hard, "take her on the honeymoon. It's never too late. I mean it. Take her, why don't you, to Niagara Falls. She's coming to see them, so why not? The least you can do, now, I mean. After all."

He stared at me as if I was crazy. Looking at him, I thought for sure he was. Or would be soon. Like everybody else, crazy. He took me by the elbow, got me up and steered me out of the room, and closed the door. The girls were giggling. He wanted the fountain. After swallowing five cups of icewater, he said, "Why are you cunts so cruel?"

"What's got into you, Harry? There's an hour to go, and you're making a scene. An irrelevant scene. Where's your sense of reality?"

"Oh no you don't! Oh yes it is too relevant! You spoiled a perfectly nice week all week playing games with me. Now you put the knife in."

"You don't know what you're talking about. What are you talking about, Harry? What?"

"Take her to Niagara Falls, she says! Take her to Niagara. How could you talk like that after this week? To me yet. You bitch."

"Look, Harry," I said, as quietly as I could say it, because he was working himself up for something. "First of all I don't know what you mean, and I don't care to know. You better believe it, too. I'm working for a living, and I've got kids to put through school. That's enough for me. Second of all, I've *been* to Niagara Falls. Once upon a time. So do yourself a favor and take your wife there. It'll give her some perspective or something. Maybe. Understand? But don't do me any favors, please. And don't expect any. I've had it. *It*."

"Sally," he said, pleading. "Sally!"

"Oh what the hell do you want, Harry Cohen. Stop yelling at me and take a look at yourself will you for a minute?"

All you can do with a man in a state like this is tell him the truth. Though it won't do him any good. He doesn't know what he wants, if he ever knew, or how to get it even if he does. He's in panic. What? Why? How? He just doesn't know. I've seen it up close once. And as I told him, once is enough. Hands, head, feet —all jerking and thrusting out like a scared boy. Or thrusting in. Same thing, in or out; they can't tell the difference anyway. Even if I wanted him, after a year without a man, even if I wanted him even, Harry Cohen, which I don't, I wouldn't let him use me. Why should I? To him, I'm just a hole, maybe only half his size, but big enough to get lost in, or curl up in and sleep it off in. I don't know. And who needs it?

You'd have thought I had slapped him again. He was silent

suddenly. He stepped back, nodding his head a little, as though both up and down agreeing with me about something, and yet sideways also, as though denying he'd heard me. Then he went away somewhere. I had no time to ask him where. We weren't children, and time was short. I went back to the models, who were decent enough not to notice the incident.

Things went off quite well. They usually do, despite everything. The blizzard held off, so that everyone who was coming to the banquet was able to get there in time. Including Mrs. Cohen. Her I met in passing; that is, she showed up by mistake at the dressingroom just before the parade, looking for her husband, who for once wasn't there. She was well-dressed too, for a woman from the Boroughs, though she wore a corsage of gardenias as though she were a local donor. It must be the Southern style, I thought, from her New Orleans years. I sent her round to the main ballroom doors, and told her whom to see to get in. She had certainly made it to Buffalo in record time; it occurred to me that she must already have been at the airport in New York when she'd telephoned. That surprised me. For a Momma's girl that was an independent kind of thing to have done. All for Niagara Falls. That shows what an idea will do. Perhaps honeymoons should be reserved for people who have stayed married, no matter what, for at least twenty years. They could mean something. Niagara Falls!

As a matter of fact, our two guests weren't married either, at present. Lusho from filmland hadn't made a picture in more than twenty years or even done the club circuits: he had so much money he couldn't splurge it all in another quarter century even of his kind of life. A starlet came along with him, as his valet, he said. After the sixth or seventh, he'd had enough of marrying them. The Bond business was just another routine, a tax loss, a timekiller; but he automatically knew enough to keep her well out of sight upstairs away from the rabbis. Since it was probably true, as you hear, that he never showed up with the same chick from one month to the next, it couldn't make much difference for all these people around here would know. She was a nice girl, and sobered up from the bumpy flight in from Chicago. She came out in the hall in her bathrobe, a flowered terrycloth down to the floor, with a towel turbaned round her head and her face creamed, to ask me if she could sit in my room and look out the window for an hour or so, while he made his funnies downstairs. Their rooms were too lonely, she said, and besides she didn't like bridal suites, which he always took, if she wasn't on a honeymoon. She wanted to save them for the real thing someday. She had a cool permanently high school-sophomore California voice and she had never before in her life seen snow. Not much of rain either. A desert girl. The other guest was a widower. Now how did I know that? I asked myself. I suppose, just by looking at him. I watched from the wings, while he spoke at the banquet in that cultured English voice, with under it the sound of Polish, or Serbian, or Rumanian something, and it came to me that he was a widower. Sure enough, five minutes later, in his speech on current affairs etcetera, he said as much. This was the man, it turned out, who'd gone ashore and snatched Eichmann out of Argentina. He was the captain of that commando squad, I guess it would have been called. He was sorry, he said, only that his wife had not survived the deportations from Hungary; he was sorry that he only had had the miserable satisfaction of seeing Eichmann at last lying in the rubber boat as they rowed back to the submarine that night. It took a strong man like that, I thought, to have had the sheer self-restraint not to have smashed his face in there and then in the bottom of the boat. He was marvelous. Harry had been right, I could see: we would get more than two million in Bonds out of this town, no matter what the weather was. The Captain was a man to admire. What a pity, I thought, that the way these affairs usually go, I would have to wait till the bitter, rushed end to get to have a drink with him. It came sooner than that, though there was hardly enough of it. Meanwhile, the fat donors' wives were slavering at him; I looked out over the ballroom and saw the chins uplifted, the jeweled hands stroking the throats or touching the diamond and pearl necklaces. No, I was by no means the only one there that admired a man. Of course they had a right to him; they had paid for him, and they were going to shell out plenty more. That started me laughing. My usual luck: I was watching the hero from backstage: they were never sent for me. Well. He'd get the shekels out of cold old Buffalo, and they'd be used to catch a little more snow-water from the mountains of Syria, wherever that is. Eichmann's captor. What did Buffalo know about Eichmann, even in retrospect? Well, he was telling them enough to make them come across with lots of Bonds. They owed him. Something for the survivors, as long as it doesn't cost too much, and gathers good interest. Something. If we could all have a chance to lay hands on the Eichmanns of this world, there wouldn't be judges enough to listen. He was *also* an organizer, Eichmann.

It all went well, as I said: pledges starting falling with the snow. It would be a big hit. They wanted to place orders on everything we had, samples, used stock, patterns, etcetera. This weekend we would be overrun. Which was really just as well, considering what a lousy town it is. If you stop to let yourself think about them, they're all pretty lousy. About two in the morning, it was snowing like Niagara. There was no wind anymore, only a muffled dark sighing of great soft flakes drifting down so thickly that the next lamppost seemed like a dim candle far off. The cars parked in the streets had disappeared nearly from sight, and looked like odd lumps or even igloos here and there. When the plow went by, it covered them over, and it had barely gone before the streets filled in again with that heavy snow. My Cap-

tain came from the bar and asked me for a walk in that marvelous weather. I had only a pair of plastic rainboots with me,
but I'd have gone with him even if I'd been wearing just my
backless shoes. On the way past the crowded lounge, I saw Harry
busily talking it up with some Assistant City Manager or other;
Harry's eyes never looked at the person he was talking to because
he was always on the make for the next higher-up. When he saw
us going out, his jaw dropped. Mrs. Cohen was standing beside
them clutching a red patent bag and smiling foolish and vacant
at the Assistant City Manager, and feeling I suppose that she
didn't belong there with her husband working so hard at that
boring conversation. She looked at me and then at Harry; her
smile closed, and she said something that must have been so irrelevant that both of them looked at her stupidly. Harry gave a
little lurch as though to walk away, but remembered that he was
working. I was relieved to get out at last into the silent dark
world of the soft blizzard, and took the Captain's arm going
through the doors.

We returned about half an hour later, having struggled as far
as we could stand in the cold, and then struggled back. Captain
never said a word, oddly enough; we just held each other tight by
the arms and took a wonderful walk, pure and simple. We came
into the now-emptied lobby, stomping and laughing; our faces
were snowed in too. Upstairs in my room I changed as fast as I
could and got into bed shivering. There was a knock.

"Go to sleep, Harry," I said.

"Listen, Sally."

"What will your wife think?" I asked from under the covers.

"Listen," he said, "listen."

I sat up. I was tired, and getting angry.

"Are you going away or not!"

"Please, I need some papers. They must be in your room."

I got up, unlocked the door, ran back to bed. He came in, dressed as usual, messy tie and all. There was a lot of the office stuff we kept in my room.

"You know it's past three?"

"Yeahyeah," he said, and began rummaging here and there like a maniac in the boxes. I guess he did need something or other. "Where'd you go?" he said to the wall.

"Out."

"In this weather? You crazy? You need Buffalo clothes for this weather, not party clothes."

"I'm sleeping, Harry. Leave me alone."

He got what he'd come for, but still wasn't on his way. I felt a little sick when he sat himself down on the bed.

"Sally," he began again in that miserable way.

"Make it short, Harry, I'm dropping off now . . . one . . . two . . . three . . ."

"I have to talk to you."

"Some other time. It will keep. Go warm up your wife, will you."

"She's asleep anyway. Three drinks and she's snoring for good. Doesn't know what to say in business anyhow."

"What business? This is not business."

"I mean downstairs, with the City Hall. Listen. Did he make a pass at you?"

"Oh now, Harry, you are sick."

"I asked you a plain question, didn't I?"

I was really surprised. The shlep was jealous because I had gone for a walk in the snow with the Captain! I couldn't help it, I started laughing and couldn't stop. I had to put my face into the pillow to keep it quieter, but I couldn't stop the laughing. He didn't say anything, and when I caught my breath and saw his face filling up with tears, I stopped.

"You got what you came for, Harry, so go to sleep. Don't make
a fool of yourself. Please."

"I'm sorry, Sally, but . . . I don't know. I must be drunk."

"Goodnight," I said again, "goodnight."

He sighed and went out carrying the papers he'd said he
needed so badly as if he meant to throw them in the first waste-
basket down the hall. I was too tired to get up and lock the door.
I knew he wouldn't come back. But if he went on like this there
was bound to be some mess round here.

The snow went on pouring down its gray and white silence all
the next morning till after the luncheon, but things rolled on;
nothing could stop the pace of this sort of weekend extravaganza.
These Northern towns are set up for this weather anyway, with
their gigantic orange plows moving night and day everywhere
scooping out the roads, and people carrying a hundred pounds
of clothes on their backs, and their cars equipped with big tires
and chains and antifreeze down to 65-below. Things may move
a little more quietly but they don't stop moving. And it was beautiful when the sun came out in the afternoon and the wind
stopped and the temperature sank to zero: the world was clean
and white, buried under three feet of snow. From my window at
the top of the hotel, I could see for miles now across the soft
white world buried under the glaring snow. Even the bare black
trees were etched with snow, and the dark woods near the Falls
were like a great thicket in a miniature forest in a Dutch paint-
ing. From Niagara came a vast mist rising like steam from the
bottom lake of Hell, a sparkling mist full of ice crystals; and the
roar itself seemed muted in the mute world of snow. I had about
two minutes to take it in, dressing madly again for the big gen-
eral-public show. I'd not had a chance all day to be worrying
about Harry Cohen or Mrs. Cohen or anyone. For that I was
grateful. Previews are one thing, the big show another.

That too went off better than we all hoped, and despite the storm there was a more than full house. About one in the morning, as the girls were putting their clothes on and I was just sitting down for a solid drink and a quiet smoke with Lusho and his baby in the corner of my dressingroom, in barges Harry with the Mrs. He was semidelirious with success: we'd made close to three million. Three million! He had a bottle of scotch under his arm: we were going to celebrate. Paper cups all around, ice and soda, and we sang a song. Lusho started a string of dirty stories about Las Vegas and we were about to have a good time just relaxing. There was a knock on the door: my Captain. We brought him in, and I made room beside me on the vanity bench. The Mrs. was watching Harry and I made sure not to give him even a light. I don't want to imagine their life together. Then the Captain had a bright idea—Niagara Falls. He'd never seen Niagara Falls. Would I go with him? Who was for a second honeymoon? Mrs. Cohen raised her hand first, Miss Lower San Berdoo Valley hers, and Mr. Palm Springs said sure why not. I didn't feel up to that, and Harry said he had too much straightening things out and besides it was meshuggah to go in this weather. But I didn't want to spoil the Captain's idea: we owed him it, to say the least. All right, we'd go. That made a sixsome, and away we went. Had I known how long we would be gone! Somehow we managed to make the complete circuit: over to the Canadian side, on the trail to the Falls, over the snowed-in Promenade that was all lit up in the arctic night by spotlights, and into a restaurant in a woodsy motel for drinks and more drinks and coffee, Lusho telling his tales of Las Vegas nights all the way with his hands working for warmth inside the girl's coat. We got stuck in a drift on the way over, and stuck again, of course, on the return, only badly stuck the second time: it took us an hour of pushing and hauling and burning tires to get the damned car out on the road again. Mrs. Cohen slipped and fell down hard pushing the car beside me and skinned her knees open and tore her stockings to bloody shreds. She was crying all the whole way back as we slid along. I pitied her. Harry couldn't drive a car in snow worth a damn, and Lusho didn't drive from way back. The Captain tried his hand at the wheel, but being a sailor from the Negev he didn't do much better with that pushbutton contraption. A mess. What can you do, starting off tired and hilarious and half-looped, if you're on an unplanned second honeymoon in a crowd of strangers? We were surely silly to have tried it, of course, since we weren't kids and belonged in bed asleep. But Niagara Falls is Niagara Falls. I was useless all along too, because I felt drunk as hell by the time we skidded off into the snowbank the second time. I was laughing because I was remembering, all too well, how twenty years ago I'd been up all night seeing Niagara, rather somewhere near Niagara, I mean, fixing a tire because a drunken man was sleeping it off in the back seat of a honeymoon car. Ridiculous things happen. Do they have to repeat themselves?

By six we were back at the hotel. So much for Niagara Falls! So said my Captain, who had a plane to catch back to Washington at nine. Instead of going to bed, we went up to the honeymoon suite of Mr. Hollywoodland and his Daughter. That's what he was calling her by then, Datter. It tickled them both, at least. He never stopped putting down the sauce, but never. With his little wizened face, tanned by the winter sun of the Palm Desert, and his eyes buried in cracks of continual jesting, he seemed like a perpetual liquor and sex gadget. Cutie didn't care what he did, where or when. She finally dropped off with her head on his lap. My Captain rose about eight-thirty, still cool and formal and very Israeli, I mean Polish-Rumanian-Serbo-English, kissed me on the cheeks, shook my hand and said Shalom Shalom. Next year in Jerusalem. Why not? Oh sure, I said. Lusho wanted to go on telling his jokes and holding out his glass for me to fill, but I had to get into my bed for a nap, or I'd never get to clean up downstairs by night at all; he could fill his own glass and talk to it—he'd be at it till he died at eighty anyhow. As far as Harry Cohen was concerned, I didn't give him another thought. He should have had enough to go off and keep himself busy with today. Besides, his wife's honeymoon, I mean. Considering everything, I guessed I'd gotten through the week safe enough.

Was I wrong! I'd been asleep an hour maybe, when the phone rang. Harry. Whispering at me from the other end. He must have been in his room. He wanted to get some more files that he said he needed to finish up for New York. He said. Later, I told him, I'm sleeping it off now. No, he insisted, *his* reports couldn't wait. It was plausible. Half dead, I got up, unlocked my door, and went right back to sleep. There was his knock, his shlep knock. I shut my eyes and sank into the haze. It wasn't deep enough, and vaguely I heard him opening and closing the door. I heard him turn the latch too. That I didn't like. He rustled round the boxes for a long while. Then it was too quiet. I sort of opened one eye, and saw him standing looking down at me. He was in his pajamas, and wore a creased maroon bathrobe of some ugly rayon. Imagine him, at that cold Sunday morning hour, after all of yesterday and last night, with that patchy stubble and puffy white skin, the bags under his eyes, with his narrow shoulders and slack chest that was like a pair of flabby breasts, and that dropping kind of paunch a man like that carries round with him.

"You're up. So talk to me. Sally?"

"I'm dying. I've been on my second honeymoon, Harry, and it was a bust. Don't take a group tour, Harry. Remember. Now let me sleep it off."

"You've been with that hero all this time, haven't you? Well?"

"Go away, go far away."

"I said, you've been with him?"

"What of it?" I said. Let him choke himself, I thought. He's just too much. "You want to sue me for desertion, Harry?"

"I had a better right than him. What's he? Some refugee? So they forgot to gas him, and he ends up in the army, so you have to go crazy? For a uniform?"

"What uniform? Anyway, he's navy, no, Marines." This was getting funny now. Was I awake, really?

"Navy, Marines. Don't crap me. He comes over here to show off what a hero he is. What does he get for it? Two hundred a month? Big hero."

"Harry, you're not mere nuts, you're getting stupider by the minute."

"I mean it, Sally. Seriously, what is he? I schedule guys like him a dime a dozen all year. And I get one thousand per month plus expenses, and you look at him like he saved the Jews from Hitler. Where's your seychl? Without me and the others like me, they'd all be nowhere by now. But nowhere. Don't be such a sucker for the uniform, is all I'm saying."

"You got what you want in here, Harry? Beat it. You make me sick. I never heard such— Listen, go on back to your wife, will you. I don't want a scene over you. Of all people."

"My wife's sleeping as usual. She's happy. She saw her Niagara and serves her right if she froze her ass off. She asked for it. Next time she should only fall in!"

I started laughing then. I couldn't help laughing. He was so confused. What could I do but laugh at him? It made him angrier.

"Don't laugh," he said.

"What should I do, cry for you?"

"Don't laugh, Sally. Listen . . . I'm unhappy. I'm unhappy, Sally."

I laughed anyway. It was too much. I'm unhappy, Sally. Oh my god, it was funny. "You're unhappy? You're unhappy, Harry? You're telling me the news: you're unhappy? Don't make me laugh anymore. Oh, oh, my stomach hurts."

"You bitch, I'll kill you, so help me," he said, grinding his teeth. "I swear I'll kill you!"

"You? You?" I laughed harder. It was a mistake, in spades, but I couldn't stop myself anymore.

The next thing I knew, he had flung the box of papers aside and was on me in the bed, beating at me with his soft fists like a child, and sobbing and moaning and thrashing and cursing. I covered myself with my arms as best as I could, but he caught me a few times in the chest and belly anyhow. For a while I thought he had me there. It didn't stop my laughter even then. Finally, he lay still, half on me, and stopped the nonsense. Poor bastard, I thought. Poor bastard. Can't even rape a tired woman who's undressed and already in her bed.

"There, there," I said to him, patting the fat on the back of his neck. "There, there. Don't feel so bad. You raised three million bucks yesterday. They'll have a nice bonus waiting."

"To hell with it," he mumbled into my armpit. "I don't give a damn."

"Look, Harryboy," I said, and started to raise him off me, "while you still have a little time and strength, why don't you go back to your room and be nice to your wife, will you?"

"It's no use, I can't," he said.

"What do you mean you can't? A woman's a woman. I don't want you in here anymore."

"I can't, I can't," he said very low. Heavily, he got up then, and his glance went down, embarrassed. There was a wet stain on my nightgown. He shrugged. "You are all the same, you bitches."

I was laughing again. "So that's our second honeymoon? Oh you pig, Harry Cohen, you pig! Three million bucks you can raise, Harry Cohen, but nothing else. Not even at Niagara Falls. You had me worried there all week, you slob, you really did," I said. "Oh get out of here, get out, get out!"

And I jumped out of bed then, I must have sounded like a nut to him the way I was laughing, judging from the expression of sheer fright on his face. Putting my hands on his belly, I shoved him back toward the door. He let himself be pushed that way, and right on out in the hall. There he stood, holding himself protectively, as if he thought I was going to kick him one too. And what do you think he said, before I shut the door in his face and locked it?

He said, "I'm sorry, Sally. I'm sorry."

Now I ask you, what can you do with shleps like that?

# AN EGYPTIAN
# BONDAGE

I had not gone to the movies in three years. Saturday morning my mother gave me my allowance, and off I trotted with the kids, getting as far as the Palace Delicatessen where we bolted hotdogs *with,* plates of french-fries, cole-slaw, sour pickles dipped in that special *deli* mustard, and swilled Dr. Brown's Sunray Celery Tonic. But I never bought my ticket. In the winter, I hung about the lobby, to keep warm, reading the garish coming-attractions posters, each in its glassed-in shrine lit up by hidden, colored, 10-watt bulbs: three posters on the right, three on the left. I looked at the glossy, cornily-posed stills of the current movies over and over again, and listened to the uproar of a million kids there in the darkness beyond the swinging bronzed doors. I heard their silly giggling with the zany-sounding cartoons, and their hushings of each other as the creepy music that introduced the chapter came on—twenty weeks of Flash Gordon crackling and zooming and disintegrating his way through outer space, twenty weeks of Charlie Chan against the Spider Men of the Yellow Tong, twenty weeks of The Shadow pitting his hypnotic guile against the clanking Master Robots, twenty weeks of Tarzan hallooing his leopards and apes on the Zombie Island . . . and then the meaningless music and speech of the two feature films: agonized yells, shots, blasts of TNT, mutterings and sighing, crisp commands, screams and pleading female voices. Four long hours I mooched around there, bored to nausea, but I never went in. And in the sweltering, humid light of July and August, I used to forsake the shade of the marquee and the cool, still lobby to lope sweating back to the hideout in our ash-heaped, weed-choked lots, gather stones for an hour and throw them steadily at the tinny billboards for the next two hours—crang crangcrung!—without stopping or breaking the beat. It was awful. And after they came out to have to listen to the grinding, point-by-point discussion of the show! "Remember when Dr. Zitho takes out the special needle and sticks it in his throat?" "Yow! and the water starts pouring in and he can't get out and they took Janie on the other ship and there's a time bomb on the engine and . . ." "Suppose he shoots and he doesn't know the Black Squad loaded it with spoiled dum-dums?" "Yow!" and "Yeah! Yeah!" and "Yow!"

Those years after ten are tedious; whatever helps them pass quickly is a pure gift to be grateful for. Yet if I hadn't taken to the delights of the movies, I had a good reason. It wasn't because I was saving quarters for anything, because, conscientiously, I spent them here and there, dragging out those long afternoons with candy and ice cream; and I was careful not to do anything useful, like reading the comic books my gang deposited with me

out of compassion at the ticket-taker's stand. No—I was testing
my will power. So, while the others rioted like Eastern flowers in
California gardens, I shriveled in monotonous passion, petrified
by the struggle between will and fierce desire which raged in renewed spasm each Saturday. Of course I did not know that the
regular small victory of my ethical will sapped my foundation,
bringing me that much closer to the defeat I dreaded. Being only
an ungrown boy, I had no fiber to support my purpose; so that
by the end of the third year I was worn out and rotten. And considering that except for the vow to resist I'd made long ago I had
no reason to carry stubbornly on, how had I been able to keep
it up?

My strength was derived from the last movie I had seen: *The
Cat People,* a shadowy film created in the blackness of the heart.
In the first of my minatory images, Simone Simon sat in her bathroom, wearing a nightrobe which fell away from long thighs as
she deftly raised a crossed leg, leaned forward and rolled the other
stocking off on her cool, slim fingers; then the robe cast itself to
the floor as she sank into her tub, tilted back her head of blonde
curls, and dropped into a tranced sleep. Then, there was a frightened man who wore a trenchcoat; his character was obscured to
me by the crush hat brimmed over his eyes as he hastened along
rain-dripping wet streets: what had he done to Simone Simon?
And the grand woman with the eyes of a lynx, who was she? And
the woman in a fur coat, who walked through the night, flanked
by a high wall of squarecut stone blocks . . . she began to scurry
on her high heels, and each time she emerged into the foggy zone
of a streetlamp she was terribly anxious; then there was an un-
earthly yowl and she ran, scared: but it was hopeless, for above
her, behind her, gliding on top of the wall, was a rippling shadow
—the silent, sleek, bestial power of a black panther stalking its
human prey. That was what I remembered, and I was no longer
certain it was at all correctly remembered; these scenes elaborated

themselves infinitely in my fantasy. In reviewing their permutations and combinations when they came again and again harrowing my heart, I could not discover whether good or evil won out. Nevertheless, during my three years' continence these images gave me the meager triumph of having kept my vow; for wretchedly puerile though they were, they suggested enough about the world. Such were the motives, they hinted, behind the doors bolted at midnight, an automatic tucked beneath a pillow or laid handy in the night-table drawer—and for the terrors of my own suffering sleep. By refraining from those delirious Saturdays of the others, I pursued purity and preserved the native innocence from which I believed the final, lasting strength might some day come. Had I not been too young for words, I could have expressed the gist of my foolish wisdom by an inspiriting motto such as, *To remain free, keep out the truth.*

*Gone With the Wind* broke me. As a birthday treat, my parents had me wash, dressed me in my first real suit—long pants and jacket of navy blue serge, starched white shirt with ready-made clip-on tie of jaunty red plaid—took me into the steaming subways, dined me downtown somewhere on dead steak and dry potatoes, stood me with them for an hour or more in a line stretching clear around Rockefeller Center under the grilling August sun, and paid theater prices for seats in the Radio City Music Hall. And I grumbled at them the whole way, fearing this exception to my record which I had let them tempt and force me into for their sake, so that they should be pleased to celebrate my birthday . . . until we were inside. The wealth of that lobby! Wurlitzer music floating like perfume in its vastitude; the mottled, creamy marbles; that piled carpeting; those braid-encrusted epauletted ushers, fit to be chosen for the President's Honor Guardians; and the breathing silence of thousands of people waiting rapturously in the violet air that suffused its immeasurable spaces before the film went on—that violet, premonitory glow which was neither glimmering dusk nor yet dreamful dark. Then color, beauty and color! Scarlett and Rhett, Ashley and Melanie: stormy love and stormful anger, melancholy torment of noble impetuosity, and the technicolored doom of Atlanta in holocaust. I believed it. That waste of riches and disgrace of manners I could never have imagined. It was a revelation of the possibility of human grandeur so terrific that my laborious, primitive disciplines cracked before it: the waters of life began to press, to seep through and wash out the crude, handpacked mortar; in an instant the last frantically thrown bags of sand and stones were swept away. I buckled and crumbled, and the seas of life flooded raging over the parching, deserted lots of my old self. And there I sat, stiff, quiet, drowning in my virgin tears.

That September the promised "adventure" of high school began. I was not deceived into eagerness by the exhortations of my friends and their teachers. While those mundane children exchanged their money for outfits for the crass mind—the clerical tools of scholarship like paper, bookcovers, briefcases, notebooks, pencils, pens, erasers, ink—and outfits for the unfledged body —combination locks, sneakers, T-shirts, shorts, socks, soap—I grudgingly gave as little as I could for the shoddiest stuff: all the rest I gladly spent on the movies, for the good of my soul. I walked to school: I went without lunch, without pie, without sodas. Yet, though I skimped and I scamped and I scavenged, I couldn't scrabble together enough to see more than three shows a week. How I bemoaned my folly and extravagance in not having saved three years' worth of Saturday quarters: forty dollars in tickets converted into unwanted crummy candy and crammed down my choking, ascetic throat! I was so despondent over the thought of my lamentable misled former life that it never occurred to me that even if I had used the money then as I now knew I should have, I would not be better off. Instead, I accused myself: You brainless, you! Why didn't you go? Because you didn't want to go and you ate to keep from being tempted to go! But why didn't you want to go? I talked to myself in this confusing circle for hours as I went from class to class, grinding my teeth absurdly in frustration. Time! I cried, Time is passing every minute! Each day without a movie was another void in my life, now that going to movies was not idle distraction but commitment to wonders of experience beyond my ken, vistas of superior knowledge that opened, perhaps, on a superior mode of life. I was appalled by the thought of looking back some year to a life full of empty holes in its weeks. I desired only to give myself over to the movies, to be so wholly possessed by them that I could feel their excess oozing from the pores in my stretched hide. I knew that to be free to enter the rare, special darkness of the theater, I must cleanse myself of frivolous concerns; so I practiced preparing myself for the proper state by withdrawing attention from the six irrelevant waking hours spent in school and the three vacant afternoons a week I suffered from due to poverty, not to mention the energy frittered away on homework, dressing, undressing, washing, eating, basketball, sleep. Finally, since there was only one way to have money for those afternoons, I began to think of a part-time job. Part time! If I got a job, where then would be my time? The logic of my situation, when I sat down to consider elementary dilemmas in the dark corner of our simple, homely livingroom, made me pant and groan. However, it had to be faced. So I sold myself, quickly and shamelessly, to Mr. E. Golden, of the Golden Pharmacy under the El, across the street from the RKO Royal, around the corner from the Loew's Imperial.

The moment I saw this man, I hated him. He was bald, obese, pasty yellow, stubble-faced. He had thick bifocal lenses that caught the light in two places. His shapeless tie was askew on a dirty white-on-white shirt with a pattern of fleurdelis; his cuffs were pulled up on his hairy arms to his elephant-wrinkled elbows. His chronic expression was a sickeningly knowledgeable smile, and he looked out at the world over his eyeglasses. His hands were dirty too, lying on the scratched glass counter and folding each other constantly or dealing out an infinitude of sundries, and taking in money, money, money. He never raised his voice, not in conversation, not in argument; but spoke questioningly at you like a rabbi. Your answers never fooled him, it seemed. I hated him as I sidled into the Golden Pharmacy and saw him standing by the cash register, pressing his pearl-buttoned, gray-smeared belly against the counter, hated him as I asked for the job delivering prescriptions and making myself "general handy" about the store, packing, unpacking, packaging, rummaging, sorting, sweeping—all for a quarter an hour, plus tips if any. I got the job right then—"But will you work good, sonny?"—and didn't learn till the end of the week why it was open: not a kid in the neighborhood would work for Golden the miser, the slavedriver, the taskmaster. I think the sort of nicknames he was given in the scrounging world of rabble boys, such as goldgrabber, kidkiller, miserymaniac, poisonpounder, soulsucker, show that he was held in awe as though he radiated occult might or perhaps an uncanny misery, even if contrary to the local superstition his piggish eyes were both the same color: gray, watery oil sloshing behind his steelrimmed spectacles. Those popular names didn't matter to me, for I was going my own way, impervious to rumor and aura and history. Besides, the Golden Pharmacy was located on a rich, exciting corner, a crossroads of that section of the Bronx; everything in the world, almost, passed by or took place before its open door or was reflected in its Ex-Lax and Feen-a-mint tattooed windows. Surely it was worth any boy's time just to be there, legitimately, to see and to learn while sweeping the sidewalk with careless industry, to snatch moments for meditation while wrapping sanitary napkins in anonymous blue paper for quick sale, and lettering them K-large, K-regular, K-small, and M-small, M-regular, M-large?

I went briskly to work for him. Again, in my proud, contrary way I was crazy to succeed where it could never even have occurred to the others. My ferocious addiction, far from the saturation point that marks the last stage in the descent to enlightenment of the lucky (or damned) person, made me that rarity, an enthusiastic slave. I hoped that by the end of the first week I might win the approval from Mr. Golden necessary to the maintenance of my life. Though he was of course only a means to my end, as any master is for his slave, I hoped to betray him into a humane generosity so that he would deal with me gently, benevolently. And I used the most obvious means to propitiate this stolid man: my goodness. But he only grunted like a sleeping crocodile and never commented on my performance. No matter how many cartons I wrestled from the pavement outside, heaved between the showcases, around the chaos of boxes, bottles and brooms back of his prescription counter, down the narrow dangerous cellar steps, and dismantled, unwrapped, sorted, washing their contents and drying and arranging them on the grimy storage shelves in his tomb-lit basement; no matter how quick I was, how neat and tireless; no matter how fast I galloped delivering pills, syrupy nostrums and custom-made medicines and beauty formulas, returning with my cheeks glowing in a fever of self-congratulation (and a cold sweat drying on my spine), he only grunted, neither yes nor no. He would glance expressionlessly at me over his glinting bifocals as he went on hieratically wrapping a package precise and tight in the way he alone knew: folding the blue paper, creasing it straight and sharp with a stroke of the long, black-nailed, wicked index finger, pulling out the green string that unrolled endlessly from the spool beneath the counter and winding it once-twice to the right, once-twice to the

left, taking an extra length and twisting it around one pinky,
around the other, pulling it taut, giving it a preliminary pflick,
once! pflick, twice! and—snap! breaking it on the third, the real
pull, and then unconsciously tying the ends with some rapid
passes and twirls that came out as inviolable knots. Well, that was
the way he was—inscrutable. I could not guess whether he was
amazed, suspicious, or downright resentful of the superb way I
was working out; he only grunted and turned to his ceaseless
argumentative deliberations, his quarrels and explanations with
cosmetics salesmen, drug and sundries jobbers, and cranky grand-
mothers who detailed every symptom down to their slightest private twitchings, and complained about the behavior of whatever
limb, nerve, or organ he was helping them treat.

Sometimes I thought he waited maliciously for the foolish
freckly grin I couldn't hold back which announced that some
chore had been accomplished beyond his most liberal expecta-
tions, to say "Nu, sonny, next! Take these pills to Mrs. Katz on
Eastchester Avenue. Quick quick! They're for her husband, he's
got heart trouble, he's sick, he might die if you don't come soon.
Here's change for ten dollars—" Bing! the cash register opens,
there is the accurate, unhurryable counting out, and bang! the
drawer is thrown shut—"and you don't need carfare, it's only
ten blocks. And come back right away, I got one for the other
side of the park." And when I'd climbed the fifth flight and stood
gasping before that unidentified door which was scratched by
penknives with hearts and initials and swastikas Xed-out but re-
engraved, Mrs. Katz would invariably be one of those late middle-aged crones who called out, "Who's there?" quaveringly
from a remote cubicle at the end of her echoing, dank apartment.
Out of breath, embarrassed by my saving presence at the scene
of some typically incurable human emergency, I'd yell, garbling
the words to save Mrs. Katz from the curiosity of her pitying
neighbors, "It's me, the druggist boy."

"Yeh? What do you want?"

I would not answer again because I despised Mrs. Katz. I could hear her come shuffling in her soggy, filthy mules, nastily, rheumatically along the empty linoleum-floored hall. She would fumble at the peephole; then her invisible face would put its rancorous bleary pupil to it. But I would be too close for her to see more than another staring eye. A little scared, maybe, Mrs. Katz would say again, "Who is it?"

Now I stepped back and declared in a voice ringing with offended simplicity, "It's only me, from the Golden Pharmacy!"

And then, Mrs. Katz changed, instantaneously, from a defenseless creature into an abused, sorrowful, wailing, almost possessed mourner at a funeral which had not yet occurred, and might not for years. "Oi! Weh! The medicine. Oi! Weh! God help me, how long you take. Oi, weh! You heartless! We're sick, dying, you bastards! Oi, weh!" And then she would fumble at the chain of the police lock in the gloom of her unlighted foyer, and then the doorlatch's lock; she would give a pull and discover she'd double-locked the police lock, so then that would be turned two or three times, opening and shutting the baffling cranky bolt. At last, the door would give, only a crack, and this Mrs. Katz would snatch her faded, greasy, flower-quilted housecoat to her in miserable modesty, having revealed the top of her gray breast, that drawn-down dug—why wasn't she ever dressed? and strike the gray hank of iron hair back from her temple, and look bleakly out at this sleetsparkling kid in his shiny, new, belted and fur-collared leather mackintosh, who stood panting with fatigue and impatience to be gone again (but first to impersonate the cherub of mercy and salvation himself so that he would be tipped, a quarter maybe, a half-dollar even—who knew?). And now, having forgotten the tedious process of her approach and opening to my summons, she would say, "Yeh? What is it?"

Unctuously then, I would resume our ritual, "I'm Mr. Gold-

en's boy. With the prescription for Mr. Katz. It's the rush order
. . . I think?"

"You're Golden's boy?"

"Yeah, the new boy. I deliver now."

"Yeh? Okay. So how much is it?"

"Five-eighty-three. It says so here on the box."

"Oi, weh! Five-eighty-three! Robber! Murder! He should
drop dead from cancer. It should eat your heart, Golden, you
thief!"

That was the payoff; that, I knew, was the end of my four-bit
dream, my vain hope to cash in on Mrs. Katz's gratitude, her
surge of Old World, courteously embroidered thanksgiving for
my miraculous messengership. Didn't she realize how far I had
come?

"You got change from ten, sonny?"

I would hand the prescription to her, avoiding the touch of
those raspy, dry fingers, and reach into my mackintosh's secret
zipper pocket for the change. Still painfully shuffling, Mrs. Katz
would disappear back into her vague, staled, chickensoupy apartment, returning with a crumpled ten; she would take my four-
seventeen and put it all into a worn, leather snap purse, and then
wait in doubt while I stood there unmoving, shaming her. An
awkward silence, until with a sly smile she said, "Oi, weh! Here's
for you, boy. A tip." Into my open, humiliated palm, she would
drop, first the two pennies, and next, as with all my power I
wished the dime away from her—at least that dime—she fished
around in the purse (oh I knew she'd put the change away first
so that she'd be forcing herself, so full of virtue, to give me her
own money instead of permitting me to keep a decent portion of
my change in my own hands), and inevitably not the dime but
the nickel would be the award. And then I squeezed out a faint
"Thank you very much indeed, Mrs. Katz" over my shoulder as
I receded down the stairwell, hotly cursing her under my breath,

her purse, her pains, her medicine, and cursing poor Mr. Katz too, whom surely she and Golden were conspiring to kill.

It was falling into November. The sooty, chilling November rain of sleet drifted through the light of the streetlamps as I stumbled back the more than ten blocks to the Golden Pharmacy through the emptied five-o'clock streets and over the black burnt-over lots. My shoes were stiff with damp, shriveling cold that broke the seams; my heels would have rubbed through my socks by now, blisters would have formed, broken, and been scarified into raw, red half-dollars of morbidity.

But I stuck to it, obstinate. Lacking any evidence whatsoever, I'd found it the more necessary to convince myself I'd proved indispensable, a wonder worker, and that Mr. Golden not only needed me but by now wanted me. It seemed to me that his business had picked up because my delivery was so accurate and prompt, that people were telling their friends to come to the Golden Pharmacy, and even bought more prescriptions than the doctors ordered, just so I could arrive grinning at their doors. How could it be otherwise? It didn't occur to me that winter made them sick. Also, Golden could never have expected to get so much out of a boy for a mere quarter of a dollar an hour: surely he would give me a raise soon? Naturally I should not ask him. How would I bring it up? He might easily wax wrathful and fire me like a shot; that was the risk I couldn't afford. Every week, just before the dramatic moment at ten o'clock on Saturday night when my six dollars and twenty-five cents was due, I fretted myself into a state of hope mingled with indignation: hope that he could count out the extra dollar-twenty-five bounty I deserved, and indignation in my fantasy that I would have the courage to blurt out my demand for a nickel an hour more in wages and be gallingly rejected. Upon which, spontaneously of course, I should tell him what a rat he was, maybe kick a hole in the sliding glass door of the vitamin cabinet and—be arrested,

sent to jail?—and quit. I quit! Do you hear me? Do you understand me, Mr. Golden? I quit! Naturally, it never happened that
way.

And Sundays I brooded all morning, standing beneath my
mother's wet, dripping wash in the bathroom, and glowering at
the mirror where I saw myself, the original yellow yellow. But in
the afternoon I soothed my anguish in the dark, people-packed
Sunday Matinee (expensive!) movies to which I went—across
the Bronx by taxi—in the immense Counter-Reformation cathe-
dral known as the Loew's Paradise. There, the mezzanine lobby
was a way station full of marble alcoves and chambers furnished
with gilded baroque furniture for those who loitered between the
blurred throngs and gray traffic of the Grand Concourse and the
ecstasy within; there, the bathrooms were Venetian delights, little
palaces wherein one was privileged to go; there, inside, far above,
the constellations moved forever past a pale Cyprian horn of
moon, and simulated clouds drifted always under that deeply
vaulted though fake sky, and far down below, the fat seats slid
back and forth instead of tilting up, the backs reclining in rhythm
with the seats. There in that house of worship I melted in filial
gratitude toward the impossible Mr. Golden, and soon forgave
him, and easily forgot him.

After two months of this strenuous equilibrium between spiritual debauch and the labor of wresting a meager living from
Golden's killing schedules, lung and limb became adapted and I
knew I could take it.

December lowered on New York, horrid with clinkered slush
and sewers stuffed with polluted snow. In the gutters at corners,
scrapings and chippings of sidewalk ice floated in two or three
inches of black, sludgy, freezing water. The northeast wind blew
virulent in your face and whistled agues down your back at turn-
ings and through the open spaces, and you went in and out of
this marrow-cracking weather, from drowning cold to dry over-

heated hallways and apartments where people had only to hawk
once and you came down with shakes, dragged in an hour from
prime strength into the suicidal gloominess of the flu. That is how
New York's exasperating winter has always gone; but that year I
was impervious to mere weather and impermeable to the invisible
creatures of the blast. As in a plague, people fell away with one
pharyngo-bronchial thing and another; yet I kept moving, god-
linglike, twin to the cardboard Hermes displayed in our store
window who bounced eternally oscillant back and forth, driven
by the miniature electric motor which was hitched to a set of
gimcrack rubber-band pulleys. The pandemic grew so intense
that I was seldom present in the Golden Pharmacy except to
touch home and start off again. In those December days I con-
ceived of myself as a pathetic, demerit-burdened minor angel
condemned for some short time to the misery of this biting, death-
ray-ridden solar system of Sol's, working off my penalty by dangerous flights through frozen space which were necessary to the
grander scheme of the central bureau. I was continually posting
hither and yon over the East Bronx, delivering Golden goods;
there was just no time left to stand and serve at the counter. I
was satisfied with my lot, and confident I satisfied. Yet, one afternoon when Golden held up a monitory palm and commanded
me to stop right where I was and take off my coat, I had a shiver
of alarm. I thought, perhaps Mr. Golden had become used to
the dustlessness and new order I'd brought to his neglected showcases, too used to freedom from the trash he'd formerly stumbled
through behind his counters. Hadn't he seemed morose now that
I was not around, a sweating and heaving, shrimpy Hercules?
Had he seen that I thought myself a free agent, a sort of self-
administered contact man between his prescription table and the
ailing who clamored for his costly salvations? Had he caught me
looking too saucily at him, as if I thought *he* was the dependent,
unable to survive without *me?* Had I been so noticeable swagger-

ing and strutting before him, like a child of the wastes and wild
places, the illiterate random Bedouin daring him to challenge his
roving habits? Or maybe, so I half-hoped, he missed me a little,
and wanted a dose of my unwashed sunny spirits ever so often
to relieve the monotony of his days at the store, that oasis and
midden where he squatted loaded down by the trivial and num-
berless civilized luxuries he dealt in, and bored by the endless
vulgar color and variety which streamed through it every day,
and which weighed on his soul in that depot of fateless things?
Whatever the reason, when I came rushing in, trying to avoid
his eye and in my self-begotten autonomy get efficiently out again,
he said, "Sonny-hey! What took so long?"

"Well, Mr. Golden, I had that order for near Parkchester, and
the other one, the package the old lady phoned for, down on
Westchester, so I took both at once and—"

"Okay, okay. Wait a minute, will you, please?"

"But—"

"What's your rush? Wait!"

"But I have this medicine to take to near Gunhill, and this one
for Burke Avenue—" and I reached audaciously into the cash-
register for change.

"No, I say! It's Friday. I want you should stay here. It's getting rush hour: everybody's coming home. You stay and sweep
up. Take these cartons"—they were three great heavy ones I'd
left plunk in the middle of the store for two days now, effectively
having wished them, in my mind at least, into invisibility—"and
break them down. Then you go and work that counter for the
girls when they come in tonight—you know, all that junk they
want for the weekend."

"But, Mr. Golden," I said righteously—really, I was a fanatic
about *running* the damn prescriptions, although I'd lost my illu-
sions about the necessity for speeding them through, having seen
that sick people either go to the hospital, die, or have someone

come to wait for the stuff to be made up— "I *must* take these orders. You said before Mrs. Schluge called twice, and Mr. Kryon is *really* bad this time."

"Never mind what I said. You stop thinking and running where you please, and get those cartons down from there."

"Well, all right. But how will those orders—?"

"Gott! I say never mind them orders!" And then, as in afterthought, he remarked casually, perhaps to mollify the spurious expression of conscience-stricken concern I wore, or perhaps to explode it, "They will be taken care of, Joey. Don't you worry." He raised his eyebrows ambiguously at me over his shoulder, "Hey! Come up here now."

I couldn't believe my ears. Was I being fired tonight? On a Friday? But why? My racing heart trembled like a melting jelly. I hadn't meant to seem that rambunctious and uppity. I really hadn't! In truth, I was still assiduous, and as faithful. Just because I left a few cartons . . . But he himself knew how I'd been dashing every minute all week. What? What? But then, I was being promoted, kind of, wasn't I? I was to put on the gray cotton jacket, wash my hands, and select sundries with such comprehension and discrimination for the girls who came for cosmetics before their weekend dating, and help the guys who asked shyly for their tins of Ramses or Trojans (just in case), and the people old and young who wanted to buy Christmas presents of toilet water, special soaps like Bouquet de New York, powder sets, fountain pens, after-shave lotion, and whatnot. And I would be working the cash-register constantly, touching and folding twenties as I liked, making change and serving so pleasantly the myriad folk who came to me needy in unending lines. And yet, I could not help suspecting that I had somehow displeased Mr. Golden, had failed him, or failed to make him believe in me. It also occurred to me right then that if he had been decent he would have consulted me about how much work there really was,

asked my opinion as to whether I could not speed up, or work
both the in and the out sides of the job by rearranging deliveries
on a systematic schedule instead of running when each order was
prepared; and that if he had done the right thing and begged
for my considered judgment, I could have told him, oh so ju-
diciously and with suggestive cunning, that he could avoid shell-
ing out two wages by having me step up my output and pay me
half an additional worker's money (which would not be *quite*
the same thing as a raise from him, but for me a raise nevertheless). So as I waited numb with surprise, chewing and swallowing
these chagrined thoughts and ruing my simplicity in having taken
my control of Golden for granted, he shouted again, "Hey, you!
You heard me? I said come here!" Now there were indeed feet
on the cellar stairs. Unhurrying steps they were indeed. Then this
other kid came out.

*God!* Where could he have come from! *Keerist!* In our neighborhood teeming with kids, how had he remained unknown to
me and my friends? What a hideola! A ratty belt several sizes
too large, the gnawed end of which dangled in front of his half-
zipped fly, barely held up his brown corduroy knickers, and their
frayed cuffs hung down his skinny shanks to his ankles where
absurdly big feet were cased in heavy, heelworn brown rubbers.
He wore a flannel shirt of rusted green plaid; over that a brown-
buttoned, unbuttoned, old man's black wool cardigan, the unraveling cuffs protruding from the sleeves of a too large, too
heavy, hairy, three-quarter coat of checkered black and orange
boxes. His clammy blue hands looked like worms in specimen
bottles; the nails had been bitten down and were replaced by
scarred palps of nibbled flesh. And his head! That face! The
skull rose to a point behind; mousy, pig-bristle hair; the mouth
was open, slack, slavering, full of tiny round blueblack teeth
which were lead-braced and hooked top and bottom by rubber-
bands; eyeglasses round as the bottom of a six-cent Woolworth

water glass behind which bulbous gray eyes swam, out of phase and out of focus; the frame of those glasses was held together where it had been broken by friction tape on the bridge of his devious, green-clotted nose—and that whole greasy and pimpled face had a gross allotment of knobby warts overrunning it, from the back of his neck on up through his scalp. My stomach twisted over with rage, and outrage, at this apparition. That *that* was what Golden was willing to settle for! That sullen, nasty kid fit to do my splendid work? What a travesty of the fine image I had of myself: the worker worthy of his work, the work worthy of the worker, evoking from him a beautiful intensity which he embodied in the swift clean responses of a dancer intuitively moving to music he has not heard before. Even were I not so trammeled in the gorgeous garment I threw about myself everywhere, I should not have been capable of understanding who that creature was or why he was there, and what criticism it cast upon my notions of what was important in the world, of what meant what and to whom. As I changed into my clerking dustcoat I watched him chew and blow and pop a wad of sky-blue bubblegum and listen absently to Golden's directions and take the money for change from him with a disrespectful, nay insulting lack of interest, and stuff the precisely wrapped medicine bottle—rolled with such finesse in its striped green paper by Golden, the top of the wrapping twisted once into a locked spill so that no string or scotch tape was necessary to seal it—into his pocket carelessly, as if it didn't matter that the bottle might slip out and spill its precious content en route. Mr. Golden for his part seemed not even to notice the rudeness. What were my ideal efforts worth? It was incredible! Callous, unrushed, he slouched out of the store; passing the window outside, he peeled a strip off Mr. Golden's Notary Public seal, and left that officially scarlet badge, that important legal sunburst, a mere slice of old tomato with a bite taken out. This was but the absurd beginning of my trouble. Right off, I caught its sensational tone: it gave me a whiff of the exasperation and horror I was in for as I dwindled into a mere butt for derisory amusement.

The next night, for instance, was Saturday. When business slowed after the dinner hour, I went down to the cellar to flatten cartons for the garbage collectors who came after midnight, and gather together the trash of wrappings and packings I'd left from my week's hectic dispensing. He was reclining down there in the murk on a heap of corrugated litter under the steps. Perhaps he thought I had cut him, as if I were yesterday's favorite vexed at feeling myself slipping into obscurity? Well, one could not let an interloper think that. I would not show my bitter temper; frank and securely genial, that would be my style. I should, since that *thing* was evidently good enough in Mr. Golden's eyes to be enlisted—and having hired me, he ought to know what a man was worth—I should not behave in any way that might impair the felicity and efficiency of our organization. After all, wasn't it probable that he was not conscious of his unfortunate appearance to others? Though he was unhappy, might he not be good nevertheless? He could even turn out rather helpful; with proper handling he might work into the job. I wasn't one to spoil things. So I planned my approach carefully: I set to work clearing the floor, fitting things neatly into each other, gathering up loose ends, making symmetrical piles of cardboard and tying them tightly, just so, using no more twine than necessary, and shifting them into stable heaps in one place. I hummed a little workmanlike tune and whistled while I worked, offkey, between my teeth, absentmindedly, to create a busy warehouse scene. After I had swept out and cleared the stage, I sat down at the table and started ranging raw bottles together according to their color, quality, size: brown heavy ones for big pills; quarter-pint and half-pint clear white bottles for cough medicine; clear pint bottles for the Special Secret Formula Golden Lotion; small brown round bottles for expensive pills, vitamins and such; and flat brown round minijars for the Mystic Golden Unguent and the Golden Sun Pomatum. Next, I had to select proper-sized stoppers and black plastic screw caps for each lot. Before doing that, I turned around for a break, ingenuously, and said, "You're the new boy here, eh?" No answer. I said, louder, "You're going to be working with us from now on, eh?"

A barely audible sigh came from under the stairs: "Huh?"

"I said—"

My polite repetition was interrupted by a bored snarl, "Yeah, yeah, I heard you. So what?"

"Well, I thought, since we have to be working here together, we might as well get acquainted, you know, and see what has to be done. Sort of have a conference and, uh, divide up the chores properly, you know?"

A shaft of giggling. I persevered. "Say, uh, my name's Joey, fellah. What's yours?"

Giggling again, he said, "Sam-u-el."

"Okay, Sammy, how's about it?" Silence. "We'll divvy up the cleaning down here until you catch on and learn how to do it quick for yourself. After all, I have to spend a lot of time on the counter up front, you know. And then, well, we can share up the orders even-steven—once you, once me—so's the tips work out pretty much the same. Uh, confidentially, they mostly stink, anyway."

"No," he said, louder still and shrilly. "No. Sam-u-el! No Sammy, hear me?" He was scrambling out from under the stairs.

"Sam-u-el? What kinda name's that?"

"Sam-u-el!" he said, glaring at me with those watering eyeballs.

"Okay. Take it easy! Suits you, suits me. Sam-u-el. Sam-u-el, okay?" I laughed, patronizingly. "Sam! U! El!" If that was the only name he'd answer to—so? A jerk, I thought; a moron.

"Now, how about giving me a hand here with these bottles?
I'll call out the size, and you get the bottle caps down from the
boxes there."

He looked at me once, curiously, and started back for the stairs.

"Hey!" I called, "Sam-u-el! How's about a hand here—it's
part of the job."

"Screw you," he said, crawling back into his retreat. A fat lot
of help he'd be! Later, taking the washed and sparkling glassware
up to Golden, I looked down between the steps and thought I
could see him lying there. One hand was in his mouth, he was
gnawing the thumb; the other seemed to be squirming around
inside his pants.

Things in the cellar were not ever to be improved. With or
without my direction, Sam-u-el had no desire to cooperate; in
fact, I came to believe he didn't intend working at all. I couldn't
imagine why Golden kept him on, for on the job he certainly was
not, responding only after long delay to the Golden summons—
one cry, "Hey, sonny!" and one stomp-stomp overhead—and
dragging along as though through quicksand out into the whining, murky-winded winter street. Soon I saw why he was so slow
to answer. He had built himself a den down there under the
stairs, a kind of comfortable troglodyte's home, floored with corrugated cardboard carton-liners and pillowed, sided, and shelved
with detective and screen magazines. In my compulsive cleaning
up, I would have to collect the photos of movie people, the
cheesecake, glamorous, workaday and recreational pictures
(swim? dance? golf? tennis? drive the convertible? lunch-cock-
tails-dinner-soirée-banquet-function?) which he tore out, stuck
up and gazed at for a minute, and then defiled, crushed, and
tossed over his threshold like so many cracked and cleaned bones.
I couldn't see the reason of his passion for those stupid, wooden
magazines full of stars and stareens, starlings and starlets all so
fit and grinning at you, when only a movie could bring them to

life so variously and so well-disguised that they became multi-
tudinously incarnate real people, instead of remaining the mere
abstractions of cheap publicity, sterile forevermore. Nor could I
appreciate why he looked at those tawdry "official" police photographs: the trampled grass at the edge of the stagnant pond
where the rusty hatchet was found, and then, a few yards on, the
battered and broken body of Beatrice Zyzwlinskzi, glared by the
flashbulb, and the same monochrome, unsolved scene shown in
daylight; or the old leather-and-ironbound steamer trunk opened
by a curious child in some rooming house attic, stuffed with the
naked honeymooners, whose matted, blood-clotted heads are just
visible twisted awry on their gory white torsos, while detectives
in blueblack striped serge stand vacuously about, confused and
bored, paunch-vested and badged and fat-faced under their fe-
doras, wondering, what now was what? I thought, at least a kid
Sam-u-el's age could be reading men's adventure magazines, or,
since it was such as he, Katzenjammer comic books; not those
dull, repetitious crime things littered with snapshots of the guns
and bullets and butcherknives and grenades and homemade
bombs and whips which had been cached in this place or seized
in that place, or the manacles from which the girl had been sus-
pended left dangling in the other place. Because I was hating so
hard, I did not understand that Sam-u-el's idea of spiritual reality
was not so different from mine; I was too full of repulsion from
that dirty scoffing, drooling, and yes, he smoked also, moronic
little wart hog. I did not recognize that the only difference between us was that he worshiped alone, a cenobite and rebel, while
I sat for three hours and a half at a stretch with the adoring,
demotic mob in my regular, thriceweekly retreats to those mixed
monasteries, the movies. Most important, I couldn't see that
though his icons were static, they were closer than mine, in a way,
to the actual, because his were private and served himself alone
there in his rooted-out cave, while mine, though enormous and

moving in their expensive temples, were ultimately utterly false. But, also, I discovered that he was deeper into esoteric wisdom than I, that he was an ecstatic with original, peculiarly depraved and bestial rituals.

One sleeting afternoon in January when it was good to be among warm, dry, dusty boxes, I heard him snuffling with what I took to be amusement. I walked over to see what was going on. At the door to his wallow, some of the packs of Camels he'd stolen from my counter upstairs had been stood together to form a small box that contained about forty or fifty loose cigarettes, while a dozen or so matchbooks were arranged around it to make a five-pointed star. He was leaning back between two burning, faintly incensed votive candles in violet and orange glasses. He looked up. "Hey, Joey, didja ever hear this song?" Without waiting for a reply, he crooned out:

> *"I took my girl to the ballgame*
> *And sat her right up front,*
> *Along came a baseball*
> *And hit her in the—*
>
> Country *boy,* country *boy,*
> *Sitting on a rock,*
> *Along flies a bumblebee*
> *And stings him in the—*
>
> Cocktail, *gingerale,*
> *Five cents a glass,*
> *And if you don't like it,*
> *Put it up your—*
>
> Ask *me no questions,*
> *I'll tell you no lies . . ."*

A stupid kid's song; it meant nothing to me. "So what?" I said. "You know something? You're a jerk, Sam-u-el." I was going away when he called out mysteriously. "Hey, Joey, wanna see something?" When I said, dubiously, yes, wishing he would stop annoying me, he motioned me to creep in with him. I did.

Spreading a pack of playing cards out face down, he told me to turn one up. I thought it was silly gambling, and immediately regretted I'd gone in only to be enlisted in some boring game like Go Fish or Casino. He lit a fresh cigarette for himself from the purple candle. I turned a card over. There was a picture on the other side. I looked at it, and was shocked. It was a photo of a fat, naked, peroxide blonde of about forty-five, eh old! blowsy-bellied and balloondugged. She was hunkered over a pot, and she was grinning inanely at me. I could see, by staring hard at the black patch between her legs, that she was peeing. Sam-u-el snortled again. "Funny, hah? Take another." I turned a card again. This one had a picture of a skinny, naked man who still wore his shoes; his socks were stretched up on his shins with garters. He had plastered, shiny hair, parted down the middle and worn like they did in the movies; he had a handlebar mustache and his face, though he looked me straight in the eye, was void of expression. The same blonde woman was bent over before him, still grinning; her baggy tits hung low; apparently her backside was pressed up against his stomach, though I couldn't see what for. "What the hell—?" I said. "Take one. Go wan." I turned up yet another, fascinated but repelled. It showed the same deadpanned man (I could tell by the socks and shoes and mustache) and two ladies now (I thought of them as "ladies" on account of their age). The man was lying on his back on an old brass bed; there was a rubber plant in the corner of the room, an old-fashioned room such as you saw in Chaplin movies. Both the ladies were on the bed with him, on their hands and knees like dogs. It was hard to imagine what they were up to. Sam-u-el must have seen the horrified astonishment on my face. He tore the card out of my numb fingers. "Interesting, hah? Lemmee see.

Ooh, that's good." He stuck his cigarette in the side of his mouth, threw his head back on the bolster of *Crime Confessions,* held the card above his face with one hand where he could make it out in the flickering orange-violet light, ripped open his fly with the other and began jerking at himself, making those little snuffling noises. I scrambled out, taking extra care not to upset his altar of cigarettes, so leery and fearful had I grown of disturbing his peculiar ways. I was dizzy, and I felt like throwing up. So that was what he did in there. That little . . . And that's what he used those full-page pictures of movie stars for, and had the gall then to throw them out for *me* to sweep along with his cigarette stubs and chewing-gum wrappers and Babe Ruth wrappers and what all else. So much I loathed him that I decided, against the clear advice of my intuition, to get him out right away. The next afternoon I went to Mr. Golden and said, "Mr. Golden, I have to tell you this"—my breath came irregularly no matter how I tried to calm it—"about him."

"Who?"

"That kid down there. He's not such a good worker—you know?" The questioning note tacked itself on to my declaration of its own accord.

"Yeh?" I didn't like the way he smiled, so knowledgeably, at me and raised his eyebrows as if he knew all about whatever I was going to say (though I myself did not) and was amused by it no end.

"And he doesn't help me clean up, or sort out, or sweep, or anything. He even *makes* dirt!"

"So?"

"Well, you know, I'm doing it all anyway, and so . . ."

"So?" The man was impossible! Why did I have to state it, when he should have taken over the line of investigation I had suggested and come to his own conclusions?

"Well—what *good* is he? You're wasting your money on him."

That stroke, appealing to the money angle, would surely do it, I thought. I was wrong.

"*Your* business?"

"Well no. But it's a shame, I think. Maybe you should try to get somebody else? I mean, if you *really* think you need two men?"

"Yeh?"

What more could I say to him? He didn't seem to pay the least attention to the importance, or the gravity, especially from the businesslike point of view, of my charge. I was baffled. Would I ever understand him? "Look, sonny," he said, after watching me change legs a couple of times, and with that sphinxy smile on his face that said nothing yet hinted all, "you go mind your counter there for a while. Yeh?" I went, grinding my molars, rednecked with shame and defeat. He returned to the sanctum of his prescription bench. How terrible, now that I was in an almost intolerable passion of disgust, to be forced to recognize that there was no other way but to suffer it, though the sight and sound of that Sam-u-el, his mere presence in the cellar, made my mouth tingle and water with metallic nausea.

For the next half hour I could hear Golden busily making up prescriptions and things, weighing, pouring, scraping, pestling away in his mortar, screwing on caps, moving gallon bottles of basics around, typing up labels, and wrapping. Frequently, I'd glimpse the light bouncing off his glasses as he looked through the plate-glass screen at me. Finally, he called down, "Sam-u-el?" The usual long silence. I smiled to myself, vindicated. "Sam-u-el!" *Stomp-stomp.* Then at last those clumsy feet climbing the wooden stairs. "Take this order to number 39." That must be in the building upstairs, I thought. Another long pause. "Well? Get going." Silence. Then Sam-u-el said, "No." Even I, predictor that I was, was surprised by that flat refusal. "What do you

mean, No?" Golden said. "No—No is No!" I was elated. That
would finish him. I stood perfectly still, waiting to rejoice when
the wall fell on him. There was no crash. Golden sighed, then
looked in my direction. "Joey! You heard me?" "Yes sir yes sir
yes sir," I said. I took off my clerking coat and went for the package. Sam-u-el stood there yet, looking mean and stubbornly un-
repentant. Golden paid him no attention. I went out, puzzled.

Though the store was on the ground floor and occupied a good
space on its busy corner, I'd not been into this apartment house
and had never noticed just how immense The Alexandria was. I
had to go two blocks, clear around two corners, to find the entrance which, guarded by a pair of unsexed concrete lions whose
fangs had been knocked off, was a Moorish archway of brown
and yellow bricks encrusted with tiny sculptures that also gave it
vaguely Byzantine echoes. Its name, The Alexandria, broken up
here and there and embellished with chalk by children, was
spelled in mosaic on the pavement of the inner courtyard just
beyond the arch; there were also potsy squares around it, a flock
of grotesque, colored, hieratic figures, childishly formal, and lov-
ers' broken hearts and names scrawled vulgarly on the pink concrete of the walk. It was an old building, one of the grandiose
monuments from the early times of the neighborhood, mannered
and regal in ground plan. The lobby had carved, blackish-brown
oak furniture, gigantic thrones and chests and sideboards with
empty brass candelabra and other useless, elaborate objects like
trays and bowls; the elevators were capacious, disguised as elegant antechambers, and must once upon a time have been oper-
ated by uniformed boys, as the dead wheels with handles indi-
cated, but had long since been converted to modern self-service
machines. There were actually four sections to this great apartment house, arranged in a quadrangle around seven rotting Lom-
bardy poplars, as tall as the cornices on the roof, which stood in a
neglected leafless garden that was not much more grassless and

dead in January than it would be in June. Each wing of the house had its own elevator, but the hallways met at the corners through low firedoors with arched lintels, doors chained open regardless of the law. Four wings meant there were four apartments numbered 39, probably all alike in layout; they were on the sixth floor: 39-North, 39-East, 39-South, 39-West. Golden hadn't told me which to seek. I didn't care for returning to the store, so I wandered along those faded, varnished stucco halls, pleased for the moment with the cavernous sorrows of these crypts cut into by deep-set steel doors, behind which reposed the bodies of richer, better people. I stopped at 39-South. What difference did it make? If I was wrong, I would move onward to the west. When I pushed the doorbell button, I was pleasantly surprised; instead of the raucous blatting of the usual painted-over buzzer, a noise that always made my heart sink because I feared it would bring me Mrs. Katz, I heard a distant set of chimes, four notes down, four up again. They were slow chimes, golden and warmly vibrant, and caroled to each other. I felt instantly calmer; why should I be upset over carrying this order for Sam-u-el? I think the chimes sounded a broken chord that soothed.

There was no answer. But Golden must have known someone would be home—he wouldn't have had a delivery made for nothing. So, I gladly set them off again: Ding! Deng! Dang! Dong! they rang, and after pausing, back up once more, Dong! Dang! Deng! Ding! they sung. Then a woman's voice called from a long way off, tunefully and slow, "Come in." I tried the door; it was unlocked. I walked in. To my eyes, accustomed to the penurious squalor of my parsimonious Katzes and Schluges and Kroynses, this was an Alhambra. Not scuffed linoleum, but carpeting from wall to wall. Three-foot-high porcelain lamps, glazed sylvan scenes depicted on them, stood on round leather-topped mahogany end tables. There were deep armchairs and couches covered with nubby silk brocades of watery-hued oriental magentas and

turquoises, citron, saffron and emerald. There were credenzas of
mahogany on which cut-crystal wineglasses stood poised. There
were real, painted pictures—flowers, ships, landscapes of the winter and summer with mists and peasant cottages and cattle—
hung in gilded, carved frames which had little lights attached at
the top to light them. And here and there painted plates, and silver and gold dishes with figures hammered in them hung on the
walls, and mirrors everywhere, ornate, glass-framed, large and
small—everywhere mirrors. Before the windows at the far wall
was a black lacquer stand, and on it a great cinnabar vase, in-
tricately chiseled with pagodas and sages and flowers, which contained a whole armful of gladioluses, as in a funeral parlor.
Drawn back, the plum velvet draperies exposed white silk curtains on which the light moved soft after filtering through the
triple-width venetian blinds. Nor were the walls one color; some
were painted pink or brown, some were actually papered, and
the wallpapers showed bucolic scenes or unique arrangements of
rare flowers in bunches two feet high. And there was, to complete
that suave enchantment of my senses, a waltzy music lulling and
lilting from a Chinese-modern ebony cabinet. I stood, gaping at
the inexpressible beauty of this living room into which one descended by four steps that were flanked by wrought-iron, gilded
railings. I drank it in. "Hello?" I called, not too harshly, to pre-
serve this peace.

"Come in, come in," she said from somewhere, whispering the
words again, singing them it seemed. I tiptoed down the long
carpeted foyer, following the perfumed echo of her voice. There
were turns; I opened some closet doors by mistake, closets stuffed
with linens and clothes, and I stepped into two bathrooms—two
of them!—big bathrooms tiled all the way to the ceiling, one with
all its fixtures pink and one green, with a green sink, green tub,
green toilet! Finally, I found the way and came to the door of a
bedroom lit lemon pale by the January sun which hung low in

the south over Manhattan, and was dropping beyond the Consolidated Edison gas tank that marked the low bottom of the Bronx.

"Come here," she said quietly. Her tone was not one of request, but expectant and sure of fulfillment. I crossed the room; the rug my unpolished, squaretoed brogans walked on was orange-brown, overwoven with green flowerets; the elegant furniture was rosewood, carved and glistening with oil; there was a froth of white and gauzy curtain cascading from the windows, a field of scarlet covered the bed. A door led to a small yellow bathroom, and another to an adjoining bedroom which was not so sumptuous as this one since it lacked the glorious thing to which my eyes were drawn: the enormous vanity table, mirror-backed and mirror-topped. All the light in the room it gathered into itself and condensed there, like shimmering silver, making the room insubstantial, unbounded by walls. It occurred to me that she slept alone in that enormous bed, and that the other room belonged to the Master of the house. Master and Mistress were the terms that came to me—straight from my complete handbook of filmic lore. And she (the mistress) sat on a pink stool before that vanity; she did not turn, but watched me in the mirror. I could not see her face, but I knew she must be very beautiful. She wore a heavy satin kimono, so white it had a shade of steel-blue in its surface, like frostbitten cheeks; it was gaudily magnificently embroidered with a rampant dragon whose head reposed in flames over her left shoulder, whose short, gouging forelegs reached rudely under her left arm, whose burning, mica-plated, flexible torso stretched the length of her spine; whose punishing lower limbs grasped her hips (one extended talon seemed to be clutching her left hip, the other was fastened into her right hip), and whose armored tail coiled over and around in front and enveloped, I supposed, her thighs. Her hair was long and of a jetblack color I'd never seen—it glowed with violet highlights. It was spread out on her shoul-

ders and she brushed it with languorous strokes, the movement
of her arms causing the great reptile on her back to undulate in
slow passion, as if he was a god coming gradually to life. I
couldn't keep my eyes off it. At once I thought of her, and was
ashamed at my reversion to comic strip puerility, as the fabulous
Eurasian in "Terry and the Pirates"—none other than the Dragon
Lady herself, that mysterious, fatal bandit and vamp of the South
China Seas.

"What do you want?" she said. Did I detect an exotic accent?
Had I come to the right place?

"Here's your order you sent for from the Golden Pharmacy,
madame." Before I could help it, I began to kowtow, but stopped
gracefully short of that and offered her my lumpy package with
just the right indication of noble, squiring courtesy.

"Golden Pharmacy?" she echoed, bemused. "Did I order anything special today? I don't think so; but . . . However . . ."

"Ah, madame, I must be mistaken," I said, meaning again to
say, ma'am, but the instinct of servility had possessed me—I
didn't know why except that I felt such a personage ought to be
addressed in that manner.

"No, it must be a surprise. Mr. Golden knows what I require.
And Mr. Golden always has it here in time."

She was a regular customer then? I wondered why I had never
been sent up in all these months. She turned around and took the
package from me. Her eyebrows were heavy and black, the lashes
long and black and gummy, the lids faintly aquamarine, like the
evening sky above the horizon. Her eyes were large; glowing. Her
face was powdered deathly white. A pale red suffused her cheeks.
Her mouth was a wide, red, enameled gash filled with large even
teeth, except for a place where a molar seemed to be missing on
top at back; also I could see gold caps on the bottom row toward
the back. The kimono was held together at the lowest part of the
deep V between her breasts by a couchant gold dragon which had

red stones for eyes (rubies, I guessed). The silk tassels of the scarlet sash lay along her legs and drooped over her knees to the floor. Her white-ankled, blue-veined feet wore Chinese slippers of scarlet, beaded felt.

She unwrapped the parcel on her lap, smiling in a pleased way as she read the labels of that assortment of pomades, unguents, creams and lotions, marbled liquids and burning chemicals—all custom-blended, as I well knew. One at a time she placed them on the mirrored top of her vanity, stretching and swiveling half-around, her hand drawing the kimono closed again, too late, every time she turned back to pick another from her lap. I was not conscious that I stared at her; I was all petrified stare. When she was done, she crushed the wrapper and string into a ball and tossed it carelessly toward a pink-quilted basket in the corner of the room. Without thinking whether I ought to, I went to put it in.

"Thank you, very much," she said. She actually had a queer accent, concealed but noticeable. "Now. I suppose you are Mr. Golden's new boy?"

"Yes, madame."

"How long have you been working for him?"

"Five months, madame."

"Five months? Why have I never seen you before? What is your name?" I hesitated. For such as she, I thought, it should not be Joey or Joe as my parents, my friends, my teachers called me, but the name I'd never used. I wondered if I could even pronounce it with conviction. It would be funny to hear it, but I took the chance: "Joseph is my name. But I'm called—"

"Ah! Joseph! A beautiful name! I shall call you Joseph from now on." From now on? In five months Golden hadn't sent me there, and now she thinks so much stuff comes twice a week! And yet there *were* innumerable bottles, phials and vials and jars collected on her vanity.

She leaned toward me. My eyes struggled up to meet hers. She smiled. "Come here, Joseph." I inched closer. She reached out and took my hands in her cool, red-lacquered, long-nailed fingers; large fingers and strong they were too. "Let me look at you." She looked into my eyes. I couldn't really see hers, I was so confounded by their painted sheen and by her suffocating scent, which I could distinguish, now that I was so close, from the fulminating odoriferousness of her . . . boudoir.

"Yes, yes," she breathed. Yes what? I asked myself.

"Would you like some cake and milk, Joseph?" she said abruptly.

"No, madame . . . Thank you, but I am obliged to eat my supper later, or my father will be angry." As if from nowhere, how such words evoked themselves formally in response to her!

"Yes, Joseph, of course." She kept hold of one hand as she swiveled again, the kimono sliding down one white and blinding shoulder, reached into the drawer and pulled out a dollar bill. I thought it was a twenty-dollar bill at least, and said, "I don't have change, madame, I'm afraid, for twenty." Then I realized that Golden had never mentioned any price for the order. "Besides, I forgot what it costs."

"Never mind," she said, "Mr. Golden charges me later. This is for you, Joseph, for coming and for being so sweet." And she folded my fist on the dollar, the biggest tip for the least running I'd done since beginning to work. This was more like it.

"Thank you, madame, thank you very much." But she had not freed my hand. I wanted to take it back, but she drew me gently closer, and before I could guess what was happening, she placed my hand inside her kimono, upon her breast. I felt the mole I had already glimpsed, and knew how much I had desired to touch that tiny stipple. A shiver of satisfaction riffled down my neck. "Do you feel, Joseph, how my heart beats?" Surely it was, and I thought I detected it, pulsing there, somewhere. She moved my hand upon her cool skin, over the large, satin-soft nipple. "So, so," she whispered, "gently, Joseph, gently." My hand, fostered and led implacably here and there around her breast, shown how to cup and stroke, began to caress her on its own. When she squeezed it against her breast in a hard, involuntary spasm, I discovered that my head ached, and colored lights burst like pinwheel rockets inside my tightly shut eyes. Then, before I could move, she was working deftly at my clothes, unbuttoning them, pulling at my sleeves—so many sleeves! and at my clumsy legs. In a few minutes I was hot and dry and stiff and naked and tingling with chills in that dimmed, purpling, overheated sweet chamber. Her hands went firmly over me, patting, slapping, pinching. I didn't know what I felt as she worked and whispered at me like a rapt masseuse. Suddenly, her living hand went between my legs. I cried out in joyful pain. "So, Joseph. So," she said. "Come here, Joseph." And still holding me with her hand she walked me to the bed and sat me down. And then, breathing over my face in a steady, sucking hot roar, like a furnace full of red-white coal, she pressed me down. And then, unclasping that hard golden dragon, she took me inside her cloak. It was dark everywhere now. It was stifling so close to her, but she folded me in and coiled around me like an iron serpent. The Dragon Lady! I was thinking. The Dragon Lady!! Briefly I wondered if I should pretend I was Pat Ryan, or only Terry, his sidekick kid. And as she directed me with caresses and fierce squeezes and constant murmured imprecations in my ear, I decided, doubtfully, for Pat Ryan, because he was black-haired like myself.

It was snowing outside an hour later when, cleaned up and trying manfully to control my tottering walk, I came back to the indifferent, safe, fluorescent glaring and cluttered insanity, that other insanity, of the Golden Pharmacy. I couldn't believe I'd been gone so long, though the lapse of time was shown obviously by the change from afternoon sunlight to storewindow-lit eve-

ning, from clear cold to an inch of flaky, crunching snow. I
hadn't thought of an explanation for Golden because I was not
yet able to accept the fact that anything had happened. That is
probably what saved me from betraying myself by a hesitant
flicker of my eyes or an apprehensive tic of my cheek. But I quite
expected to be zeroed and brought to bay against the wall of con-
fession; I even feared I would break down with the first question
focused at me from behind the glare of Golden's accusatorial
glasses. After which I would be fired for laziness and incom-
petence. Golden passed me over, however, with a shaft of raillery
that missed its dumb and quivering mark, and let me creep to the
cellar to recover myself. My escape was, I granted, sheer, fortu-
nate chance.

He said, "Hey! Look look who's here. Joey, where you been
in the snow without your coat?"

Stupefied, I answered, "Delivering an order. Not so far."

"Yeh? You know what time it is? Quarter to six. You went out
half past four. What kind of delivery is that? Should I pay you
wages, Joey? *You're* Joey the firefoot, the efficiency expert?" I
looked at him with false amazement.

"But, Mr. Golden, you forgot to put a name on the package."

"So? I gave you the apartment number. Dumbbell!"

"But Mr. Golden, you never told me there were *four* number
39's."

"So? You couldn't come back to ask?"

"Well, I figured it would be easier to try a few doors. You
know what I mean?"

"So what took you so long?"

"Well . . ." I paused, and it came to me. "I went to the North
Building, and the elevator was out of order. Up and down: six
flights! I went to the East Building, and the same notice was up:
Not Working. You know?" I was scared; this was going to be too
obvious, but I hoped to bore him with tedious detail. Anyhow,

that's what I *had* been doing for five months, climbing stairs, and a lot he'd cared. I went into a complete routine, panting out my wanderings, in pantomime, up and down the vastness of The Alexandria, and I felt the release of the passion of my accumulated fatigues, and purging of the many disappointments I'd suffered from his clientele of Mrs. Katzes—for they had tired me the way I was worn out now. "And you know something funny, Mr. Golden? I went to the West Building and the elevator there—"

"Joey, Joey, not again. Please! I'm busy. You gave the order? Good. You got a good tip? Yeh? Fine. You're no better than Sam-u-el. Stupid! Why couldn't you pick the right building on the first try? Go away. Don't wear me out. You'll tell me the elevator's broken there, too?"

"Well, as a matter of fact—"

"No, no," and he lifted a mock fist at me, though for a second I thought he meant to strike me in earnest, and I flinched.

"—that one's working." A little truth to season the lies. He let the cuff fall jestingly on my shoulder as I ducked behind him. Affection from Golden? That *was* something. I crept down the cellar steps, relieved that he had not caught me and so thankful for the fatherly blow of blessing that I could have fallen and hugged his knees with mawkish gratitude.

Once below, I sat down at my table, exhausted, and drooped into thoughtless torpor. After a while I heard a rustle and a slobbering sigh behind the stairs. I went over to look in on Sam-u-el. He seemed to be quite asleep there in his sepulchral shadows. I nudged his foot. He was asleep. I went back. There was further rustling. A match was struck and flickered momently; some puffs of smoke drifted out and thinned through the basement. I watched the vapor dissolve in the stillness.

"Joey?"

"Yeah."

"Didja go up there?"

Putting on an annoyed, gruff voice, I said, "Of course! I had to—you didn't want to go. Why not?" He did not answer my question.

"Didja see the tickler?"

"*What?*"

"You know, the tingaling?"

"*What?*"

"Ah, come on, fella. You can't be that dumb. Did she show you the twitcher, fella? It's full of teenchy little teeth that go chip-chop! like in a chicken's mouth. They grind together, sorta—you know?" He let loose that scoffing giggle of his. I was mortified. What did he know about it? I was sick with sudden anger against the little beast. I got up ready to kill, and strode over to him. But then I controlled myself, partly because I was ashamed for her sake, whoever she was, at her being in the lurid thoughts of this Sam-u-el, this thing, and partly because I was frightened by what had happened to me up there. "You pissy little pyoick," I growled, "shut your ignorant mouth or I'll—"

"What?" He laughed.

I gave him a good kick in the leg. He yelped, and began crying like a girl. I was glad he had the sense to keep it low. I ran up-stairs, shut the door tight, and clerked away my hour.

During the next two weeks, I began to feel oppressed by the coming on of the future. I didn't know why this sorrow crept over me, but it was dreadful. I had a dream that I was roaming down an endless narrow street flanked by endlessly tall, feature-less buildings, their even rows of opaque windows concealing menace; they were buildings without entrances; forward was the only direction I could go. What I feared, I realized in the morn-ing, was that I might be sent to number 39-South again, and that it was just a matter of time. And, while I waited to go, I dreaded even more what I would face at my return, Sam-u-el's cruel gibes, the mockery of that foul mouth dribbling dirty words expressive of the distorted, livid images he constantly held before his eyes, and the dirty laughter that made my uncertain limbs shudder, not in recollected pleasure, but in eager, empty lust, as if I were recently dead yet wanted to walk abroad again. I was sure he knew nothing of what I had done; his questions were off the track and revealed themselves as guesses and mere ugly imaginings of besotted, private gratifications. Yet he knew enough from his maniacal, self-involved and self-abusive lechery to make me feel in my own fancies as bestial as he, and make me hate myself as much as I did him, as if I were some untarnishable metal subjected, for spite, for aimless folly's sport, for nothing at all, to an unbearable green flame. He grasped that reaction at once, and teased and tortured me by obscene remarks and grotesque gestures. When these were not enough to please him, he took to planting his fetishes and his wastes for me to stumble on or open everywhere—pictures, cigarette butts, condoms blown up like balloons and lettered with foul words that were disfigured by expansion, and so on and on. I began to call myself the innocent and blameless and ideal-loving Dr. Jekyll, and him Mr. Hyde, my shambling, bloated, irrepressible, irresponsible and unappeasable, monstrous shadow. In that narrow space in which my working life of suffering mortgaged hours was spent, I had no way to escape him, to hide from that homunculus Mr. Hyde. Late in the days, when I'd had about what I could take, he would let up his jeering and gibing: he saw just how to keep his game going. I was caught—but good. You would have thought Sam-u-el knew every bit of that Frederic March-Mary Pickford picture; knew how Mr. Hyde's brutish psyche, clothed in its ghastly physical emanation, gradually took over and dominated the idealist Dr. Jekyll; knew how it ended: Dr. Jekyll's committing suicide to escape. The comparison was close enough to occur to me, but too disgusting, and too painfully complex to contemplate. But it kept coming back, no matter how hard I tried not to think of that fog-obsessed, night-obscured nineteenth-century London, the horror in each Limehouse lane and blind alley. How I longed for escape!

Before the month was over, the cause of my anxiety became real, originating in the same events as before. Sam-u-el refused to go up; so Golden sent me. I wished he would reflect, recall how long it had taken me last time; I wished he would give me warning, better still, an express command to come right back— some pretext to protect me. But he picked a slack hour to make up the stuff and ship it by me, saying only, "You know the way now?"

Again, I had to ring twice; again, I found my way down that simple maze of foyers; again, I stood at the door of her bedroom. She must be in there. The water stopped. Was she getting out so soon after calling to me to enter, or just stepping in? "Joseph?" I didn't reply. "Joseph, come here." Her voice, cajoling, brought me helplessly across the room.

"Come in, Joseph." I walked into a cloud of lavender steam. She was in the tub, behind frosted glass that went nearly to the ceiling. "Sit down."

"Madame, I'm sorry. I must go back. I'm busy. I have orders to return . . . right away."

"Yes? Sit down, Joseph. Keep me company—for just a little while?" What could I do? I wanted to stay. I took off my warm leather coat, which I'd put on to challenge Golden's questioning eyebrow, and also because I'd thought in a muddled way that I'd need a uniform, some sort of armor to indicate to her when she opened the front door that I was busy in the cold streets, full of orders and urgency, that I couldn't possibly linger. I looked hard through the glass encasing the tub, hoping to see where her dark regal head was, but distinguished only a mass of foam moving and making languid, washing, dripping, soaking, fuzzy noises. Her voice in this closed, tiled chamber was not the same as the

Dragon Lady's. It was bright, though still sweetly low and coo-
ing; younger perhaps, or sprightlier. In a way, I was happy not
to have to look at her. She must have known that, because she
took the advantage to ask me questions: how old I was; where I
went to school; how I liked working for Mr. Golden; why I
worked so hard; what I did with the money I earned; where my
father was, what my mother was like. Finally, so flattered was I
by her interest, and so curious to delay and maybe see her get out
of the tub, I revealed to her what my movie schedule was—what
day I went to the Royal, what afternoon to the Imperial, how I
treated myself on Sunday to the Paradise. When she asked me to
repeat that last one slowly, I was immediately sorry I'd told her.
She sat up then, and I saw I'd been talking to the wrong side of
the tub. Her blurry form began soaping. She told me to leave my
package on the bed and take a dollar from the vanity table. There
was a bowl on it full to the brim with fresh quarters and half
dollars, straight from the bank they looked. She called out,
"Joseph, good-bye. And come again." Come again? Did that
mean, when I was sent or should I just come? How could I do
that? *Come again.* Not me! Lingering at the bedroom door, I
heard her open the glass gate. She sighed deeply. I saw her bending over, completely enwrapped in a white terrycloth robe and
hood. As she straightened up, the hood slipped from her head.
This woman's hair was short and brown and wavy; I thought I
saw a snubby, pert profile, a small mouth, perhaps freckles. She
was humming a gay swing number. I dashed fleeting out on tiptoe. I certainly would *not* come back.

There was no need for that. Two days later, right in the middle
of the crisis of a risky, misadvised safecracking job, when a light
had to be used and the alarm, set off by accident as in a night-
mare, was blingblanging away, and you could just make out the
siren wailing in the distance, and the most important tool in the
kit turns up missing, someone sat down next to me. I knew who

it was by that velvet, soft and seizing perfume. I tried to concentrate on the work in hand. This was the moment when months of planning should pay off, I knew, because the action was not much different from a hundred jobs like this in a hundred other films, except for the precise details: they'd be surrounded: that weak character they shouldn't have taken along (the skinny guy with the sweatful, hollow face and the hacking cough) would be shot down making it to the car; the gray geezer would manage to scramble in the last instant, leaving the door flapping open dangerously; the tough guy would curse through compressed lips frayed with cigarette shreds, and reach out, dead-pan, slamming it closed while spraying the coppers; the fat fool would be driving with wild skill and tenacity, revealing an unexpected potential for heroism (which explained why he had been included in the venture), and the calm grim hero, though he had a couple of desperate slugs in him and was bleeding from the mouth, would be in the front seat directing the driver and keeping himself conscious through sheer guts . . . and then the improbably successful getaway, followed by complex evasive maneuverings as the gang broke up and quarreled tragically over the distribution of the loot. Yet those varied details of the hackneyed story—this brave one's flicker of yellow fear, that one's impassive, brainless courage in defiance of stony law, the other's long-expected stool-pigeon quailing in the clutch—these were the touches that mattered, and I always watched for them as if they were omens and I a diviner entrusted with the fate of the city. However, her perfume put me off the film's track, and I sank into it like a patient into undesired anesthesia, fighting for my life—realizing at the same time how helpless I was without an irrelevant cliché such as this one from my concise encyclopedia of movie clips—fighting for my life against the enchanting, mad doctor who intends to practice the strangest surgery on me. Far off, the coppers' tommy guns were counterpointing with their vivid life the midnight sharp brasses of the tumid score as I turned away to look at her. She was watching the screen, wide-eyed and youthful, a bobbed and banged, chestnut-haired sweetheart, an ingenue. I saw a small, round, brown head, a tan polo coat worn on the shoulders, a pink cashmere sweater molding her chest. Still, I couldn't have been positive who she really was except for that spiced and oily perfume, and her ears: large, deeply convoluted ears whose lobes seemed an inch long, and were pierced and stretched like a belly-button's gash by heavy earrings. Though these signs woke in me that anxious distraction I knew her by, I had to see to be sure, and there was not enough light from the crime-black screen.

So I put my hand out, accidentally, where I hoped hers would be on the arm. It came alive, clawed and ringed, as soon as I touched it, and grappled mine like a peregrine's swift talon. Caught! A laughing whisper, "Hello, Joseph. Surprised?" She transferred her other hand to mine, put the near hand up on my thigh and held me fast and cunningly. I couldn't hope to think about the rest of my picture. In the parts I wanted to watch hard, she would be tickling my ear, whispering I don't know what; in the romantic, boring part, when the hero was being nursed back to health in the country by his moll (still hemorrhaging, however), and the farmer's daughter falls for him and they walk and talk by moonlight, she leaned back intent and silent, sucking her lower lip, watching as if I wasn't even there—just at the time I, moviebug though I was, would have been happy to be disturbed. I couldn't take it; she had spoiled the movie. I wanted to cut out and go home. I rose but she pulled me down. "Joseph, will you come with me? Please." Was she asking or telling me?

"No, I don't know who you are. And besides, I have to go home."

"You haven't seen the whole show yet, so you don't have to go home. Anyway, if you are not sure, why not come and find out? Please?" What the hell did she mean? I had only meant to be

polite when I said I didn't know her: I had just got that line
from the stenographer in the D.A.'s office who was being picked
up by the fast operator, the one with the Menjou mustache. It
didn't seem I could say an original word to her, I had so many
rotten, used scripts to refer to, though I had already noticed she
never responded logically to the gambits I threw out, but seemed
to have another set of lines in mind. I knew I had no control over
the situation.

Stalling, I said, "Where can I go with you?"

"Why not try The Alexandria? Number 39-South." With that,
she chirped coquettishly, let go my leg and arm, and disappeared.

I sulked in my seat for a few more vapid scenes. Finally I got
up determined to go home, or something. That something took
me straight around to 39-South. I rang the chimes twice; fast.
No answer. I tried the knob. Open as before. I didn't quite like
the feel of the whole thing, and registered this doubt to myself
in the voice of the ancient crook warning the impulsive, young,
ambitious gangleader (son of the ambushed master-hijacker).
My reservation and my rash resolve both resulted from having
been so rudely awakened by her handy presence from my medi-
tative exercise, of having stepped out into the still daylit street
long before my customary hour, and of my unauthorized presence
here on this day—after all, I had nothing to deliver. Shaking the
sage one's apprehensive head, I went on in. I crept cautiously
toward her bedroom. No one was there. I peeped into the bathroom, and to make it complete, into the empty, spotless and featureless bedroom of the master of the house, whoever he was. I
had halted, puzzled, wavering between fearless youth curious to
find out and heavy experience nervous to clear out, when I was
startled by a blast of jazzy music from the living room. I raced
back down the long foyer, a route I knew by now, having unwillingly traversed it in my mind many times during the last month,
sort of practicing my lam. Nobody was there either; the console

roared. I stood there for a moment, and I lost my chance.

She came jitterbugging in from a door at the opposite end of the room, carrying a round plastic green tray with two abominably tall glasses of milk and a couple of giant chunks of chocolate cake. It was Jean Arthur, slightly youthful: curly, light-brown hair, white socks and brown-and-white saddleshoes cutting the rug, a short tartan kilty whose accordion pleats ballooned way out as she swirled, showing off white, tight panties. Her pink cardigan came down on her hips; it was open at the top where a round dicky blouse collar came cutely out. She had three or four ropes of fake-looking pearls on her neck, and fat pearls hanging like weights from her ears; she had lots of orange rouge, and orange, cupid lips.

"Come on, Joseph, let's dig it," she cheered as she slopped the tray down on one of the fancy leather endtables and came bouncing, lindying at me. I didn't think I could ever dance like that.

"I'm sorry," I said stiffly, "I don't dance."

"Oh yes you do! C'mon, let's try." She tugged me stumbling down the wax-glossy steps, tore off my leather coat, and put me into her routine, letting up from the frantic jittering for a few seconds only while the records changed. In a short time, trapped into that frenetic whirl, and glad not to be too close to her dazzling, glass-bright and round Betty Boop eyes, I picked up her beat and capered about as she wished. When the player stopped, I sank to the floor. She skipped away to turn the stack of records over, and I glanced at her narrowly. Was *that* the Dragon Lady? Only, perhaps, in the muscled calves and too-full hips, the sinewy, long-nailed and orange-tipped fingers, the thickish, square shoulders. I thought—I couldn't tell what. The noise crashed on again; she yanked the drapes to, throwing the room into dusk, and came back and sat down with me, her legs drawn up in front of her so she could hug her smooth, tanned shins and rest her cheek coyly on her knees. She made me drink the milk and fed me the chocolate cake, eating fast herself. As soon as that refreshment was done with, I mumbled some words about good-by, but she jumped to her feet, laughing a shrill, girlish, silver laugh, and held me down. I had no speech for her; none was necessary. Tapping her foot and swaying her skirt to the beat, she sang to the Benny Goodman record playing now,

> *"Joseph, Joseph,*
> *Won't you make your mind up?*
> *Joseph, Joseph,*
> *I'm in love with you . . ."*

Then she flung herself, squirming and jumpy like a fevered filly, upon me. And only then did I feel sure who she was: it was no girl's light and bicycling body upon me, but that compulsive, channel-swimming, woman's strength.

"Joseph, Joseph," she hummed as she swept over me, "you remember now, don't you?" I did; yet I couldn't accept my former fantasy (it came to me, all right) that I was Ryan, or rather, young Terry now, lost in the western reaches of China and dreaming of cokes in the haystack with Mary Ann Jones back in the heart of Iowa in harvest moon time. If I wasn't Terry, then who? Swinging there on the thick, spongesoft carpet to the rhythm of Ziggy Elman's trumpet, that nutty Yiddish jazz which filled the whole banal Bronx with its wild screech, I began to think that, maybe, in the end, I was truly her "Joseph, Joseph."

For the next two months, this heavy, jangling, voracious woman intruded herself into my only life; she sought me out in the Royal, in the Imperial, and on Sunday, in my last refuge, the Paradise, where the downtown shows played, and where I hoped that the crowd would hide and defend me from her. Yet no matter how I slouched into the shadow of my seat, or what uncomfortable and awkward angles in back, on the extreme sides or down at the distorted front I chose, sooner or later she would arrive, that impossible bobby-soxer with jewel-framed, harlequin, Hollywood-blue glasses, her pendulous coral earrings, her silk scarves and pearls and rings, and surround me with nervous rustling and pressings and confusing chatter. She knew nothing about how to watch a movie; she was unaccountably blasé during the hottest Indian chase, asked silly questions about horses and ranches, the aiming and shooting of guns, and about whose side who was on—she was unable to tell the good guys from the mean and bad, indifferent to the problems of heroes—their survival, their honor and revenge—that strung together these axle-creaking and leathery wilderness dramas. She held me down, petting and scratching my thighs and my head tenderly during the big scenes, just when I needed freedom to feel and thrash and jerk with the showdown fights when they were punching and gouging up and down the saloons, round hotel corridors, through doors and over balcony railings, smashing furniture on each other, hurling bottles through mirrors and windows and demolishing with their falling bodies the most expensive, imported gambling equipment and rare Eastern-style, Wyoming apartments. But whenever there was that dull and silly mush where the man and woman yakety-yakked about nothings and kissed it up till you wanted to shout a warning, Get out before they catch up with you! It's a trap!—then she watched, half-amused, and made me sit holding my breath, absolutely still and twitchless. And I couldn't prevent her. How I reviled myself for having blurted out my movie routine to her that afternoon. Yet how should I have known that someone who wasn't interested and couldn't understand would even go to the movies? The worst of it was I had no other times when I could go; and nowhere else to go and nothing to do when I was free.

For two months I persevered, keeping up with the minimal amount of homework in school—how nothing that was—and running my orders and counter silently and efficiently for Golden.

I had become a settled little career man for that morose and heed-
less chief, that arcane, pharmaceutical priest whose presence I
tried to avoid by remaining downstairs as long as I could. As for
the lousy Sam-u-el—I threatened to bash him if he so much as
looked at me. And I persevered with her, too, trying patiently to
instruct her inattention; although, by letting her stay there in the
dark with me (as if I might have done otherwise!) I gave away
my mental solaces, my mental furbishings and delights. All for
what? Usually, I had to give in, and I did it with bad grace, and
follow along to number 39-South, where the afternoons passed
with dancing and pauses for refreshments, into that arduous, in-
satiable and crazy hour of hers in which she took the rest of me
away; that hour which seemed never to be led up to directly—
unless it was by our ritualized, formal struggle, that apparently
coincidental yet mysteriously fatal reacquaintance in the obscurity
of my theaters—and which each time, that is, twice a week, and
to my utter disbelief, exploded on me after I had closed the door
and searched for her as stealthily as I could manage through that
apartment in which she always trapped me. And no wonder I
couldn't find her first: for when I had passed the cement lions
guarding The Alexandria my mind stopped grinding; it neither
dreamed nor figured but went into a light coma as I moved, automatically quick, toward the correct elevator, punched the button
for the sixth floor, and then slunk down the hall to number 39,
where I stopped only to hear her chimes sound up and down,
waited, out of courtesy, for an answer which did not come, and
then set them off again to cover my opening and closing of the
door.

So our unvarying program went for eight weeks, and each
time it was like going to die. Nevertheless, toward the end of the
second month it seemed to me that I was going willingly on my
own, for I no longer fretted and fought to delay, making myself
repeat garbled, inane equivocations in the attempt to forestall

that passionate moment in the movie house when she would whisper, "Joseph? Will you come with me, please?" I found I was waiting for her to press my arm, lean to me and nibble at my ear with those words. In fact, one Thursday, we had hardly gotten through the first reel of the first feature when I wanted to clear out on that sunny, silly, country romance in which Laraine Day was leading on or being led on by some smooth guy—he had the usual creamy convertible coupe and there were studio trees and studio cottages and cardboard moonlight—and I almost told her so. But I couldn't bring myself to it. I brushed my free hand over her wrist. She shook it off. I put it on her knee, modestly, not too high up. Her legs squeezed together rejectingly tight. For an instant, I fancied that this time, it was actually the wrong woman, and made as if to sneak away. Of course it wasn't someone else: who but she would have my hand so locked in hers? I glanced at her; she had on a kerchief which covered her whole head and was tied tightly under her chin and tucked behind into her raised coat collar. I was amazed to see tears furrowing her cheeks and leaving tiny scars of clotted powder and mascara. "What's the matter with you?" I hissed. "This is a silly picture and you know it. The next is the good one." She shook her head. Was she saying she didn't know why she had those tears, or was she angrily asking me to shut up? "Come on, grow up, will you? Crying at this corny crap!" She shook her head again—sadly it seemed—and said nothing. I begged in a whisper, "Ah, please! Cut it out." Her crying made me feel a little hollow in my stomach. "I'm going," I said.

"Wait for me, Joseph, please!"

"What do you mean, wait for you?"

"Upstairs," she said. Fumbling in her baggy coat pocket, she brought out a key. I took it without even thinking of the next picture, a Humphrey Bogart, which a few weeks earlier I could not conceivably have missed for anything, for anything! But I got up and went out.

I had sworn a lacerating oath not to return to her today, but I ran straight there. And once in, I remembered to leave the door unlatched—my mind was working well now, though on nothing at all—and went to the bedroom. I sat down at her vanity, and started counting her collection of bottles and jars as if their labels, all Golden Pharmacy, would spell something for me. It also helped me not to see my face in the mirror: I did not know what expression I might find. But their myriad shapes, qualities and sizes only baffled me. I heard the door open and close far away. How well I had come to know her scurrying saddleshoed step. I looked in the mirror, over my shoulder, as she went by. She held a handkerchief with both hands to her face, which must have been mauled by her tears. She crossed quickly to the bathroom. What *was* the matter with her? The lock snapped, she called, "Joseph, I'm changing. Go out and wait in the parlor . . . Go on!"

I went. I don't want to be here, I thought. I don't! I could still get away safe; I could even hustle back and catch the Bogart film. Yet I wished to stay. I can kill the three hours here, I told myself. What else did my life leave me when I wasn't suffering squalidly at school, brutally busy at the Golden Pharmacy, or sleeping and eating like a dead one at home? And I had to concede that, anyway, I should have come after her later on this afternoon, oath or no oath, as soon as she loused up my Bogart. I went down the hall, opening and shutting all those doors to crowded closets which hid nothing but incomprehensible quantities of costumes, colorful clothes for every season and mood and occasion. In the living room, I pulled out some albums at random and decided on quiet music. I put a pile of records on, foxtrots and tangos, the strings of Kostelanetz and Gould. I tried to think what she might like, so I drew the drapes to as was customary for that room. March, though still biting cold and wet, was growing brighter, and this early hour didn't go with twilight music. Then I took off my leather coat, plumped into a corner of the down-pillowed engulfing couch and waited for her appearance.

I don't know how long I waited, because I fell asleep. I awoke, startled by the silence. The last record had played, leaving behind only the faint electronic hum of the speaker. Then, I heard her in the kitchen. Had the noises she made as she worked been in a movie, they would have told me what to expect; nothing in a film surprised me anymore, for I was an adept in translating even the title blinking on the marquee into the unreeling simplicities of celluloid fatality. I certainly would have guessed that there were high heels afoot in the kitchen and drinks being mixed. But I had no title to go by, and I felt merely dully real; I didn't discriminate the sounds. So, when she came through the door, I was smashed into a wonder of speechlessness such as only the unknown and totally unforeseen can cause. Carrying a square silver tray which had on it twin long-stemmed crystal glasses filled with the palest amber fluid just barely bubbling, and a silver cocktail shaker, she was dressed in an evening gown that enclosed her from her ten gilded toes to just above her formidable breasts, like the cold stalk of an artificial flower. It was a scaly sheath of hammered and sequined gold. Diamond bracelets, or what looked fabulously like diamonds, gauntleted her wrists, and a diamond-glittering, platinum collar yoked her throat. Her sharp, drawn-out nails were gold-flecked and her fingers bristled with diamond and topaz rings. I looked down, where her white-ankled foot stepped shyly forward, hobbled, from the short slit in the sheath, wearing a gold-mailed, backless and toeless and spike-heeled slipper; I looked up, and failed to remember her face, for the face I saw was framed by long, thick, straight, golden-white hair, rolled under at the ends. That hair shielding the right half of her

face—it was . . . Gloria Grahame . . . versus . . . Bogart?
Even her eyes seemed to glow gold, liquid gold as in a fraudulent
alchemist's ladle; and her mouth was turned down at the corners
in a contemptuous sneer; and there was a bronzeflaked beauty-
spot penciled high on the left cheek. Her radiant perfume pre-
ceded her toward me. I had been set to bound away in terror,
but that scent I knew; it kept me still. "Joseph? No milk and cake
for us this afternoon."

"No milk and cake," I said.

She stopped to place the tray on the morocco-topped cocktail
table hovering voluptuously over it so that I might goggle my fill
at this apparition of the svelte where there had been a jitterbug,
the sultry, swank and demimondaine where I had grown perhaps
too familiar with the hot fudge sundae from over the next white
picket fence, my elm street and maple avenue American jukebox
girl. She pulled a gold-and-silver threaded hassock over and
seated herself to face me, her knees almost touching mine and
that so plushily sophisticated and nightclub visage gazing seriously
at me. She gave me one of the fragile, diamondcut glasses, took
the other up and, clinking them, said in husky toast, "Joseph,
these are champagne cocktails."

"Champagne cocktails."

"Let's drink, my dear Joseph, to our special friendship."

"Friendship," I followed stupidly.

"And drink to us, that we may continue to be loving friends.
I don't want to quarrel, Joseph dear."

Loving friends? Quarrel?

"Drink up, dear."

She sipped; I drank. My father sometimes let me taste his shot-
glass of whiskey before Sunday dinner, and it went down like
mercurochrome; I'd never tasted anything like this. This was
good: sour-sweet, and strong. She opened a little golden casket
that lay on the cocktail table and took out a very long cigarette,

goldtipped. I hadn't seen one like it behind my counter at the
Pharmacy, though Golden said he carried every brand. "These
are made to order for me," she remarked. I flicked up the lighter
for her, gallant Bogart waiting out the dame to learn what her
racket was before he let her have it . . . have what? Well, anyway, this sort of glamour is sure to be dangerous; there must be
silky crime, money, dead bodies behind every word of hers—that
was the notion bubbling through my Bogartish brain. "Do you
like it?" The smell of that Eastern tobacco was oil-heavy and
plangent with bored lusts; it floated slowly away through the
room in thin layers of languid cloud.

"Yes," I said, shrugging. What next, what next! She poured
another glass for me, half a glass for herself, and then sat dreaming, sipping, smoking. I couldn't stand to look straight at that
solid, utterly new face and hair, so I searched shyly for the mole,
the mole I thought I knew, on her breast. It was, I think, still
there, though so faint, as if touched by a whitening cream. Okay;
your move, baby, I heard him say in my foolish forehead.

"Joseph . . . Joseph, you do love me? You know how I feel
about you, don't you?" This vibrant, crooning voice just could
not be happening, I thought, not really for *real*. And to myself, I
said in warning, None of those corny lines now, and tried to reply.

"Now wait a minute—" Her enormous, phony eyelashes
dropped—I hoped she wasn't going to start in crying again, not
*this* babe, this babe could take it straight from the shoulder—
"Let's be frank with each other. Let's lay our cards on the table,
okay?" My God! My God! I kicked myself.

"Yes, Joseph. I know. You don't really love me. And I don't
want you to say you do if you don't. I wouldn't want you to lie
to me." She put the words in my mouth and then took them
right out again. I was lost in her presence, always lost. She was
always playing out of bounds. It wasn't fair. What was it I really
wanted to say?

"Joseph, you don't really love me, do you?"

"How can I love you? You haven't even told me your name."

"What difference does that make?"

"I don't know. Plenty."

"Don't be silly. We have so much else between us."

"I'd like to know your name, that's all. You see what I mean?"
And I confessed what was bothering me: I had too many names
for her. I told her that at first I had called her the Dragon Lady.
She laughed at that, the low, undecipherable, exotic Dragon
Lady laugh. Then, I thought I'd known her as the Country Girl:
Jean Arthur, Laraine Day, Irene Dunne even. She tittered.

"Are you saying you'd love me, Joseph, if you knew my
name?"

"I don't know what you mean."

"Well, just supposing."

"How should I know?"

"Then you won't." She turned her head away. I took hold of
her shoulders, quite surprised at myself.

"I will. I will love you. I promise. I do now, right now." I
leaned over and kissed her cheek. She sighed, but said nothing.
"Well?"

"No, you won't want to love me when I tell you."

I crossed my heart; I held up my hand; I promised over again.
She didn't tell me her name. She only turned back to me, strong
and fierce and hungry. Her determined mouth had a hundred
talents; her lips were creatures possessed; her tongue was a snake,
a ship, a battering ram, a flower blossoming red and many-
petaled. I tore away and ran to her bedroom. I was beside myself
to be back in that deep place her bed again, instead of whomping
and rolling around on the floor and over the furniture like kids
at a blackout party.

She gave me the wealth of women: various, abundant, sweltering like a fanatic even in this glacial disguise of hers with which

she welcomed the mild, modern spring of the treeless Bronx. And, terrified, I responded to her with a lover's filial awkwardness, as if she were all I had to look forward to in life. At first she had overwhelmed my body in a consuming rampage. Then what had been my spiritual food, my ambrosial movies, she had gradually soured, curdled, and then dashed away with her irritating, ignorant attendance at my side, her vacuous erratic attention to the false, her carelessness and lack of interest in cinematic truth, and her banal, undiscriminating enthusiasm for slush. She did not know how to suck the bones in which I believed the essence of our human existence was concealed; she seemed to want only the diluted juice so easily squeezed from formless fat. To my way of thinking at least, she was fooled by the outward appearance of things, and just like a female, followed and changed with every fashion, adoring and adorning the plastic and perishable body. Now, lacking a will of my own, I'd become the worshipful, worshiping victim of its most paradoxical phase—idolatrous, I served the bitch.

But not willingly. The affair, because of her latest incarnation (there was no other word for it), had become too complicated to sustain much longer, too intense and exhausting. Not physically —she was somewhere between thirty and forty, and I was fifteen, growing fast and full of new, well-exercised muscle—but exhaustive of possibility, so high had the incredible illusion she created been pitched. She had once been that Asiatic temptress, an erotic reptile; and then had abandoned the role for that of my madcap adolescent playmate, my friendly, sexy little sister, that brown bunny with electric fur, hind legs of steel and sharp teeth that could nibble you to death; now she was a woman, the desirable, yielding woman of tender violences, dressed in this hard, most gorgeous costume. True, she'd been driven to it by circumstance—hopeful youth betrayed, given to hard men's use—until

by sheer unbreakable drive and ruthless intelligence she had
emerged invulnerable; true, she was cut from the domestic poetry
of ordinary loving in an ordinary frame house for which she still
wistfully longed, but it made her the more valuable and capable
when at last she gave herself to a true and innocent lover, myself,
the only one who saw the original, virginal she secreted within.
It was a pity though, that unlike her magnified silver sisters, she
did not intend to die faithfully with me when the gross man who
kept her returned from his business trip into the racketeer's out-
lawed unknown; and a pity that I, who had given up everything
I believed in and was for this fatal queen, would have to accept
that approaching disaster all by myself. And it was coming to
that, even though I was, in my true conceit, furiously unaware of
our true situation.

Nevertheless, my defect, the astigmatic flaw in my besotted
perception, did not derive from this corny and abysmally low
scenario I'd concocted to explain what was happening; it lay in
the fact that I too had been driven remorselessly into the last
deadened street of self-deception by a disinterested and witty
doom. I call it "witty," because I think it worked out to inform
me for my own good, the only thing no one sees for himself. For
I'd forsaken, many years ago it seemed, my primitive country,
where I should have had an eventless evolution, and bound myself to drudging serfdom in the Golden Pharmacy for a sufficient
reason: the movies alone satisfied my craving for higher knowledge, the deeper experience of that greater civilization that lay
beyond the stony nomadry of my brethren of the streets, the
Bronx boys. Because of that I had fallen into the hot hands of
this multiple, mutable lady who, although she seemed so much
like those who governed the destiny of my filmic heroes, was
strangely different: for she was both essentially unknowable and
grossly real. And when at last she deprived me of the movies, I

no longer cared to support with my green strength and principled loyalty Golden's fruitless, commercial necessity. I had nowhere to turn.

And yet if I still went on working at the Golden Pharmacy, it was because of her. On one hand, I was afraid of having more time to devote to her; on the other, I needed money now to buy the small offerings she didn't want. She repeated every other day that she needed my love, and that I could not bribe her with junk. But I had no way of telling her I loved her except by writing what I considered rather elegant and exact notes of affection, and wrapping them up with the paltry Persian shawls and Indian Paisley scarves, the two-dollar-ninety-five rings, earrings, necklaces, and silver-filigree, chain-linked bracelets I picked out with agonizing connoisseurship at a dingy shop with broken plaster on the walls and a rusty whitewashed flowerstamped tin ceiling, an ex-grocery store down on Tremont Avenue, run by a sallow, haggling Armenian in a wrinkled, black, pinstriped suit. She said these presents and declarations meant nothing; she said she'd know when I loved her truly. I swore at her that I loved her; I tore my hair at her to prove the intensity of my love. In a choking exasperation, one Thursday afternoon, the last Thursday we were together—my blood-sweated gift rejected once more in that stubborn, unbelieving, hardheaded and yet intuitively practical female way—I reached out and slapped her, pretty hard.

"You *know* I love you," I yelled. "I show you I love you! I come to you, I stay with you. I go on working like a dog for Golden. And what do I do—spend it on myself? go to the movies? No—I bring you beautiful jewelry. And you refuse it! What else *can* I do to show you how I love you? You're driving me crazy!" It made no difference to her. She held her hand to her swelling cheek, and smiled at me.

"You shouldn't force yourself, Joseph. You don't love me." Was there no way to demonstrate love to her? I slapped her on

the other cheek—harder, backhand, even!—leaning into the
blow with all my strength. And then I fell upon her with a fren-
zied, lover's fury. Later, she leaned over me, drooping her hair
over my head and kissing my face with feathery kisses, her knee
thrown leaden over my trembling thighs, and her woman's sand-
heavy breast resting on my shoulder, "Joseph, I don't want you
to force yourself to lie to me. It doesn't matter."

"But it does!"

"Why, Joseph?"

"What am I doing here then?"

"Pleasing me."

"I want to please myself, too."

"Ah, Joseph, don't dream of it. You can't make yourself do
that. Believe me, I should know."

"Oh God! What do *you* know?"

She smiled and kissed me again. I lay locked under her. It was
no use, even if I burst my heart in anger. I felt like socking her.
I looked at her face, blurred and featureless without makeup, her
shoulders, not white but yellowing and liverspotted; under my
palm I felt a rippling roll of fat on her flank, and the coarse
matted hair of her groin. Suddenly, I knew she was right. I gave
up. "All right, all right, I'm lying. God damn it, you old bag,
you— All right, I don't love you. You're perfectly sure you're so
right. Well you are! I hate you, in fact. I spit on you!" She
merely smiled again. Oh that smugness, that condescending mothering wisdom. I struggled to get up.

"Joseph! Don't go."

"You know so damn much? Okay, okay. Choke on that
smile!"

I managed to dress without looking at her. But, tying my shoe-
laces, I glanced up and saw her quietly watching me. That hard
yet famished gaze nearly cowed me, but the smile lingering in the
corners of her mouth drove me on. My head was breaking, liter-

ally breaking apart with frustrated thought and feeling, hatred and love both wrestling and throttling each other to death inside my head. Not looking at her again, I ran out, leaving my coat behind.

I had no idea why I'd carried it all day, except that I'd started out to wear it in the morning, and then I'd cut school. It was the kind of useless vagary I'd been capable of these last four weeks. Well, I hated that heavy leather coat anyway; it was much too warm to wear now in mid-April, and it attached me to intolerable memories of the whole winter past, which I regarded as a season of most hideous suffering, happy though I'd believed myself to be all along. Good riddance! I raved back over my shoulder as I slammed into the elevator, good riddance! You can keep it for all I care!

Yet I didn't actually believe it was the end. I was dying only to get out of The Alexandria and walk, walk anywhere until it was time to go home to wash and dress up. That night the holidays were beginning: my father, and all the other fathers, would be home early for a change, and we'd go up to my grandparents' where the clan would trek in from all over the Bronx and Brooklyn for the annual feast commemorating deliverance by the Angel of Death, the only person in the Passover ritual I liked besides poor, frozenfaced Pharaoh who couldn't seem to help his accursed spite. When the elevator jerked to a stop, I threw open the door and bumped right into Golden. Behind him was Samu-el.

Golden grabbed my arms. "Hey, hey! Look who's here! Joey, you don't live here." I was astonished, but still coherent enough to say nothing. "What are you *doing*, here?"

"A friend—I got a friend in this building."

"Yeh? Sam-u-el, you know his friend?" What was he asking that loathsome little bastard for? He knew we didn't talk to each other; he knew I hated him, I'd as much as told him so. Indeed, what were *they* doing here? It hadn't come to me yet, the answer, but it would soon. Sam-u-el, standing well behind Golden's thick back, sneered, "He's got a friend here, all right."

"Yeah? How would you know, you filthy pyoick, you!"

"Hey, hey, Joey!" Golden admonished, as between kids quarreling.

Then Sam-u-el yapped, "Smell him, smell him, Uncle Eli! Smell him! Go on, smell him!"

Golden held me tighter and sniffed at my hair. I couldn't resist him; I was limp with confusion.

"So, Joey? You got a friend, yeh?" Now I *was* scared. Golden his uncle? So that was why he'd hired him and stood for his crap! I was beginning to understand. "Come here, Joey. Yeh?" Sam-u-el had already dodged behind me to hold the elevator open, and Golden backed me in and pressed me against the wall. Sam-u-el pushed 6, and stood there with his brown-coated tongue out at me, mocking, "Nyaa! Nyaa! Nyaa!" until Golden told him to shut it up. I was quaking now. The unbelievable was happening and I couldn't think what would come next although surely, surely, I must have seen it.

"Mr. Golden, Mr. Golden, let me go," I said, mustering a stern indignation. "I have to go home. What do you think you're doing? You can't do this to me. You're crazy. You can't get away with it. What's the matter with you, you listen to that dirty Sam-u-el?"

"Yeh, Joey? Let's see, no?" he backed me down the long corridor quickly, never relaxing his grip on my arms. I stumbled and hopped backwards to stay on my feet. I think he would have been glad to stomp right over me if I'd fallen. Sam-u-el opened the door: number 39-South, and Golden called out, driving me steadily back down the long foyer. "Hey! Goldie! You're home, Goldie?" I could see Sam-u-el's unspeakable face, grimacing with glee, bobbing behind Golden's shoulders, right, then left. Golden shoved, paying no attention to me, as if I happened just to be in his way, and mattered nothing to him.

When we all tumbled into her bedroom, there was another surprise waiting. The place was a mess; it looked as if there had been a real movie struggle in it; whereas when I'd run out five minutes before only the velvet bedspread lay thrown in a heap on the floor and only the bed itself had been upset. Then there was an anguished, rising and falling wail from the bathroom, and she emerged from it holding my leather coat out before her like a trophy. I could have been ready to protest with my life that it was another woman I saw. Barefoot, she limped out, squat-looking in a pink chenille housecoat which was ripped apart under the left armpit, a full-length, awfully pink thing she clutched together heedlessly at the waist. That glittering platinum hair which had electrified me when I first saw it was savagely disrepaired, straggling and hanging down every which way, as if she was a mourner who had been tearing at that splendid coiffure. And her face, mottled with purple blotches of emotion, was swollen worst where I'd struck her cheeks. And her blank, streaming, redshot eyes. And that greasy cold-creamed skin, going dead, in which, even from across the room, I saw that Mrs. Katz's wrinkles would be graven in ten years' time . . . I didn't know that contorted face. Her voice shrieked hysterically, a pushcart harridan's. "You caught him? Good. Kill him, the dirty vantz, the little bastard. Kill him kill him!"

Level and judicial, he said, "Goldie, what's the matter now?"

"What's the matter? What's the matter? Where do you get these boys! He comes in here like he has an order for me. He doesn't bother himself ringing. Just because I gave him cookies and milk once, he acts like he lives here—he comes right into the bedroom. Did you ever hear of such a thing? I never!"

Sam-u-el collapsed against the wall by the door, cackling. What the hell was so funny?

"Yeh, Goldie? Joey, you came here today? Why? What happened, she called you?"

I was about to take my chance and say, Yes, when she started ranting again. "Kill him—or kill me! So help me, I'll die. Look at me, Golden!"

"Goldie, let him—"

"I was resting. I was taking a nap—I can't even nap without your kids coming in, Golden—and there he is. Not enough he's got no business here, he wakes me up. You know I need my rest. And, look at this place! Just look! He—that schvantz, that little bastard—he jumped on the bed with me. He—he—he tried to—Golden, Golden, I can't say what happened."

"Yeh?" Golden rattled me so hard my joints cracked.

"Mr. Golden, I swear I—"

"You shut up!" she howled. "He'll fix you: he'll kill you. You, you—! Don't leave him for the police, Golden. What he did to me! Look at this place, look what he did to my room."

"Wait a minute, Goldie. You're sure you—"

"Sure? Sure I'm sure! Am I crazy, Golden, you fat pig, you stupid ass! Move already! Look, I held on to his coat when he tried to get out. So? What's his coat doing here?"

Sam-u-el was gagging laughter. "Oh! Oh! Oh! Oh! Oh!" This was a madhouse!

"Now, Goldie, Joey's a clean boy, I tell you. I know him. Even if his coat . . . ?" He looked at me with those weak gray eyebrows of his raised, not, as I'd always thought, quizzically, but puzzled. He was pretty slow, after all. I saw now that he didn't think his way through things but felt, gropingly, painfully, afraid to step, yet impelled to, by squealing, squalling, screaming voices on every side of him. He was not the prescient wizard compounding cures for everybody, but a sorrowing, confused old chemist; rich, yes, but merely a servant ministering impartially, for good money, to the vital and the trivial needs of a clamoring world at large. Poor Golden! Poor, betrayed Golden. There were more sides to it than I had ever imagined. "Goldie," he sighed, and took a timorous breath, "maybe you—?"

"Oh, my God in Heaven, Golden, I'll die of shame from you! Look at me, will you! What more do you want? Look at that nephew of yours, just look at that little animal! He's like the rest of you. Oh, I'll die, I'll kill myself. I swear it! I'll kill myself right now! Golden!"

"Joey—?" Patiently, Golden was beginning again, "Joey, you—?" But she threw herself shrilling upon me. She smelled terribly, sweaty and musty: it was not her smell. Seizing my face between her strong hands, she ripped at both my cheeks. I yelped with the pain of it. Though she wasn't the woman I had known, those were certainly her proud, raking nails.

"Goldie!" He let go of me and ran clumsily after her to the bathroom. But she'd slammed the door in time. She was in a fury. "I'll kill myself. It's too late, Golden, you pig! I can't stand it anymore. I swear I'll kill myself!" she wept from behind the locked door. There was a fearful crashing of glass.

"Goldie!" he roared in misery. "Goldie, open this door!"

I bolted, halting long enough at the other door to bash that Sam-u-el right on the top of his crooked, cheesy skull, muttering, "For you, you—!" As I went past him, he stuck his foot out. Sprawled on my face, I heard his mean laugh behind me. I scrambled up. Down the foyer and out the door I went, leaping the cheap marbled flights of stairs, three steps at a time, and hurdling banisters wildly until I came out into The Alexandria's meagerly leaved, drab courtyard.

A pale afternoon sun warmed the sky. The local flock of pigeons, started by my headlong flight, scattered fluttering round the quadrangle, and a burst of sparrows chattered in the shabby untrimmed privet hedges. Outside on the street, cars and delivery trucks passed in their usual traffic. Some little girls were playing hopscotch at the archway, and a couple of little boys leaned on the handlebars of their bikes, watching them skip through the chalked-out and numbered potsy squares. Nothing much was doing, as usual. Breathing in my panic like a broken-winded runner, I made for the cement lions, but had to stop short. I had a stitch in my side. My face smarted. I put my hands up to wipe my burning sweaty cheeks, and cried out from the pain. It wasn't sweat but sticky blood that covered my face. That horrible cat had gashed me. Blood was dripping on my shirt; now that I had noticed it, my face began throbbing and flaring with the etching fire of pain. Yet now I was laughing too. My blind fear was melting in laughter and tears and blood. I realized I was free. I was free!

# JACK THE
# GIANT KILLER

---

"Sixty, sixty-one, two—"

"Sixty-three!" she said.

"Where's sixty-three?"

"Over there. The briar."

"Damn them." He began a formal malediction. "Damn Sir Montagu Burton Limited, the mass-producing firm of master-craftsmen. Damn the clanking looms of Harris and Lewis and Uist. What are they doing up there—a million yards of muddy tweed! And damn these sixty-three clerks and navvies and tellers and travelers all wearing the same botched coat and all on the same 'fortnight' strolling at the end of the goddamn Europe—"

"Sixty-four. And look: five, six, seven—look, won't you?" With each tally she pinched his arm because he was pretending to ignore the four men in identical Harris coats who were standing propped by their elbows against the rail, observing the row of fishlines hanging in the sapphire pool of a harbor. But he saw them, he couldn't help keeping count, and he muttered, "Six, seven . . . Hell, you look at them. A lot of good this walk is, I won't be able to eat."

"We'll have a couple of drinks," she cheerfully suggested. He crossed his eyes and stuck out his tongue to show what he thought of that offer. "Really," she said, "can't you see the joke? The thing only cost you fourteen dollars; besides, no one will have one like it when we get home."

But he wasn't listening. "I'd like to squash them," he said. "If you'd let me buy that Beretta in Florence, I could have walked up to these guys one by one: 'See here, my good man,' I'd have said, 'take a look at yourself, will you, chap? It's got pinching padded shoulders, a wasp waist, and it buttons up on your chest so that your buckle shows. As for these short-cuffed schoolboy sleeves, they are, sir, an outrage. No, I'm veddy sorry, it can *not* be allowed.' And then I plug him right in the middle of his vestytumtum with my little blue steel Beretta." He became inspired: "I drag these sixty-seven browncoated bodies together. What a heap I make! I set a match to the pyre—horrors! The noxious, hideous stench of that greasy smoke, that slow and rusty fire of sheep's wool. Naturally, it burns and burns—for sixty-seven days."

"Naturally," she agreed.

"Naturally. The Cornish Conflagration, they call it in the books: 'Yea, behold! and he went forth across the seas to Penzance Town, even unto the Promenade thereof, and he found there seven and sixty of that cursed tribe, sons of the giants of Cain's clan from before the Flood, and lo! he slew them in their iniquity, even so that hairy pelt, that uniform which was by them flaunted—an abomination—and so with his tiny automatic pistol he slew all that were there!' How's that?" He gestured grandly, eyes flaming, nostrils distended.

"Louder, please. Everyone for two blocks hears you as it is. They think we're quarreling," she commented.

"But you do see that I get the joke? Only, it's on me. Easy for *you* to laugh," he exclaimed, "you don't have to wear it. But every time I raise my arm to put it on, I'll be seeing, not sixty-seven but thousands, thousands in England, in Scotland and in Wales, raising their right arms to put on the same jackassed jacket. I'll look in the mirror, and there they'll be in an endless diminishing recession, snickering like you. Mockery! With my prophetic eye I see it far in the future, even over the Western Sea: I'm doomed. It's coming on already. Here, feel my forehead." He seized her wrist, brought it to his brow. She shook him off and walked faster. He kept up as they went along the stone-flagged Promenade. Her face was averted; when he tested her elbow she pulled away. "What's the matter?" he asked.

"Absolutely nothing."

He seemed surprised by her tone. "Are we arguing about something? Of course, my jacket!" He struck his forehead in dumb amazement. "It's the curse of the Laird of Harris and the ancient crone who sits at the peatfire in his kitchen stirring a kettle of usquebaugh." He dropped his voice to a wheedle. "Please don't fret. I'll give it a chance sometime. Maybe. How's that?" He put on that innocent smile, that charmer, and she found herself grinning back, her eyes moist with angry joy.

"You think you can brazen your damn way through every time you're in the wrong," she mumbled.

"What say?"

"I said, 'I love you.' "

"Yes?" He squeezed her shoulder.

They walked on toward the bandstand, a pink octagonal cage of Victorian scrollwork blistered and gummy with fifty seasons' paint. Since it was a late Sunday afternoon in August, a fifteen-piece band was seated in it. The players wore scarlet costumes stiff with brocade; their epaulets were gilt, their bursting buttons glowed like new brass, their instruments gleamed like the horns of angels. Old folks dozed on the benches ringing the little pavilion, scattered couples pressed knees together and whispered with eyes, children chased each other up and down between them all. They stopped to listen to the oompahpahs of the monotonously gay waltzes and marches, played just so. Gulls skated in the mild blue sky; pennants flapped in the soft airs down the street of houses painted with bright southern colors—blue, coral, green, yellow— that fronted the harbor. A model seaside town, small, perfect, peaceful. After a while they moved on toward the west reach of the Pier. There Penzance ends; the land breaks into low cliffs and coves which swing south, protecting the harbor from the Atlantic swell. They found a jetty where folk sat, facing the length of the town. They perched themselves on the low stone wall over the water, lit cigarettes, and smoked in content.

She couldn't help it; she just had to poke him. "Sixty-eight! Now don't stare." If it wasn't the same ill-fitting coat of tawny tweed. Yet in the light of the falling sun the thick cloth took on a ruddy warmth, fuzzy with golden filaments—it was really hand-some, in a way. The man who wore it looked like all the rest of them, and quite as suitable for number 68 in that infinite series, except that he had a pair of enormous black binoculars slung from his neck. As he came their way he glanced frequently and curiously at everyone. Finally, he halted right next to them, leaned forward on the wall and began gazing intently out to sea.

In a couple of minutes, she thought, it would begin again, it was inevitable; so she prepared herself to watch, and to be as in-different, as reposed as the afternoon. Jack fidgeted; he turned around and craned his eyes over the harbor. The man responded by casually inspecting his binoculars, fussing with them and whetting Jack by his ritual: he breathed on the lenses, gently rubbed them with a large blue handkerchief. At last he brought them up and commenced sweeping the horizon, twiddling the focal screw professionally. Jack was stiff with interest. At last the man left off scanning, caught his breath with pleasure, made delicate adjustments. She braced herself, and looked away as Jack broke out, "Excuse me, is there anything there?"

Without lowering the glasses, the fellow spoke coolly. "You're Yanks, aren't you? I expect you'll be taken by what's to see. One of your big aircraft carriers is moving past. She's a cruiser with her."

"Really?"

Of course Jack badly wanted to look through the binoculars; he wouldn't directly ask a stranger, but his twitchy eagerness was laughable. He was made of curiosity and it always gave him away; still, pursuing it down to the usual disappointing end was the only thing that seemed to make him happy. So far it had not struck him to build nonsense out of it: he had given up the idea of heroic expeditions, grown almost civilized. But he had not stopped insisting on going to the end of the line—as if there might somehow be something yet undiscovered and untroubled, a place of power, devoid of people, where a pot of gold squatted. So he always had to find where the city ended, in villas or slums; where cultivation ceased and woods grew; or, walking through humus under the dark trees, reach the barrier of tumbled boulders where the mountain began its sheer ascent. Most often, he wanted to smell the salt on the ocean wind: every long promontory was an invitation; not the habitable shore where houses have already arrived but the very last mile of broken cliff, beyond the telephone poles—the final beach without animals or trees, with nothing but water and sky and a few crumbled shells. That's what it came to, his traveling, in Baja California and Monterey, at Gaspé and Florida, in Sicily, at Cadiz, Bergen, in the Hebrides, at Holyhead. So now they were near Land's End with nothing in particular to see or do. Well, because it was good to be with him, she let herself be pulled along on these crazy sidetrips, reciting to herself, *Jack be nimble Jack be quick Jack jump over the candlestick.* Sometimes she puzzled at her patience . . . Watching out of the corner of her eye, she saw the man point the direction, hand Jack his binoculars; heard her husband say, "Who'd have thought they were there? Ah, there's the destroyer escort; he's just come over the edge. Say, how do you know they're ours?"

The man squinted, greeneyed, and answered, "They've your flag, can't you tell?" The instant she heard Jack's reply, "Well, yes, I can make out some kind of flag, but—you're certain?" she felt a shiver of clairvoyance and recalled what a fool, what a gullible fool, he'd been last week.

They had stopped in Tavistock, a town of heavy gray stones and cobbled streets, because they wanted to see Dartmoor. Hiking east in the morning, they climbed some hard miles on a road that cut through snug farms until it ran out on the high wild table of moors swept by that eternally fresh, grayblue breeze. Once on top they aimed for the inn marked halfway over on their map of bogs and granite tors. They intended to find the British Stones . . . "Menhirs and dolmens, dolmens and menhirs," he'd chanted on the way up. When they had gone three of the six miles to the inn and were supposed to be smack in the middle of an archaeological city of hut circles, they stopped. Not a car had passed during their walk: the gray macadam strip fell westing behind them and dropped again to a deep-troughed valley before. There was nothing on either side of the road but great scattered rocks sunken in the soft grassy fields. She said that this was the area marked on their map, but Jack, in his usual fit, insisted on marching on. On they finally went, though the random boulders gave way to straight heaps of stone fences: "modern" cattle pens, said their fifty-year-old Baedeker. She was vexed and growing tired and wanted to turn back, even if the road ahead did rush downhill, when a hale man and the young woman, his strawblown-haired, flat-gray-eyed daughter, came pushing their bicycles up to meet them. They talked with them. The man poohpoohed the very notion of hut circles. He said he had grown up here on a farm before going off to the mills in Birmingham. They showed him their map, a recent government survey item; but he only snorted: it was all foolishness. There never had been anything hereabouts. Why, just look at all the stones strewn about—when he was a lad they'd sledged them together to build fences. Farmers had been doing that for hundreds of years. And then bookish people who came blathering supposed what was left scattered around to be some vanished civilization. A good one that was! Jack was sobered. It seemed likely; it must be true. They all went back to the high ridge. There, the man said, was what they were looking for, and there he had labored twenty years ago. He and his plain daughter, stocky and silent as stone, mounted their bicycles and coasted away. Jack's stuffing was knocked out of him; he sat down to mull this one over. But she, with her investment in his precious imaginings, and a stubbornness fostered by her new contempt for his habit of taking poor exchanges from any stranger—a handful of shriveled beans for his meat and milk —stood up for him this once more on the crown of the road and looked again. Suddenly, as though she had been regarding the wrong side of one of those trick drawings of cubes, she blinked: they *were* there. The field was full of them. She counted ten rings right below them, and turning north saw whole blocks of grouped stones on the downs. She cried joyfully. Jack trudged up to see, discouraged, still dubious. And though she pointed, he didn't see them. Exasperated, she ran down into the meadow, planted herself in the center of a ring and revolved slowly, pointing and

counting the old roughhewn rocks like a chanting Druidess—
"One, two, three, four . . ."—mysterious and proud, delighting,
flabbergasting him. They were really there. Once he could believe, he trotted from one circle to the next; at last, over the rise
hundreds of yards from the road, they came on circles with slen-
der stones standing nine feet tall in their centers. Dolmens and
menhirs. They took pictures. Then they made their way up one
of the broken conical hills, King Tor the map called it, ate their
box lunch, and on a swatch of moss between two great granite
blocks made love under the pale sky of scudding clouds. Later,
seeking their way back to the road, they found themselves floun-
dering over muddy peat, ankle-deep in drowned grass, into
clumps of manure, and returned long hours later to Tavistock
with ruined shoes . . .

"Fine glasses, aren't they?" the man was saying.

"They must have cost you something," Jack said.

"Oh my yes, that they did. German, you know, Zeiss. I expect
some chap picked them up from a Rommel man: look here, see
the inscription? Arabic. It reads, *Zeiss*. Sent off to Africa, I
shouldn't wonder, in 'forty-two it would be."

"Where did you get them?"

"Oh, that was after the war. They were in the Jew's in Ports-
mouth. That chap really wanted money to pawn things like these.
Thirty quid, I paid."

"Wasn't that a lot of money? I mean, that was before devalua-
tion then, wasn't it?"

"Yes indeed. But they're my only vice, you see. I don't smoke,
thank you—" Jack was offering him a cigarette "—I don't drink,
I'm not married. If you live like that, I mean without luxury,
you know, what you can save for better use adds up." He contemplated his binoculars, a shade regretfully perhaps, and added,
"I live quite pure. These are my one weakness."

A little embarrassed, she glanced at the man. But Jack went

right on: "I wish I'd had these yesterday at Land's End. Even from that height I could barely make out the lay of the Scillies. I've heard the islands are a mass of flowers the year round."

"Are they? I've not been there in a good while," he said as if talking to himself. "And where are you off tomorrow?"

"We're going to St. Michael's Mount." Jack pointed east along the shore where the hill rose out of the shallow sea. She wished he didn't always tell everybody where he was going.

"Are you really?" the man said, looking at Jack oddly. "That's where the giant Cormoran lived once, isn't it? Here, have a peek."

Jack took the binoculars once more. She felt the man watching him with his green eyes as he described the woody slopes crowned by a black castle with a forked standard flying over its tower, watched him in a way that made her feel a silly anxiousness. The man said, "That would be that Lord St. Levan's flag, now. The St. Aubyn family has been there a fairly long time, too, at that. Before them, as I recall, some clever hermit fellows took it over. You know, I'd like to see the old place again. Tell you what, suppose I meet you two tomorrow? You won't mind? There's a bus leaves from Market Jew Street and runs over to Marazion. You know where to get it? In front of the station, then? Ten o'clock? Good, then. That's settled. You shan't miss me." He nodded, whirled abruptly, and disappeared at a brisk pace into the people moving down the Promenade. Alarmed, she turned to Jack; but he was gazing off at Mount St. Michael.

"I must urgently request the ladies and gentlemen to obey all the rules. You are about to be admitted to a private residence, not a monument belonging to the public commonalty . . ." They were gathered in a group of sightseers on the threshold of the St. Aubyn house, waiting for the guide to rattle off his adjurations. ". . . and though you are permitted and may take photographic snaps if you wish or so desire, do not touch any of the objects and articles of furniture in the rooms through which you shall pass. Entrance to these grounds is a privilege enjoyed only on condition the proper decorum appertaining thereto is observed . . ." Jack was peculiarly restless, or exuberant, this morning. She was relieved that he had at least agreed to take the nine-o'clock bus so that they could evade "Old Tom," as she'd dubbed the man with binoculars.

At Marazion there was a stone pier whose steps went down to tideflats extending their sandy fields a good half-mile beyond St. Michael's Mount. They walked over on a cobbled causeway, their steps squelching a foam of brine out of the greeny-brown seagrass covering it. The islet was an almost Mediterranean paradise: grand oaks and pines and monkey trees shaded its sides, and the narrow red-brick path that wound up and around to the castled peak was bordered by flowers and rhododendrons in full pink and white bloom. The air was warm and moist, thronged with flitting, chirping birds. It was a place to be at peace in.

They traipsed with the other tourists through a series of rather smallish rooms which were all packed with old furniture, some elegant French, some dark Spanish, some massive Jacobean. Everywhere hung paintings of the St. Aubyn ancestors or portrait photos of recent members of the family. There were cabinets of china; silver services; porcelain vessels, European and Chinese, tasteful but hardly extraordinary or even beautiful. "Clutter of junk; loot from the civilized spots of the world." That was Jack's muttered refrain, a complaint the same in every house, museum, and public monument they had ever visited, as if he personally had been insulted.

"What do you expect to find?" she whispered, trying to keep him from disturbing the others in the file of visitors.

"I don't know. It's never any different. All that marble stuff, those scraps of dead Egyptian kings in the Vatican Museum, and

that depressing collection they keep on top of Hadrian's Tomb:
dress uniforms, Garibaldi's shredded shirt, broken bayonets and
rusty Swiss blunderbusses, hacked bloodstained swords, all those
medallions and medals and letters. Napoleon's bulls to someone
or other, this document, that fading parchment, constitutional
and preconstitutional and protoconstitutional banality: all the
State's boring properties."

"What do you want?"

"I don't know. Something precious that I'd recognize right off.
Maybe something I know could have belonged to me once. I
don't know."

They had lagged behind in a trophy room filled with a fine
collection of armor and weapons from everywhere. The blades of
swords and daggers gleamed with thin films of oil. She went on
amiably. "What do you mean, *belong* to you? People like us only
have the things they use."

"I know that as well as you do, but—"

"No buts. That's the way it is. Why should you want something
special? There's nothing like that in the whole world."

"But I *feel* there must be. If it's a hunch, there must be a basis
for it. I must mean *some*thing," he argued.

"Jack, it's not out there. There's nothing out there but ruins.
You're forever saying that yourself."

He looked away from her eyes, dejected. "I know. I know."
Coaxing, endearing, she touched his arm. "Don't be miserable.
You're special for *me*. That's all there has to be—it's enough,
isn't it?"

He considered that, smiled crookedly, and answered half-
pompous, halfhearted, but got it out anyway, "Yes, but . . . you
must realize that I couldn't love you half so much, dearest, if I
didn't, well, you know, love honor a little more."

She let it pass. He had started to examine the pieces in the
room, hefting knives, picking up and flourishing a sword. It made

her uncomfortable to see him violently handling these things, so she went to the window. It gave out on the causeway and gray village of Marazion far below. As she looked at the people moving in the idle streets, she pondered Jack's "honor." Honor! she thought. What honor? Whose? Where? Who did he think he was? She looked and saw a square brownish figure way down at the end of the wharf. Did it seem familiar? Suddenly its arms lifted and there was a flash of light: it was looking up at the castle through field glasses, right at herself in the embrasure. She couldn't actually see *him*, but his image appeared before her eye: the man's shaggy, ashblond hair, his green eyes, hard as agates, stained row of long yellow teeth, his red neck and throat, leathery and wrinkled as an alligator's skin, the stooped shoulders which, if he straightened them—she stepped back, startled. The guide's voice sounded behind her, and his head peeped into the room, "Come along now, we're going out."

In the courtyard the guide pointed out some old figures carved into the tops of stone columns at the corners of the porch. A foot high and crudely weathered, lords or ladies or bishops, he called them. Wizards and witches and demons, they seemed to her. And at the foot of the stairs there was a rough granite outcropping from the castle's wall itself. This was part of the house, it was said, in which Cormoran the Giant lived once upon a time. It was said, too, that St. Michael blessed it for St. Keyne, the first pilgrim to come to the hill after the giant had gone away or been killed. If one touched it with both hands and wished on it, the wish was sure to come true. The tourists filed up and pressed self-conscious palms to it. She did too, and made her wish. But Jack passed by, stroking it flippantly with one hand—the other was in his pocket. That was just like him.

Then the tourists broke apart to dawdle in the sunny court, posing for stiff pictures and hanging over the parapet. Jack, usually the last person to leave such a place, wanted to go down immediately. But she decided to stay. "Let's be ordinary like the others. There's plenty of time yet, and it's so nice in the sun."

"But the tide's coming in soon, you heard him say that. Let's get out of here."

Irrelevantly she said, "You know, you have a vice too."

"Huh?"

"I said," she repeated in a loud voice, "you have a vice too."

He glanced around to see if anyone heard them. "What, for instance?"

"You talk in your sleep," she announced so shrilly he jumped.

"You don't have to scream."

"Now who's embarrassed?" she giggled.

"Why all this just now? What kind of vice is that anyway? But for God's sake, why vices, why?"

"I don't exactly know . . . Oh!" Her hand went to her breast. "While we were upstairs I saw that man who was going to meet us."

"Where?"

"Down there." She pointed to Marazion.

"How do you know it was Old Tom?"

"He looked right up at me through those binoculars."

"My God, did he see you?"

"I guess so. He scared me, anyhow."

Jack chewed his lip. "Let's clear out," he said. But now most of the others were on their way down and they had to fall in with them. Some stared curiously at them. Preoccupied and trying to hide it by glancing nervously at the rock gardens or up at the leafage, he was going too fast. He trod on a woman's heel and took her shoe off. The woman accepted his confused mumble as an excuse and went goodnaturedly on; but she held him back, saying, "What is the matter with you!"

"Shhh, I'm thinking."

"Thinking! Why don't you try watching where you're going for a change."

"For God's sake, girl, will you just shut up for a few minutes!"

When they had at last descended, it was too late. The sea had rolled up over the tideflats and the road they had walked on two hours ago lay under a yard of pale-green water. A few rowboats were sculling out leisurely, making for the spot where the road came out. A few minutes later she was about to step into one of them when she realized she was alone. She drew back. Jack was in the midst of a bunch of the tourists standing at the door of a stone cottage where a whitecapped crone kept a picture postcard display. He was hunched over, his back to the island, his face wearing a sly expression. She saw why: the man in the brown coat was stationed at the foot of the hill and appeared to be waiting impatiently for the rest of the party to straggle down—he was peering past the gate and up the hill. As she watched him, perplexed, someone grabbed her arm. It was Jack. He shushed her, jumped into the dory, staggering because his hand was still in his pocket, and yanked her in after him.

"Easy there, matey," the fisherman said. "It mayn't be but three foot deep, but you'll find it cold and wet once in." Just as they had settled, they saw the man in the tweed coat rushing toward them. Jack put out his free arm and shoved the boat off.

"Hey there!" the man shouted. "Hey there! You, Jack!"

"Row us away now for an extra two shillings," Jack ordered the fisherman.

"A friend of yours, matey?"

"No, for God's sake! Just pull away, man."

But he yelled from the edge of the jetty, "Hey there! I was waiting for you." He pointed at Jack and tapped the binoculars in his hand. "I saw you up there. I'll catch you up later, don't you worry!" Jack shrugged and turned aside in the boat.

Landing in Marazion, he strode off quick and quiet into one of the lanes angling between the shuttered houses, and she had to run to stay with him. When she noticed that they were heading not to the bus station but toward the flinty strand stretching west three miles to Penzance, she stopped.

"Come on, let's walk it," he said.

"What's the matter with you today?"

"Nothing. I feel like walking back, that's all." His eyes glowed with queer laughter.

"No," she said stubbornly. "First tell me why."

"I will. Only follow me now."

"It's not that strange man, is it?"

"Maybe."

"But why? He's only a crank."

"Maybe. Maybe not. Who knows?"

"Jack, I won't take another step unless you tell me what this hurry is all about."

He surveyed the empty streets, and paused mysteriously. Then, furtive, yet grinning triumphantly, he took his hand from his pocket and showed her what was up his sleeve: the cold blue wavy blade of a royal kris, its great haft of dull carved ivory and gold resting in his palm.

# FAT AARON AND
# THE NIGHT RIDER

## I

Fat Aaron was a bloated angel. This is what the mothers called him, winking that smile about things you weren't supposed to know. Mothers, aunts, they would have been sweetly right to have put it this way—you couldn't be supposed to know *yet*. Then their secret might have been washed down safe with coffee and buttered rolls; then their innocent suns would have careered unswerving and unspotted above the summer, neat and simple over the rolling haymeadows golden with birdsong and buzzing clover in that good morning reserved for children since the night

Adam covered Eve, for children, who are set apart romping in an idyll, and growing quiet as appleblossoms in spring.

In such dumb warm August nights the Holstein bull over the next hill bellowed black and white through the hours of that teeming darkness; he rattled the steel chain ringed in his mist-snorting muzzle, and the clanking links of his celibate bondage rang out through the roar that yearned out of the pink giant skinbags swollen between his shanks, and burst from the organ pipes of his heaving chest, thundering over the valley to rattle the boards of the sleeping barns. And the fields seethed with chirruping crickets, the heavens dripped meteor milk, there! there! A hot wind rushed up from the panting earth; flowers, berrybushes, wheatstalks of grass burst their skin; the ground reeked with the rank musk, juice, and scents from the wrestling bodies and mixed sweat of things. In such nights you squatted round the gloam of a weenyroast fire as the spuds pulsed, idol eyes hot in the ruined embers of a jungle temple, you looked up at those bombinating skies, you hummed songs and dabbled fingers with freckled brown girls whose mouths were fruit, moss their hair, and downy arms baskets to cradle your soft melon head. While far below on the porches of the clumped cottages the mothers mumbled over cards and tea, or strolled the road, their flashlights glimmering like squids' eyes beneath a tepid sea.

And yet there I was in that August, untaught, a rough boy camping on screes in the shabby tents of childhood among the stone mountains of a no land. I had trekked out willynilly from Egypt with all its wealth. I had escaped that plentiful slavery of old Nile's beastheaded wizards; my garden memory was a starveling now: palaces and towers, those cities of daisies and barley where we played with blocks, gathering straw to make the bricks to make the temples and tombs—Rameses, Luxor, Heliopolis, Pithom, Thebes—distant now, fading hieroglyphs the sands in their whorling drifts scrabbled away. And the new scrolls, inscribed with new chronicles and new behests of blood and tears, my clumsy hands could not unwind nor my shaggy eyes read. Though there was a black thunderhead beckoning in the dog days, and an arm of stuttering fire by night, there was no voice in that furious music. Until I heard Fat Aaron's. And I knew him to be the arcane, masterful rabbin of that season.

Fat Aaron was the bakery man. He delivered to the bungalow colonies. About eight in the morning the truck would bounce, bang, hurtle up the driveway, that sassy horn tooting, and skid along to a rest as if it had no brakes and no driver. The women would collect at the back. Then he trundled out of the cab, puffing and heaving, pawing and pinching his way through them to the doors. Once at his station he dispensed breads, rye and pumpernickel and wholewheat and white, sticky jelly buns, cinnamon buns and cupcakes. They dribbled from his fat fingers into the paper bags, endlessly fluttering doves of dough, miraculous with each sweep of the arms. And like the greatest of Magi palming the eggs of milk and honey, he kept up his pudder all the while, with every bagful a daub of smut. The long rolls called saltsticks he called "pacifiers," and "Wednesday husbands"; cherries in the pie he said were gathered from the hotels clustered around Swan Lake; the plain burntsugar drynutted coffeecake was "Ol' Sarah."

I never heard enough of his pitch to make sense of it from the outside, and I was never allowed to push through the harem of housecoats. There were the heads all pressed together, pronged with those big aluminum curling pins, from among which the gray tendrils of cigarette smoke threaded up into the clear mountain morning. I'd hear his mumbling treble mutter. They would knee each other in their blueveined thighs, wallop one another's loose rumps, and screech with laughter. He was giggling too, burbling rather; the chortle foamed out of his lungs and coughed through the tight fat channel of his throat as if they were tickling him. And, though their ringed hands, their strong bonyknuckled, longnailed, fishchopping, meatslapping, carrotscraping, redpainted fingers picked at and patted and poked him, could he have felt anything through that blubber massed on his breast, blubber that came under his arms from his broad back and rolled down over the lead vat of his vast belly? When they had their day's bread the knot broke; each went clopping back in her slippers to her bungalow for breakfast, grinning. Sometimes one raised a word of raucous warning that Fat Aaron had had for another, "Sadie! If you can't sleep, don't try to beat it. Go see the big specialist down at the bakery!" At which a chorus of chokes and sniggles racketed through the screendoors from half a dozen coffeemugs.

I puzzled about Fat Aaron's being a bloated angel. He weighed three hundred pounds. He had the whitest lily skin, a great round head of golden curls, moist cupid lips of wet pink, and downy cheeks red as McIntoshes. His skin was white and smooth, white as the flour on his baker's trousers. A cherub without wings I glimpsed in him, but not a seraph. Surely, he was not pure, not refined from all sensuality, a mature specimen of any of the host, not one of the thrones, dominations, princedoms, virtues or powers. But even cherubic there was something terrible about him. Not the fatness, though he was something like those chubby hovering infants with their gold heads and disingenuous expressions: not baby, yet not adult, yet more naked somehow than the grand naked women sprawling on velvet, more naked than the holy fat child in its mother's lap. Maybe it was his blue eyes, chunks of lake ice they were; maybe the frizzled cigarette burning always in his mouth of sharp white teeth.

## II

It was near twelve Sunday night. The town still woke. Buses and cars yapped south to the city: happy people rested in the juices of the flesh were driving to their week's sweltering work. The prison gates of the rancid theater grated shut at my back and I stood in the dusty threshold of Main Street. The ache of murder was in me: my heart lusted after payrolls and molls. Warner Brothers had marked me a snarling four-reel con; my eyes were gorged with blood, my nose was pulped, cheeks and skull scarred by pistolwhippings, my feet dragged the irons of a spirit brought to book. I took desperate bearings for our cottage and cut out of town.

Then, climbing the sharp hill that led my way home, I came into the cold native air blowing from the stars. Where the sidewalks gave out, the last houses were humped snoring shadows. I stepped onto the westering macadam road for the two miles. A young moon floated at the end of it, just above the dark world's edge. It was the sire of the Holsteins, the wonderful metaled horns of the father of bulls, who cropped whole forests in his grazing meditation. The thin arc of the young moon was a boomerang brandished by the hunter of king kangaroo, who was stalking into the long Pacific combers of the night sky, the last of the aboriginal pride. It was a Viking galley; the road unrolled toward it, wavering over a blue tundra, the track upon which the wolfpelted plunderer marched. The young crescent was the mythological brow of the silver queen: the grassroot congress of katydids fiddled her virtues night long, the cottontails mumbled praises as they munched their silver salads, the owls swooped on silver fieldmice for her sport, and in deference to her virgin nudeness most creatures dropped their eyes and slept.

I topped the rise and glanced good midnight to the town sputtering out below. A truck careened past me going downhill like the yellow ghost of a comet. It was the Manna Bakery's. I turned and walked after it. There was a crossroads a few blocks back where the bakery loomed; when I came to it the truck was parked for lading against the sliding doors. I sidled up to them and stuck my nose through to get a look at the plant.

The air inside was hot moist and delicious with the aroma of baking dough: hot poppyseed, hot sesame, nuts, nutmeg and ginger, cinnamon and cloves. At the near end were tables loaded with baking trays; on the floor the great wicker baskets were lined up, some already filled with breads and heaped rolls. In the center of the vaulted room there were grouped the mixing machines, coated with flour dust, all fumbling and churning, their pronged steel arms plunged in steel cauldrons of golden batter, revolving this way and that, backward and forward and around. Far down was the bank of roaring gas ovens, and their attendant, Fat Aaron.

He was the only one there. He was ladling loaves out of the black maws of his ovens with a twenty-foot pole. His shirt-sleeves were rolled up to the bulging elbows; a linen apron stained with the stiff goo of white icing, splattered with chocolate and the blood of tarts, draped from his neck to his ankles like a white caftan. He was monumentally brisk. A dozen breads at one scoop came out on the tongue as he stepped back, balancing his staff, and tipped them into a basket. After some hundred, he clanged the last little door to and turned around. He walked deliberately to me as far as the center of the hall, holding the long heavy shovel lightly upright in his right hand, and stopped mid the cluster of his thumping dancing machines, where he planted the regal ash of his baker's scepter. His left arm swung out to invite me in. He smiled. In his high reedy voice he laughed, "Shalom, sonny! Come into the ark of my tabernacle."

He waggled a derisive wrist at the ceiling. "There's nobody else here tonight to keep me company but the living god: Baal-Berith, the lord of cookies and cupcakes; Baal-Zebub, the lord of leavened loaves; Baal-Phegor, the lord of the little broken hardon. Adonai must be lonely; he needs a quiff to keep him company. You should have brought a girlie with you. We'd tickle some cunny juice from her: that makes good cake."

The batter had begun to thicken; he adjusted the mixers to a slower stroke. I was set to filling a tray with cupcake paper. After a while he switched off one of the machines; when he pressed another button the arm drew up out of the sucking yellow stuff in the vat.

"Take a taste of this," he said as he stroked the vanes of the beater. Batter dripped from them and diffused in the rest of the mixture. I ran my thumb over an edge. I said it was good, and it was better actually than after it was baked.

"Dropped from heaven," he sighed modestly, lolling a pious head to one shoulder.

"What's in it, vanilla?"

"Sure, sonny. Vanilla, and a little flour, and some scraping off the floor; ten pounds of butter, a squirt of machine oil, and a little spit." He giggled at the expression on my face. "You don't believe? The baker's spit is good: the breath of life, the smoke of ruach, like God's in the mouth of the gingerbread Adam." He hawked, and spat a nicotined glob into a pot still on the mix.

"Come here and hold this sack." He handed me a coneshaped linen bag that had a wooden nipple at the apex. I held it spread open; he tipped the cauldron and poured the stiff batter into the open end, shoving it over with his palm. Then he slipped a ring over the gathered ends and knotted them. The whole sack went under his arm like a suckingpig to market. As I laid out the paper molds, he squeezed the dough through the nipple with pressure from his arm against the sack as it rested on his hip, and with two fingers flipped each gobbet neatly into a cup.

We worked fast. "What about the icing?" I asked when we were done.

"It's already made for this batch. Next time, sonny, you'll help. You're young and pure. It's a boy's sweet seed I got to have for icing. That makes it good!" He squealed, drumming his belly.

I helped him load the baskets of bread into the pungent truck, and we went off full gun. Fat Aaron drove with his belly, so tight did that girth press into the wheel. One arm lazed out the window, the other was dropped comfortingly on my shoulders: the roads were his, he did as he pleased. The Manna truck had been so tinkered with, the muffler magnified the blast of each cylinder's stroke, groaning and boiling on the upgrades with a monstrous catarrh, and letting off slobbish dysenteric grenades as it zoomed down slopes. The nightly passage of this dragon through fifty miles of countryside was wanton; it expressed the joyous contempt and abandon of the driver who plied the gas pedal of the highballing thing. The slipstream dragged sparks from the cigarette in his mouth. He handed me one from his shirt pocket and I lit it from the tip of his.

He said, "This is one of the beautiful facts of life. You don't know enough to like it. You're still a kid, cabbage is the leaf of your heart. Look at you, you're skinny with innocence. But me, I deliver the staff of life, I'm round on all sides, white bread and dark bread and nutty dough."

I laughed at him. He pulled over and stopped on the peak of the spur of Walnut Mountain. "And here's another fact." He drew a bottle of whiskey from under his seat, drank, and passed it to me. "It might burn at first, but drink it."

It seared; I swallowed bravely each time he urged me. We walked to the edge of the road. "Look at that country," he said. "Soon it's going to be all yours; but you won't like it."

"It looks all right to me," I said.

"Yes, from here that quilt looks like a bed of delights. But once you get down there for a good whiff it's all small, it crawls with scurrying sucking people. They're vampires."

I didn't say anything. From that height I made nothing of it. Yes, a bed, heaped and various, of hummocks and pastures and glacier-rolled valleys, stands of trees under starlight like patches of black broccoli, ponds and lakes where there was darkness visible, and simple scattered blocks of guileless habitation. What could he see, I wondered, in that lambent void which was to my vision mere massy landscape?

He drank and continued, "Look over there. Swan Lake. We'll drive to the hotels, The President, The Ambassador, The Swan Lake. That's a world chock full of girlies. The lights are still on in their rooms. You know what they do all night? They dance and they swizzle. They stand by the windows naked, and they comb their hair and look at the stars. Lovely. What I see in those bully buildings you couldn't imagine. Let's go, sonny."

I leaped to my saddle in the truck and he squeezed in behind the wheel once more. The road coasted around the south end of the lapping waters of Swan Lake and descended between ranks of maples and poplars. We ran down and turned into a gravel strip that led to the rear of The President. Most of the windows, line over line for five stories, were dark. We lugged several baskets into the quiet kitchen. In the vague light the long galvanized tables gleamed dimly. The stoves and sinks and dishwashing machines were empty, quite dead; the floor was a holystoned spotless deck. Only an old white tom hissed, stretched himself, and shuffled away.

While Fat Aaron scribbled the bill, I went outside to look around again. The buildings seemed asleep; there was no life of the night to be seen. I strained to see something. There, it might have been the glimmer of a languorous form; no, there, what I thought was a lifted arm and the nubile ivory of a breast, a delicate hand caressing the rondure of a young belly. No. Yet they must be there behind the bluey sheets of glass; any moment a shade would roll generously up, or a ripple of cuddled laughter would sound. But the night brought only the sough of summer through foliage, the clunk of rowboats against the little wooden wharves a hundred yards off.

We stopped at The Ambassador, The Swan Lake. We de-

livered orders. Fat Aaron whispered of what he'd seen just the
night before; he pinched me and prophesied wonders. And, yes,
there were some lights, there were momentary insignificant shadows that moved in rooms; there were some murmurous voices,
the tinkle of a dropped tumbler, gushes of water in hidden
plumbing; but no music, none of the promised cries of ecstasy,
no noises of pleasure at all.

Each time he came from the kitchens he asked me what I'd
seen, and I shrugged in disappointment. "It's there," he insisted,
"you're blind, sonny. The world is too cunning for you." His eyes
brimmed conviction as he flapped pictures with his obscene mag-
ical fingers. "But wait, we'll go up to Miriam's at White Lake.
She keeps the gold calf. I'll show you what's what."

By that time my brains were flaring. We bowled along in the
skies, plunging and rearing with the contours of the earth. Fat
Aaron cursed and laughed and sang words I couldn't distinguish
in queer tunes that never were, and he made the truck skitter at
sixty miles an hour.

Then we were there. I stepped down in front of an old four-
square frame building sided over to simulate logs. It was a tavern
backed by the lake: The Harvest Moon. About a dozen cars were
parked off under the trees. Inside, the lanterns over the bar were
dimmed; the front door was locked, but the lights on the second
floor glowed through drawn blinds, and a jazzy hullabaloo was
blaring upstairs.

He rattled the door. No one came. He kicked it, and sent me to
hold down the horn of the truck. Finally, a shape appeared and
moved along the bar. "Miriam," he whispered. The door was
opened to us. They grappled on the sill. In a bassoon throat as
deep as his was high she boomed out, "Angel cake! I thought I'd
have to have a party without you. Come on in, virgin, you're on
time; the joint's jumping. . . . Who's the man of the world?"

"Sonny? I was shorthanded tonight, so I snatched him from his pisspot of a mother. He's pimply, but he looks already at home with that bottle."

"Doesn't he stare!" she rumbled, and, latching hold of my ear, yanked me to her. "What a sweet present, Aaron: a ladyfinger."

Miriam, cased in green satin, bangles and bracelets of gold on her arms, loops and rods of gold freighting her ears, was as big and as fat as Fat Aaron himself. Her hair was an auburn mane: without pins or curls, it parted from the middle of her brow and cascaded to her shoulders where it fell as it wished over her bare arms, down her back, and down the freckled expanse of two breathing monadnock breasts. She crushed my head between them and I smelled the thick richness of the living body of an orchard. But when she bent her head to kiss me, it blew a west wind of gin.

The stairs climbed to a posh parlor beneath whose scarlet ceiling swayed clouds of a strange sweet smoke. In the center of the room an ivory babygrand was surrounded by clubchairs in which a trombone, a clarinet, a sax, and a trumpet slouched. They made music that no leg or heart ever beat to. I slumped in a couch.

There was a throng in the house who drifted in and out of the music joined head to knees in a kissing sigh. Like smoke they came and they went; doors banged down halls; there was singing, laughter, men growled and shouted, women shrilled in delight, in pain, in anger; there were muffled chants such as I'd never heard, though human voices made them. And the music played on and on, slow and cavernous, so slow it barely moved, or whipping, looping in the eyes so swift it dazzled like sheet lightning in the muggy glow of the room. The buzzing place was rank with the writhing and kicking of naked ruddy arms and legs.

Suddenly the trumpet flourished a clarion fanfare. I was yanked to my feet by a hand of long nails and rings twisted in my

hair, and dragged to a ring where I swayed between the hips of
two tall women whose arms were hot around me. The music had
stopped. Then, with lonely hooched chords it began again.

Knees dipped, arms wagging loose before them, their bellies
grinding and bumping, Fat Aaron and Miriam snaked to the
center of the circle. Their faces shone with sweat; their eyes blank
and orbed, they approached, gyred, retreated. The music stepped
up its rhythm and the crowd clapped and stamped in time, shouting, "Go! Go! Go it!" The dancers thumped their backsides,
bumped stomachs, swiveled, pressed and bumped, faster and
faster. At the moaning climax their hands grasped each other's
hair, the auburn and the gold. I joined in as the chorus yelled,
"Go! Go! Go!" and I heard his whinny and her contralto laughter sounding over the music.

### III

I knew in my stupor that I was back in the truck, running
through mists. As we farewelled for dawn, simple years of prince
and princess crowded cheering to the banks of childhood. I was
aware of the wet road, the cool dripping gray trees and the dank
fernery past which we rushed. He said nothing all the way. When
the truck slowed on the last hill I stumbled from it with a loaf of
bread under my arm. It never stopped, and as it picked up speed
Fat Aaron's pinkwhite arm fumbled out and slammed the door
shut. With a last sneering blat of exhaust, it disappeared over the
russet crest of the hill into the jubilee of dawn.

I stood on the shoulder of the road breathing the dew-washed
day. Rank upon rank of air in light, grain in the fields glinting
against the first shafts of the fresh sun and rippling in the blue
breeze, the grapes bunched from the green arbors, swallows bar-

reling over the treetops, the hawks spread in the upper skies. As I walked down to the colony across the wet lawn to the white cottage, the sun shone full hurrah for victory. So this was Canaan! The green flesh of the world, that solemn land, was mine.

# KILLING A MOUSE

Last night I killed a mouse. A simple domestic event. No doubt. Yet this morning, in the middle of my walk to the bus stop, it occurred to me it was enough to hang a case on.

I asked myself suddenly: Who needs an enemy to engage his life, when he has friends enough to do it for him, let alone himself and his domestic ménage (a double redundancy)? Why should that wee, sleekit, timorous, cowerin' beastie have thrust himself upon me, too? Why did he come? The answer is simple and domestic. He came for the dog's cereal, a tasty wheat and corn and soya preparation in five-pound waxed double bags. What was I doing with seventy pounds of black poodle? Answer: I had a wife, and a new child. The dog and child, we had reasoned, would get along wonderfully. Simple and domestic—wived, childed, and dogged. No real cause for fear and trembling.

When I was in college a friend of mine, a beginning poet, used to read Kierkegaard and talk about Angst all the time. He didn't need anxiety because he should have had enough to do learning about poetry. Yet, a year ago he'd given up his sad lyrics to worry about the blurred image of his own face in the age-speckled mirror of his Barrow Street tenement. He probably had mice aplenty because he left his garbage around for weeks. But he didn't care. All the same, they took him away a few months ago and gave him a round of shocks. Not a tragic case, certainly. But he didn't care, and not caring he shouldn't have had his anxiety—at least not according to his classically modern thesis. It seems it makes no difference: he had no choice.

I didn't know for a while that I even had a mouse. I'd pour the dog's cereal into his dish at dinnertime, and there'd be drippings on the floor. I was surprised at my clumsiness. I became a little anxious. But the third time it happened I saw there was a real cause: a neat bullet-sized hole in the bottom of the bag. Only one thing could be responsible, but for a few days I wavered, loath to draw that deduction, until my mouse (a city mouse) was such a damn fool as to dash out of the cupboard across the kitchen floor in the middle of a Saturday afternoon. He could have been more patient or less guilty or braver. Even then, he ran so fast I thought I saw just a blur out of the corner of my eye. I wondered if it was a mouse. But I knew it really was. And I cared—I didn't need him.

So I went for a trap. For fifteen cents I got two simple snappy things. He seemed to use either of two runways on each side of the sink to break for his goal. I say he, though it might have been a pregnant she, because I think of him as a bachelor. I set the springs (the silly pup curious about it all) and baited them with a sprinkling of the food he liked so much. What, I puzzled, could that apocryphal tycoon have meant in pronouncing that a better mousetrap would bring the world to your door—could anything be simpler, cheaper, or more effective than this little piece of wood with its delicate tripper and its smashing spring? I pushed them carefully up his two narrow runways. A mouse would know little about the pleasure principle: he would be all hunger and desire, unable to pass temptation by in the middle of his journey to paradise without stopping to take what he could get. He would not be warned by the human smell on the trap, living among us people as he did. He would be neither cautious nor safe. Best, he would never know what hit him. Nor would I— and that is the best way to do a domestic killing.

But as it turned out the best-laid plan is not as simple as one hopes. About four the next afternoon, we were all in the bedroom playing together when—snap! The sudden lock of the trap was accompanied by a series of small shrieks of pain and anguish. My wife didn't want any part of the filthy job, though she'd been quick enough to ask for the traps. I went to see the result; I was excited, and full of repulsion. One trap was nowhere to be seen. I fetched a wire clotheshanger, unbent it and poked it up the runway. There was a frantic rattling and squeaking. He was struggling back there behind and under the sink where it was impossible to get at him. He seemed to be dragging the trap after him, unable to wriggle into his hole. He squeaked when I wiggled the wire about. It was a frightened little sound—For the love of God, Montresor! And I thought, Poor Fortunato! Finally, when there was no more response, I gave up poking. Maybe he was dead; maybe he was just keeping very still. I went back to the bedroom and explained that he must be dead. What are you going to do now? my wife asked. What can I do? I said. He'll dry out, I think, he won't smell, he'll crumble to dusty fur and little dry bones, he'll be just a ghost of himself. She didn't like that. But what could I do? I took a deep breath, composed my mind, and forgot about him.

In the middle of the night, journeying through a light, agitated sleep, I awake. Squeakings; rattlings of chains. Fortunato lives still. Shivering in pajama tops, my feet cold in cold slippers, without my glasses, I steal back to the kitchen and turn on the light. The rattling comes, desperate now, from behind the stove. Has he gone back to get at some cereal for his last supper? What is the pain-crazed creature thinking of! I search for a pair of pliers. The twentieth century is pitiless: I can't risk touching him, for the lice on mice may be as fatal to me as I shall be to him; thus the compassionate heart is hemmed in by hygiene. Of all centuries to play it safe, and with a mouse—we who have bombs and strontium 90 ticking in our marrow, 30-second nerve gas (odorless, colorless, tasteless), and virus rarities to drop in the enemy's mailboxes. Carefully bending down, and peering around the corner of the gas range, I see the edge of the trap showing. I reach in with the pliers, pincing subtly. I have it! I pull gently, and with the trap, scrabbling futilely on the linoleum for a hold, squeaking in terror, comes my poor Fortunato.

After all my guilty imaginings, he's only a tiny, really tiny, little, little mouse. Caught by his left hind leg. Why didn't you gnaw it off, the way wolves do? But wolves are wild and free; my mouse is a gentle, domesticated creature. I hold up the trap. He wriggles terribly for a minute, then relaxes because the blood has rushed to his head. His heart is beating quickly, a panicky pitta-pattapitta. His bright black beady eyes are rolling. The dog approaches softly, wary, curious. I let him sniff the mouse without violating its helplessness. Sanitarian and Utilitarian; my hope is that the dog will act up if he smells another mouse some time, though of course he must be as used to the smell as the mouse was to his.

What to do? If I release him, he'll only rush for his hole, lame

or not, and I'll have to hunt for him again. What will I have
suffered for then? But I need my sleep; in a few hours I have to
get up and go to the office. I must do something with this di-
lemma now: I am freezing in only my pajama top. Decision is
the only answer; yet before doing what I shall do, a few alterna-
tives no longer possible come to mind.

Suppose I were very much younger, say an unhaired boy, I
might play scientist. Play! Empirical boys drop cats from sixth-
story windows to test their reflexes; they strip flowers and break
branches from trees to make sure nature still retains her fabled
regenerative powers. A boy might take down a kitchen knife,
summarily hack off the mouse's head or pierce for the heart.

Suppose I were not so young, but adolescent, I might pretend
to be religious, a Jainist perhaps. At that age, I'd still be so stark
scared of death and of living's impractical imperatives that I
would grasp at any opportunity, relevant or not, to assert the
right of all things to go on. I would even call this madness a
reverence for life. A pseudo-heart, generous, full of fresh blood,
seeking charity for suffering in the name of love's absolute, and in
this lovingness agonizing over the mouse. There would be reasons
for this heart to find: even to eat rice we must kill paramecia,
hence . . . O youth! health gone ascetic, unreconciled to the
necessary fist, pride and power restrained from their imperatives.
I might, being so rapt with my sensibility, even say, "Go on about
your mousy affairs, mouse, you too must live as best you can." A
philosophical dogma to rationalize the luxurious waste of youthful strength on dreams of equity: this liberal adolescent will be
stunned soon enough by the unexpected depression of his thirties.

But being where I am now, today, what did I do? I looked at
myself, my householding self that groaned in its chains like the
sea. I must have my shirts clean, my food clean. I have a wife, a
child, a dog, yet I stand here with a doomed mouse who hangs
upside down, his heart ticking faster than any bomb, dangling

from a pink hind leg with its pink little fingers of toes, minuscule human-seeming toes, from a dirty little trap, the trap from a pair of pliers, the pliers from my steady hand.

It is chilly at four in the morning. In his last years, Dylan Thomas woke fretful and sick in the morning. He had his mouse. I sighed, I shivered. I went to the bathroom, opened the toilet. I didn't want him swimming about in the bowl—too much to allow even Fortunato—so I plunged the trip quite down. As he hit cold water he squeaked for the last time. And he struggled, he tried to come up for air, his little paws dabbling upwards. But after all. Only little bubbles blew from his mouth, a tiny stream of bubbles issuing. There wasn't much air in him. I held him under for a few more moments as he gave his last twitches. Then I released the spring bar of the trap and flushed him down. Once, twice, again. I waited. He didn't come back. I dreaded his coming back—it has happened. But he didn't. I hoped he wouldn't stick either. I didn't want the plumber coming to fish him out, and the landlord saying, Who the hell puts mice down a toilet? Where else in the middle of the night, where the hell else?

Then I went back to bed. The dog curled up at its foot, yawned once and fell asleep. My wife turned over in her sleep, embracing me, never noticing how cold I was from the waist down. The child in her room slept right on. I think before long I must have fallen asleep too.

# A ROUND OF GOLF

The day was bright and warm. An intermittent breeze down
from the north blew companies of fleece clouds across the skies,
and their cool, brisk shadows marched across the hills. It was
almost noon; some of the players were still down in the dining
room, a few were lounging by the great stone fireplace in the
clubhouse at the top of the hill, drinking pop and gossiping with
the Home Pro while they changed their shoes and had their clubs
looked over by the shopman.

The hotel was holding its Fourth of July Golf Tournament at two
o'clock. Ten professionals had been booked to play for a gold
cup to be inscribed with the winner's name, the date of this con-

test, and the name of the hotel. A stake went with the cup, and another prize to the man who beat the 7-below-par record for this course; besides, the contestants were offered a fee just for coming up to play the round. This tourney was the event of the season; it climaxed the local Damon Runyon fund-raising drive for cancer committees. Ed Sullivan in person was expected at the clubhouse party.

Across the road a man was driving balls down the practice fairway. He was a hulking blond dressed in powder-blue slacks, a cleated pair of white and black saddle shoes, a short-sleeved silk maroon polo shirt laced loosely and open at the throat. His smooth-shaven face was flushed hectically; his blue eyes, blood-shot and strained, couched above puffed cheeks; his tow hair, damp now from the warmup in the noonday sun, was mottled with gray. Those powerful shoulders had brought him a reputa-tion as one of the longest drivers in the country, but he was get-ting beefy, softer every year; his breath came short, he wearied easily: laboring over a mountain course like this one played hell with his game. Too much liquor does that for you. A single man gets bored, and rough going's no joke against younger men, al-ways younger men. He had to sweat to see prize money that didn't stay with him very long anyway: every time he hit into some cash he needed more expensive stuff just to stay with it. It was a shame about that cashmere coat he'd lost in Reno; it cost him a hundred and fifty in Frisco only a week before—dice were getting tough to beat, too.

He was irritable, already tuckered; yesterday's hangover was still with him; he couldn't knock them out at all. His eyeballs pained. He should've taken the visor with him. He paused to wipe his head and neck, and put on his aviator's sunglasses. Then he teed another ten balls in a line on the beaten patch of earth. He gazed down the fairway at his caddy stationed in the distance below; the figure wavered in the gummy light shimmering up

from the grass. The kid was bending languidly for balls and dropping them into the canvas sack. Where'd they gotten him? The
boy looked no more than sixteen: slight, Spanish type, brown
eyes, straight black hair, that beardless swarthy face, soft as all
his brothers who swarmed through the white sporting world
around Tampa; they were so deceitfully pure-seeming, even in
their abominable lives so indifferent. Here among strangers in the
North that kid was trying to seem a quiet, aloof, proud little bug:
when he'd asked for a shagboy, he'd picked up the bag of clubs
without a word—"Mr. Johnson's bag is over there, kid," said
the shopman, flicking his thumb—and he'd glided over and
picked it up without even glancing at Johnson. No crowing for
the luck, none of that scraping grin of caddies who expect extra
tips shagging for their man before the game. It meant the kid
would get his bag to tote later on. But he merely took it up,
fetched the bag of practice balls out of the trunk of the yellow
dusty convertible, and walked out toward the tee uninterested as
you please. Why didn't that kid show he knew who the hell he
was? And what did he think he was doing out there anyhow; he
wasn't even watching him hit. Was he shagging balls for him or
not? He must have lost a good half dozen already. Always stuck
with a kid too cute for his own damned good. Couldn't they give
him men with a little respect for the game? All he wanted from
that young frog was ordinary caddy courtesy and he wasn't getting it. Suddenly Johnson found himself muttering and angry.
He'd better watch who's hitting them out if he wants to stay in
this racket another day. Why doesn't that spic look at him?
Where the hell was he looking anyway? He'd see who he was
shagging for if he had a few drives dropped on his skull for him.
For sure he'd nail the brat out there.

The boy must have been thinking he was out of range, so he
turned away from Johnson at the top of the fairway there to idle
at the sky and the herd of hills running around him. The boy

ambled over the stiff clipped grass, picking up balls it seemed only when he stumbled on them. Suddenly one struck next to him and skimmed on down the slope. He watched Johnson swing, but lost the ball in the sun; it whizzed past an instant later. He saw him swing again. A low drive came lining at him in a terrific slide following magnetically as he began to stumble sideways; the white dot mushroomed into a big ball in that slow-motion curve, breast-high, while a fascination stopped, held him; he saw it spinning leisurely at him until he threw himself below the busy whirling whir of it, and, falling, felt the sigh of its passing and saw out of the corner of his eye the round white diminishing speck bounding away. He was so scared that on the next stroke he stood quite off the side of the fairway, having decided to pick up the balls later. The drive slammed down at his feet and bowled away. He couldn't see anything at all after they went up into the sun. The pellets rose slowly from the man into a long arc, lost themselves in dazzling glare at the zenith, descended at frightful speed. The boy retreated to the other side of the fairway. Uncannily the ball dashed the canvas bag from his hand. Every shot had nearly clipped him, as if the man up there was gunning for him. He shuttled back and forth across the fairway, shading his eyes with his hand, straining to follow the flight of every hit. The balls still fell around him, so he moved up close to stand short inside their arc and watched Johnson narrowly; if he was trying to clip him now, he'd have to switch to a short iron. The pro, however, went on using his wood.

When Johnson had run out of balls he was all sweated. Even this ordinary workout was too much for him today. The back of the maroon shirt stuck to his shoulder blades along two black streaks that ran to his belt; his armpits glistened with black patches. He panted for breath, feeling a little sick as he stood looking down at his boy who gathered the balls dotted like daisies over the field. In a confusion of remorse and exhilaration

over what he'd just done he waited, anxious for the kid to look
up. Finally he had to call to attract his attention. When the kid,
carrying shagbag, driver, and some short clubs, came up the walk
to the clubhouse, Johnson was sitting on the porch. The man's
watery-blue squint peered at the young brown eyes and saw the
flicker of pain. Unwittingly, Johnson half smiled.

By two-thirty a crowd had assembled about the professionals
at the first tee to watch them go off by twosomes. The people
flowed out from beneath the striped canopy to embrace the tee,
which was roped off by a squad of idle caddies who leaned their
backs rudely into the press. These pro caddies, seasoned gamblers
and horseplayers, worked the golf links in Miami during the
winter and drifted north with their cracked burnt skins and
veterans' squints in spring. They talked the game forever and,
knowing this course pat, were to guide the visiting pros, advising
on distances and the lay of various holes. The guests of the hotel,
dressed in jaunty golf clothes, trailed their favorites; the caddies,
who had the inside dope, lorded over these little councils and
made bets on the side as the tourney began.

The photographer was bustling on the tee, posing the golfers
in the stance of lining the ball, or crying, "Hold it!" as they
reached the end of their backswing. Other caddies percolated
through the excited throng which clapped when the Sports Director, barking out long lists of titles and prizes, introduced the
champions.

Johnson was first off. He leaned nonchalantly on the shaft of
his driver, smiled at the admiring crowd as the Director read out
big wins of years ago. He nodded to their applause and teed his
ball with the smile on his face still broad, eyes twinkling.

"Ladies and gents! As you know, Mr. Johnson is one of the
world's longest drivers. You'll put it right on the first green for
us, won't you, Al?"

"Sure," Johnson drawled.

He turned from his contemplation of the crowd—in the heat the women's painted faces were beginning to run oilily—to glance down the fairway at his caddy who was heading for the green, the weight of the trunk of clubs jouncing into the small of his back. The newest split-cowhide, embossed with flowers, offering separate compartments for four woods. That damn kid better wipe their faces after he used them and pull their mittens back on. His eyes were drawn to the boy's back and fastened between the delicate shoulder blades.

He lined the ball for the flag. The crowd quieted. He looked again at the boy, who'd turned, shading his eyes and shuffling backwards to watch for Johnson's swing. As the pro addressed the ball his smile was gone; lips compressed, face flushed, he swung. A long, perfect drive; the crowd cheered bravely when the ball dropped just five yards short of the green and rolled up on the apron. Johnson flashed a new grin at them, waited for his partner's shorter shot, and left the tee, to stride down the fairway surrounded by a large group. He stood out yellow head and shoulders above them as they strolled toward the green where the two caddies leaned on their trunks. As they neared them, Johnson on a wild impulse tossed his driver to his boy. It caught him off guard; it was a bad throw; the driver landed short, bounced up sharply, and the clubhead struck him on the mouth. Johnson loped over and put his arm round his shoulder, saying loudly, "Sorry, kid, did it hurt you?"

"No, that's okay."

The boy pulled a handkerchief out and held it to his mouth. Johnson tugged a putter from his trunk and stepped to the pin, casually pretending to survey the lie of the cup; but he trembled inside himself. As he came back to the ball he lit a cigarette. Though he missed the chip-up from the apron by ten feet, he managed to sink the putt for a par.

At the next tee when he asked for the driver the kid stared at

him plaintively; one hand pressed a bloodstained kerchief to his
mouth, the other held the driver as if in supplication. Johnson
looked morosely up the fairway, teed his ball and hit.

As they moved rapidly along the course through eight holes,
Johnson kept close to par. These first nine were shorter than the
next in yardage, but the ground was tricky: there were too many
traps and the fairways curved around clumps of wood and up
and down ravines. The ninth hole was almost straight up the
side of the hill at whose summit the clubhouse stood. Johnson
had been sullen with the fans who started out with him. The
ladies grew bored with his unspectacular game; his failure to
give back or at least listen to their repartee didn't help. His partner had two strokes on him at the end of six, so most of the company followed the other man. Johnson was vexed by the throb in
his temples and the white July heat. His caddy hadn't said a word
since that first hole mishap, trotting ahead most of the time, not
even looking at him when he came up to pick a club. And still he
held that bloody rag to his mouth. The next nine holes would be
the long ones. Johnson thought he would recoup the strokes lost
getting out of the traps with some long driving which might spare
him those damned short irons. His irons were miserable today,
though for that matter not worse than they'd been for a long
time. He just couldn't bring the ball to the cup; even when he
did he two-putted all the same. It was murder! and those damned
women made too much noise. He couldn't bear their screams
and titters, or their grinning coos and goody-goodies when he hit
his stinking drives. At least most of them would drop away after
the ninth; the hill would beat them, and they'd stay in the shade
of the veranda drinking cool drinks, making their noises, giving
each other the once-over, and he'd have peace. Maybe he'd do
something on the back nine and come in at the head of the field
with a low score—if the heat and the climbing loused up the
others too.

The pro ran to catch his caddy toiling on the ninth fairway to tell him they'd stop for a breather. Johnson said, "What's your name, anyhow?"

"Tommy."

"Kid, I'm sorry about that bad throw back there. How's the lip?"

"Okay."

"I'll take care of you later for that. You say you wanted Coke?" Tommy nodded.

At the top of the hill Johnson found his second shot a yard from the cup and sank the putt for a three. A bunch of people who came out to see the players shoot at the ninth from below gave him a round of applause for his birdie, his first birdie in nine holes. When he went inside he found Tommy had already had his without waiting for him. The shopman was rubbing vaseline into the boy's lip, so all Johnson could do was watch, have the Coke alone and pay.

When he went off the tenth tee he was accompanied only by the boy, match partner, Barnes, the other caddy, and shreds of the former group. He'd shot 35: one above par for the short nine. As usual, lately, no good at all. He needed 37 on the second nine to par the course, and 29 to beat the course record. Ridiculous. He was pooped already. The slight wind was dead now. Four-fifteen: the white ball of sun hung half down the west and the heat was terrific. Not a sound anywhere save his own heavy breath in his throat, the clump, clump of his spikes on the turf. Hell, was it any use pushing for low score?

During the last eight holes Johnson tried to draw his caddy into talk, but the boy remained taciturn. Then he gave that up and kept the boy behind him as they walked so that he wouldn't have to look at him all the time. But he would choose a club for his next long shot before they came up with the ball, then fuss over it, asking a lot of questions about the ground, and change it for another, not even waiting for the words choked in the caddy's throat. He dubbed drives and swore at himself. He putted all over the greens. He mopped his face constantly, finally knotting the polka-dotted kerchief tightly around his head to ease the stabs in his eyes. Barnes was a tomb and, worse, shot clean and steady as Johnson's game grew wilder.

The caddy stayed out of the way, cowed by the big man's fierce, bloody face and the blue eyes that were clouded over with mists. And toward the end Johnson walked so fast the caddy could hardly keep up with him; the tremendous bag of clubs was getting like a ton, and his shoulders were raw from the stiff new strap.

By the eighteenth tee the pro had a 38. The last hole's green was directly behind the clubhouse; like the ninth's, the long straight fairway that led to it was uphill. Johnson's burly figure surged ahead of his companions. He was grim. He had muffed the last drive and sliced his second wood stroke to the left of the green. He found it in a trap with a bank six feet high.

"Tommy," he yelled, "bring that wedge up here!" The kid chugged up the last yards, the trunk clanking against his backside, his face strained white with the effort. Savagely Johnson yanked the wedge out of his hand and tossed the spoon behind him in the sand. It took him two shots to blast out; the second, however, rolled the ball to within a yard of the cup. Christ, he lay 42 for the last nine!

And then Johnson missed his putt. He didn't move as he watched it run wide past the hole. His caddy was standing way at the edge of the green, holding the eighteenth flag. The sky had turned purple as the sun dropped to the horizon. A throng was collected a few yards off at the fence to watch the players as they came in and to compare their scores. In the failing light Johnson's soaked shirt took on a shade that made his face a grim mask. He crouched over his putter for what seemed a long time, staring at the ball. Suddenly he straightened, whirled and ran at his boy, ripped the driver out of his trunk, shouting, "You son of a bitch's bastard!" and threw it down at the fairway with all his might. The driver fled over the earth in elastic cartwheels, its shaft flashing. The startled crowd recoiled. The kid dropped the flag and cringed behind his bag of clubs. There was a hush. Johnson said, "Go get that club," and when the boy hesitated, screamed, "Get that goddamned club! Get it, I said!"

The kid dropped the trunk, darted down the hillside and fetched the driver back. Johnson waited with his arm stretched out in anticipation, fist opening and clenching in spasms. Seizing the driver with a strangled yelp of fury, he bent it over his knee, crammed the folded ruined club into his bag and ran off the green through the hushed spectators into the clubhouse. When he had passed, they poured past the gate, led by the anxious Home Pro, and gathered around Barnes and Tommy. Everyone shot questions at them simultaneously.

"What's the matter? What happened?" Barnes shrugged and handed his putter to his caddy without bothering to reply. "What happened, cadd?" the Director of Sports asked. The boy's features were taut, his lower lip had split open freshly and blood trickled down his chin. He stammered, "Sh-shot 79."

By six-thirty the rest of the players were in. No one had bettered the course record of 65, but the prize went to Barnes, who shot 67, 5 below par. Ed Sullivan was due any minute for the ceremony, and many more guests had come up from the hotel to see the cup given away. Meantime, white-jacketed bartenders were hustling a buffet and bar into position before the fireplace, while a combo settled its instruments in a corner. Everyone milled around the tables, smiling as the liquor began to flow. The hotel's pro made a speech from the chair; flashbulbs popped as celebrities entered.

Over in a corner against the oak-paneled wall were a few

of the tournament caddies, grinning generously at the hubbub as they drank from beer bottles. The boy leaned in the shop door, his face expressionless, except that pain and bewilderment twitched in the corners of his dark eyes. He was afraid, swamped by fear such as he hadn't imagined. He was staring blankly at the blond head of Johnson where he stood at the bar propped on his elbow, drinking down scotches. The pro clutched to himself alone a bottle the harried barboy had thrust at him. He looked detached, uninterested in the hustle around him.

The cup and prize money were given away. Sullivan greeted them all with patter and a new young songstress and the country club swung into its usual Fourth of July Tourney Dance.

When Johnson finally heaved round from the bar he saw his caddy's eyes on him. The boy was absently polishing the head of a driver. "That goddamn kid," Johnson muttered, "I got to pay him too." Clasping the bottle, he shouldered across the floor, his eyes seeking the boy's. Though Tommy's eyes never left Johnson, he continued to polish the driver.

"Want a drink, kid?"

"No."

"Lip still hurt?"

"No."

"Everything's okay, isn't it?"

No answer. Johnson lowered at him. "I said, everything okay?" Tommy was silent. The big man passed his hand through his hair vaguely and set the bottle on the shop counter. He fumbled in his pocket for a roll of bills from which he fingered out a ten and handed it to him. His voice was gruff.

"Five for the shagging, five for the tournament. Everything okay now?"

The boy took the bill, put it in his pocket, still said nothing. His mouth was stretched open, tense, the lip cracked, bleeding; his breath was jerky. He gazed at the man vacantly. Johnson swayed closer. The blue eyes were bloody; they were welling with tears. Suddenly he gripped the back of Tommy's neck, pulled his face close to his own, and whispered, "You don't give a damn, do you? You don't know, don't care, and don't want to know, do you? I could kill you, you little punky spic . . . Well, is everything okay or isn't it?" He shook the silent boy as if he were a doll; and then, gently pressed his palm on the bleeding mouth, turned, picked up his bottle of scotch, slung the bag of clubs on his shoulder and stalked from the dancing tumult in the clubhouse. The boy stood motionless, watching the pro until he disappeared.

Once in his yellow convertible Johnson wiped the blood off his hand, tilted the bottle high, and drank off the rest of it. Then he turned the key, drove down the hill away from the golf club and sped out on the highway to New York.

# THE GREAT
# PYRAMID

Their meetings took place in a tiny hotel apartment a block or
so off Times Square. Every Saturday night, the two dusty, overheated gray rooms filled with women. They came from their seats
in the dim lobbies of decaying hotels like this one or out of their
dim warrens in dreary brownstones. Each possessed, or was possessed by, some notion that revealed every word of the language
as significant, a key to an obscured world of meanings, occult
meanings reserved for *those who knew.*

They were Mentalphysicists, Theosophists, Christian Scientists,
real Rosicrucians, or often as not novitiates in something new.
There was, however, the common interest: spirits, prophecy,

miracles. They were onto things the government would like to know; they had information, they slyly chirped, that the millions of the masses of mankind could never even suspect . . . Secrets of History . . . the Future of the World.

These aged ladies were adorned with fancifully wrought, old silver pendant earrings, dull gold brooches of filigree, great cameos of delicate ivory and coral, massy bracelets, noisy ropes of pearls or amber or onyx or jade; rings with great carbuncular pink or brown or purple stones clung to their broken fingers; layers of powder, various in hue and texture, caked their cheeks and coated their throats and liver-spotted bosoms. They used too much fulsome perfume. The large ones strapped themselves in creaky corsets, every joint of which, every hook and eye and string, was visible through their musty silk dresses of faded flowers; the small ones, the birdy creatures, came clothed in worn woolens, and accompanied by younger companions who were nervous, suffering through their climacteric.

These women doted on their host, the young student of prophecy whose shirts were foul, raveled at collar and cuff, and whose hair was never cut or combed. On one wall in the front room, next to his framed *Oxon,* he had hung the Certificate of Honor conferred on his mother by Mary Baker Eddy. A few years back he had published a treatise on Nostradamus, an excruciating explication of Things Yet To Come making up the bulk of its pages. Now, he was bubbling with news about what had really become of the Ten Lost Tribes of Israel: that is, they had in modern times been transmogrified into the invisible citizens of what he termed *Anglo-Israel.* Even the Irish, he said earnestly, are Hebrews; they are descendants of the Tribe of Dan, the Seafarer. Didn't everyone know that Gaelic was rooted in Hebrew? Or that the Basques, so proud of their blond hair and blue eyes, are Hebrews—are there not inscriptions made of Hebraic characters on their oldest tombstones? And, as for the British Lion—had not descendants of the Tribe of Judah reached England? And was not the American Nation, originally at least, and culturally of course, very largely descended from Judah, in consequence? Hence, Anglo-Israel!

Bright in his esoteric ways, avaricious for new suggestions, he was a scholarly and almost indefatigable researcher in the hidden vales, and frequently hinted that he had, as a matter of fact, but a few details to clear up before he would be ready to reveal a triumphant exegesis of the prophetic mysteries of *Finnegans Wake* itself! But for the restraining influence of his male ac- quaintances, mostly his seniors by two or three decades, he might have tried to integrate all the doctrines, various as they were, so earnestly, so beseechingly propounded by the females who came to him. But these gentlemen were seasoned skeptics, and scoffed at him for being rather gullible, and even interrupted frequently, rudely enough, when they saw him listening with that certain logical light in his dreamy gray eyes. They were, after all, scien- tific; even though they followed up the least reports of psychic doings, and traveled to attend any *good* séance within a hundred miles, they denied believing anything whatsoever—perfectly gen- uine photographs of ectoplasm, such as they had been shown last week, notwithstanding. Mr. Brett, their dean of physics, Mr. Brett with the white goatee and gold pince-nez, for example, had spoken last week and summarized the results of sixty years' work in probing the World of Spirit: he himself, after sixty long years, had had to confess his evidence preponderantly negative . . . of course, he had also gone on solemnly to maintain that he could always tell a good medium from a fake, and a real presence from the false, and of course the men in his audience, the scientists, agreed, while most of the ladies thought sixty years' worth of negative conclusion meaningless, even pathetic, in view of their knowledge, and their feminine sensitivity.

Tonight promised to be most interesting. They had a guest

lecturer, this night. The two rooms were filled early; some ladies sprawled awkwardly on the rickety beds, others squirmed on camp stools or perched on the few pieces of furniture or stood with the gentlemen at the rear wall. At the front of the larger room, over the unused firedoor, hung a chart fastened to the wall by little colored tabs of scotch tape. Shortly after the talk had started, one or another piece of tape would peel away from the wall, that corner of the sheet would curl over, obscuring the diagrams and forcing the speaker to return to it. But he continued, talking back at them over his shoulder as he grunted, reaching up to press the tape laboriously to the wall, in what was an obviously futile effort to secure the chart.

This Doctor Bowler who addressed the group had long white hair, a red face, and wore a black serge suit. He stood with his fingertips splayed on the pamphlet-littered table before him; a heavy and gnarled cane was hooked over his left arm. His deep voice issued from the leathern throat of a public speaker. The subject was the Great Pyramid at Gizeh, whose cross section was displayed behind him. The old man spoke quite impressively, pausing at frequent whiles to look long at this figure before them all and to reflect upon it with them.

"Yes," he was saying, "this whole thing is a *pro*phecy. As sure as I stand here, you will see that what I am about to reveal to you must come about within the *next* few years. You keep your eyes and your ears open. This Great Pyramid of Tutankhamen's is *all* a *pro*phecy. Entirely. Only a few greatly learned and devout men have succeeded in deciphering the mysterious writings and unraveling the *pro*found significance of this Pyramid's architecture. Just look *here* now."

He walked slowly back to the wall and pointed the rubber tip of his cane at the entrance to the Pyramid. "This is the door, yes, but a *sec*ret door unknown to all the tomb robbers, plunderers of they knew not what. It was discovered by a friend of mine, a world-famous English archaeologist who left me private letters saying that he firmly believed in the truth of what I am about to reveal to you people here tonight. Now look here at this—see how one passage leads straight down and down away back down into the bottom of the Great Pyramid? Now look how it stops dead in this little room here—and I saw it with my very own two eyes there in Egypt—from this room you can look back, and way up there back over your shoulder is the entrance: a faint glimmer of light about as big as a five-cent stamp. And day and night, night and day, do you know what is visible, shining down through that little tiny hole? Yes, the sky, *and one star*, ladies and gentlemen; and that star is the North Star! *Po*laris! Day and night, always visible, always shining there, *Po*laris.

"And, you remember that I said before this here Great Pyramid is so vast it covers almost *four*teen *square* acres! Think of that, and then think of that star, the North Star, shining down always through that tiny hatch up there . . ."

He paused, significantly, to let the weight of that settle.

"Now I'll tell you what this passageway means. You know from the Bible how Ham, the Son of . . . the Son of . . ." He seemed to hesitate in doubt an instant.

". . . The son of Noah!" was proffered eagerly by a gray wisp of a girl who had joined the group recently and who always placed herself at the elbow of the young student of prophecy.

"Thank you, thank you, Miss. I see someone knows her Bible," he said mischievously, and continued, ". . . how the Son of Noah, Ham, was driven out from before his father's eyes? Well, now, he and his children and his children's children, and all on down the line of that descent were cursed, and they went on down this slanted tunnel, down this passage to this dead end, this dead-end, empty room. *A*way, *a*way from out of the sight of the Lord, out of the Lord's sight! They got damned, you see—and they can't turn around, and they can't go back up because it's *too* steep, and *too* late! And the Children of Japheth too, and the Children of Shem! All lost, all lost down this long tunnel." He shook a mournful head, his venerable white mane, and contemplated once more the path of his doleful words. Finally, he said: *"Indeed, in*deed a great shame."

Then he resumed his guided tour of the Great Pyramid. "Let's go on away from that foul, dismal hole, that tomb and sepulcher of Ham, Japheth, and Shem, and let's start over again. Back at the entrance up here now, there is, you see it here, a path that goes upward: it goes climbing up and up until it reaches a division, a fork, a separation, a parting of the ways (all this happens deep inside the Great Pyramid, you know), and then it levels off. We have come now, therefore, to the year of the birth of Jesus Christ. *By* the by, my dear friends, all these steps here that we have been climbing up are numbered; only you have to be able to figure out these mysterious hieroglyphics on the wall that give you the right correspondences. Now, according to this ancient *pro*phecy, the key to which was discovered by my English friend, Christ was to be born Easter Week, Four b.c. And what does historical evidence say to this prediction? Historical evidence, the rectification of the calendar by science, shows us *the very same thing!*

"We walk straight along this tunnel, level now with the ground *out*side the Great Pyramid, and we come to a room which is called The Lesser King's Chamber. It signifies the Messiah; but it, too, has a blind dead end, so it's *not* the *true* Messiah. I'm sorry to say, but Christ was not the true Messiah. No, *in*deed, and not by a long shot! Many people thought back then that Armageddon would come soon and then the Kingdom of the Lord would be set up on the earth, *for*ever and ever. But it never came. Of course, the Great Pyramid could have told them that! Had they but known, had they but known its secrets!

"Let's walk along back to where we met the fork, now. Here

we are, yes. Now you can understand why all those poor people who have followed Christ—who was just another prophet, that's all, like Moses or Ezekiel—those poor people followed him down that blind passageway. But you see how they can still be led back. All those poor people everywhere who believe that Christ was *the* Lord, or the Lord's Son, the *real* Lord, when he wasn't, could not have been *at* all" (his voice grew plaintive here) "when he was merely but another prophet. A big one, I *freely* admit it, I am the first to admit it, but, well, not *the* Lord! So then, we can lead all those people back just the way we came, toward the separation of the ways in the Great Pyramid, and on toward the *true* Messiah.

"Now let's go up these numbered steps—each one stands for exactly a hundred years—that lead to the *real* King's Chamber: The *Greater* Room! On these last steps, we must go carefully and slow. Ah! here we are: the Twentieth Century! And allow me to remark that all the big wars we have had since 1800 are predicted there on the walls of the Great Pyramid—with their exact dates. Here's 1914, and up another half-step, look carefully now, ah, the last step—here's this last war. These things are down there, carved into the wall: you need only the eyes to see. The Great Pyramid tells it all. All!"

His eyes glittered. "We turn a corner and we find etched in hieroglyphic symbols, the year 1968, right on the wall as high as my shoulder here. This is the big year. September of *Nine*teen-Sixty-eight. It's down, it's foretold in the Great Pyramid. That is the year of the Angel Michael coming to announce the Armageddon. And big things will be happening in Nineteen Hundred and Sixty-eight. Just you watch and see!"

The women in the room looked at each other knowingly, anticipating the pleasant surprises of the secret, which was really no secret at all to them, as adepts. And the speaker's pitch rose more shrilly, and he turned from a deep meditation over the Great

Pyramid's runes toward the people awaiting his words. He raised his right arm and clenched his fist till it trembled with anguish.

"*That* is why, my friends, I cannot see all that business over there in Palestine, with those unfortunate folks from Europe working away and taking over the Holy Land, and the Arabs still trying to stop them. First, the English, and now the Arabs; and all that bloody fighting and bloodier truce, year after year without cease. Why, they can't stay there even if they do keep it, because in seven years, *fatal* years, after the *Arma*geddon, the world is going to be run from there. It will be the Headquarters of the Kingdom of the Lord! None of the Arabs will be thrown out then. No, they will be brought into the fold; they will have the land again, and it's no use, ladies and gentlemen, for *those* Jews to fight to hold onto it, for it doesn't belong to them, never did. The Great Pyramid says so." Suddenly, he took another tone.

"Now, did you know that England and America are the homes of the lost *and* scattered tribes of Is*r*ael?"

"Yes, yes! They are, they are!" called out a rapt voice from the back of the room. It was the student of prophecy. Doctor Bowler nodded quiet thanks, went on. "They are the Anglo-Israel nations. And they will be fighting at the side of the Lord. All those folks away down down down in that black pit below— they, *they* are the lost people! The tribes of Ham, of Japheth and Shem. Truly lost. No way for them in the sight of the Lord. All the Negroes of Africa and India, all those Russians and those millions and millions of Chinese and Japanese and Burmese and Javanese and whatnot, ragtags and remnants . . . those poor, poor people down in that black hole . . . It's too bad."

He shook his sad white head. But, he then looked hopefully up and said: "But we have got to try and help them. We have got to show them the paths of light and of brotherly love. They are our brothers, after all; and we must do our duty by them. We

have got to try to raise up those poor lost people. Our poor
brethren of long ago.

"And look here now, too—aren't there also millions of foolish
folks walking the streets of this very city of New York here, and
calling themselves Jews? Why, they're not any more *He*brews
than those poor damned Chinese. They are not descended from
the Tribes, the true Ten Lost Ones. *I* know! I can look into a
man's face anywhere in the world, and I can tell you if he is one
of the Chosen Ones."

He glanced over the faces before him. "Do I see anyone here
who's *not* Chosen? No. I am Chosen. For most of my life I truly
believed I was Gentile. And so I thought I was utterly forsaken.
But then, after I learned the secrets of the hieroglyphics, I was
able to trace my heritage back, and so discovered that I am of
the tribe of Judah, the Lion, an im*per*ial Hebrew. You know, my
friends, it isn't what a man *thinks* he is, but what he's *born* as.
You have to be *born* a Hebrew!"

Sternly he looked them over again, drawing breath deeply for
his peroration. "Now for this Great King's Chamber. There is a
big stone step just at the threshold. It's all inscribed with mystic
signs, and it's the last word the Great Pyramid has to tell us."

The rooms stirred and hummed with low excitement. Doctor
Bowler's voice rang out: "That means the King's Chamber is
the Kingdom of the Lord set up on earth after the Day of Judgment. It says that *Arma*geddon will come upon us in Nineteen-
Seventy-five! Yes, another war, and it's going to be the biggest
war ever fought on this earth."

He spread his arms over them. "The Third World War! The
battle in which the forces of Evil will be vanquished and the
Angel Gabriel will appear on earth to set up the Throne of *the*
Lord in Jerusalem! And you see, ladies and gentlemen, it's got
to be that way! It's there in the Great Pyramid, and nobody, nobody on earth, can stop it. That's why I say to you that what's

going on today has got to fail, the United Nations and such, all that useless diplomacy. It's just no use, ladies and gentlemen. Just no use, no use at all . . ." Doctor Bowler leaned intently across the table for his final utterance. "There are thirty million people in this here country who will lead the armies of *the* Lord, who will be the Chosen Ones for the Kingdom of the Lord on the Judgment! The Armageddon approaches. Seven years, seven *fa*tal years—and then the last war in the year Nineteen-Seventy-five. The Armageddon! There's only a short time left now to prepare!"

He stopped, his face and neck scarlet, glowing between the black of his suit and the white full head of hair. Evidently he had finished. Quietly, he asked if there were any questions.

An enormous woman, her breast covered with rustling bric-a-brac, tremulously begged to know if she was of any of the Lost Tribes, any one of them. Others also pleaded. Doctor Bowler referred, somewhat vaguely now, to the chart of the Great Pyramid, to its tunnels.

They were eager too about their fates after Armageddon; and he seemed rather reluctant to say exactly what was in store for them.

There was a commotion at the rear. A man rose up, drawing a sheaf of papers out of his coat pocket. Dressed in a baggy, patched and fraying herringbone suit of indeterminate color, he set his grizzled bony head forward. There was a stern smoldering look in his eyes; he spoke quickly, in an exaggerated sardonic rasp, once he got started.

"Doctor Bowler, I'm not sure I know what the gist of your talk was about, but some of my old friends here seem to be getting excited about it. Perhaps I might be able to offer a few words about your background which might cool their brains a little?" He unfolded his scribbled-up papers and read hurriedly. "In 1928 you were arrested in Illinois as a Kleagle in the Ku Klux

Klan. Then you joined up with Gerald L. K. Smith's gang. And after that you were one of the boys in that America First outfit, and also in the German-American Bund. After that, you went around preaching about Moral Armaments!"

There was a buzz of wonder.

"I . . . I don't know what you're saying," the old man stammered.

"I remember. I saw you myself. Before the war, I saw you in Yorkville at Bund meetings with that man Fritz Kuhn who they put away in jail. And here you are again—eh? What do you say?"

But he didn't stay for answer; he went on reading vehemently from his list, garbled names and dates. His message of warning, gripping him suddenly, he flared into a tirade against the guest of the evening.

Doctor Bowler stared amazedly. He seemed hurt: "But . . . but surely you can see how it's all in the Great Pyramid? the signs, the millennia . . ."

The man shouted the louder at the Doctor, demanding to know, for instance, whether he, Abe Jensen, was blind or something. "I saw you there, here and there and everywhere, you liar, a coupla times, I say: I saw *you*. Yes, and what about the KKK? What do you have to say about that? Ha! Don't you worry, the FBI's interested in you. I know, and I just happen to know they been keeping an eye on you all along. Bet you didn't see that in your hieroglyphics. Ha! I could tell you a thing or two, yes, sir— that *I* know. World War Three! Great Pyramid! What the hell, I'm sick of war, and I'm sick of the goddamned Hebrews who always start wars anyway. Who needs the goddamned Lost Tribes? Who needs the goddamned Hebrews? What the hell are you up to anyhow, you Judah the Lion Hebrew, you?"

But Doctor Bowler, stunned, mumbled he must really be getting along . . . something about another engagement. He fumbled with his Great Pyramid, disconcertedly got it down and started rolling it up.

The rooms were in a small uproar, Abe Jensen yelling at everyone by turns. He bawled out that *he* was going to *take* the Floor, that he would conduct the Forum and answer their questions, because Doctor Bowler un*fort*unately just *had* to be running along—ha!

The skeptics at the back, seemingly always saved by providential disorder, stood impotently grinning at the commotion and the ruffled bumblings of Doctor Bowler. The young student of prophecy, agonizingly disheveled at the throat where his nervous fingers yanked and pulled at collar and tie, clammy thin hair falling over his shining eyes, darted and stumbled through the confusion of female bodies until he reached Doctor Bowler's side. He began to pump his hand and thank him for coming up this evening. He begged the old man's pardon—terribly. With hesitant, hopeful smile, he apologized and apologized, tenaciously holding onto his elbow, while Doctor Bowler pulled away and tried to get out through the jammed fire door.

The women in the middle room had turned in consternation from the evening's apocalyptic lecturer to the fiercely gesticulating Abe Jensen, his words conveying hints of a world of secrets more secret than any secrets they had known, and by his attack on their inspiring, frightening, thrilling visionary Doctor Bowler. They did not in the least comprehend what he meant by the curious record he had declaimed; they were scared of the words "Federal Bureau of Investigation," scrawled in blunt blue pencil over the crumpled sheets of paper he now thrust at them, for them to see, *just see* for themselves with their own eyes: the evidence, the evidence!

Doctor Bowler, having been helped on with his forgotten coat, was at last permitted to back through the fire door. He looked down at the buttons of his shoes and murmured he was sorry to have to leave, but that his time was so short. He had grown smaller, and seemed very old.

The host scrambled about the rooms, pushing the women back to their places, trying to soothe them. Abe Jensen had now stumped forward to take over the Meeting. Waving his arms about over his head, he shouted: "I've got the Floor now, I've got the Floor! Are there any questions, anything you want to know? I'll answer any questions from the House. Come on, come on, ladies and gentlemen—any questions at all!"

# THE DOWRY

In those days a ship's cargo was people. Eighteen million bodies were carried across the sea between 1900 and 1930, having themselves freighted over from the "old country," which during those thirty years was mostly Southeastern Europe. Their pasts were dim, reaching not two generations back. The elders had no fine tales of old times.

There is some recollection of a great-grandfather, a mighty man with a red beard, who buried five wives, a poor tailor in the ghetto of Biera-Berzhan, one of the gang that collected corpses still warm and carted them off to the undertaker's. Redbeard specialized in children: a terrible sight they say it was to see him stalk out of the stricken house with a piteous limp bundle under one great arm, swinging a bottle of vodka in the other and pausing at the doorsill to tilt back his flaming top and drink a health to the parents from their gift. Plied on their rounds, the body-collectors were a roaring bunch; as there was always death, always were they drunk. Should some of the most miserable pay no tithes to the synagogue, their dead were left until dues were done and poultry won to grace the tables of the undertaker's men.

But that is all there is of this red giant. His son, the grandfather, the *Zaydeh,* was a tailor after him, sewing for a clientele of peasants their suits made from flour sacks. He too was of great strength in youth: a man who brought the dead weight of flour that made a winter's bread to the house and tossed it into the bin like a pillow. He was poorer than his father since he carried no corpses; so there was, and this is remembered most clearly, seldom a winter's sack of flour. In his time Rumanian soldiers came into this territory and warred over the land of Bessarabia. The Rumanians habitually machine-gunned the people in the ghettoes; when the Czar's Cossacks fought their way back in the country they too machine-gunned them. The emigrants escaped to America; their memories shut away this past; and they came with almost nothing.

The Zaydeh sent his oldest son and daughter over first. When money was mailed back in a few years the other children clamored to go, but he said, tapping his chest with his thumb, No. You are staying here. I am next to go, for if you went you would become rich and idle and forget about us here, and we your mother and father be left forever.

He spoke wisely; they would have forgotten him so far off, sure. His sons found it pleasant, so good to walk around New York, free, no jobs, without trades, big radicals, their sisters in the dress factories, making money.

By the twenties the entire family had come to America and

all the daughters been sucked into the sweatshops, basted with Lilliputian threads into innumerable garments by the chattering deft machines. Their father was an old man on his arrival, his eyes too weak for his tailoring trade, and himself suddenly too aged to hustle to the shops. How suddenly he declined, withered, and his wife, the *Bubba,* with him. Transplantation had exhausted him; or perhaps, like an Old Man of the Sea, he had clasped his legs tightly about the necks of his brood far back in Bessarabia, been carted across oceans with his chattel, to remain seated on their necks in the New World. Though his sons and daughters slipped out of the house to marry, one after another, they settled near the old people in flats in the same building or on the next street. One daughter brought her husband to live in one of their rooms. As naturally close they were as seedlings holding tenure in a circle round the bole of an old tree, too old a tree, and they struggled in the master shade for footing, clinging to the great stony roots in the strange forest; entangled; vying with each other for life's simplest portion in this hungry acre.

When the family lived downtown on the lower East Side there was commotion, a houseful of people rising at five and preparing for a day's work, moving around the cold dingy rooms of the apartment in the weak light of the yellow bulbs; noisy at breakfast, crabbing at the efforts of their mother to fix bags of lunch at the pace they demanded. But this bustle died down in a few years. Only the furniture remained, the dirty worn linoleums covering the floor in every part of the place; the mountain of trunks and luggage settling into ruin and dust in one obscure corner of the long entrance foyer where they had been piled in the first days; the massive carved dining-room table with its company of stiffbacked knobby chairs, and the tattered satin pillows flung on the swaybacked double beds to complete the bedroom suite: bureau, vanity-with-mirror, spindle-legged bench, and extra chair. The windowshades flapped torpidly against the streaked panes; silence drifted through the tenement rooms, condensing on the old people alone among these cheap and ill-arranged things, while the clock in the brass tiller-wheel, held firm in the grip of a brass Franklin Delano Roosevelt, ticked, ticked time from the dining-room sideboard. And the Zaydeh sat and listlessly looked down out the window at the traffic moving on First Avenue; the Bubba lay somnolent on a bed; and the husband of one of the daughters, staying in the room with a glass door, played solitaire all day long.

Until the *Girls* came home. In the family they were called "the Girls" not because they were young, but because unmarried. There were two, one perhaps ten years the elder. Because their heads ached they shuffled nights through the rooms with their stockings fallen down around their ankles and lay abed weekends with white kerchiefs bound by tight knots constricting their brows, frowning.

The older one, Bella, short and somewhat bony, had drawn features, eyes dull brown, and dull-brown mousy hair. Her skin glistened. It was oily and pimpled with eczema. She would be rubbing cream on her hands, her wrists. She was a quiet woman; but she could complain morosely how little money her brothers and sisters gave for the old people, though the Girls lived with them and had the advantage, as the others said, of the Bubba's keeping house for them while they went to work and made lots of money. Bella's shrewish tongue was a plaint of despond: she still flailed the air though she had long been down and fettered and knew it. Everybody else knew it and wondered how long she could keep it up. Though she was still called "one of the Girls," they had no hopes for her.

Her younger sister, Tessie, who said she was much younger, was the glamour girl. As short as Bella, she was raven-haired and plump. Her complexion was smooth, so she used lipstick, very red; she rouged heavily, patted her face with crusty orangeish powders; her black eyes were as a gypsy's should be. She wore tight dresses and high heels, sometimes white socks and slacks with her high heels when she was at the hotel in the country, where she put on a big straw hat and smiled at tall men so that a dimple in one cheek showed. She was what, laughing and laughing, they called "the glamour girl." Tessie went out with boyfriends. She left Bella with her mother and the ancient Zaydeh who sat after supper by the table and said never a word, for all that could be known never thought anything, because one of his eyes was full of blood and hanging out and the other eye just stared, and his lower lip hung down and dribbled onto his vest. Bella would glance at him and jump up with one of her screams, and dab at his shirt.

"Why can't you wipe yourself? Do I have to do everything for you? What are you good for? Sits, and sits, and says nothing ever, and drips and pees on himself. Why am I stuck night after night? Go to him, momma, I can't stand it!"

And then she would go hollering up and down the kitchen while the old people just stared at her, bemused, almost not knowing what ailed her as she gabble-gabbled away in bits of Yiddish. She'd fling out and come scowling back in her stained housecoat with the dirty old clout about her head, and rubbing the creams into the backs of her hands. After a while she just sat for hours looking at them until her parents drifted to bed. When Tessie's high heels clacked up the last stairs to the apartment and entered, Bella would be waiting for her to say:

"Why don't you ever shut the light and sleep, idiot! Go to bed. Don't sit waiting for me there with your stinking hands. You have to work tomorrow."

Then Bella would sneer:

"You go straight to hell. You have to work too."

Sundays, the family came together for dinner; all there, daughters with husbands, the sons with wives: none of them had personal affairs which could supersede the gathering of the central family. The three sons brought their own little groups to the board for Sunday dinner. Childless, not absorbed by families of their own, the five married daughters who still went into the shops vaunted themselves young simply because the Girls, being mates, wanted only too obviously. The Girls resented their sisters' smugness; it was unwarranted, especially since they were all proving barren. Who were they to be proud? The dress factories had claimed them every one. And indeed, the whole line of sisters was rapidly aging: middle-aged, stout, hair withered like straw, wrinkles and puckers in their faces coming on just like the deep, etched creases of their parents. Almost no longer distinguishable as the children of these parents was the group sitting at the table with them Sundays, but looking like siblings, all, a single generation of men and women.

In this acrid atmosphere explosions were the natural order. Sunday dinners inevitably jangled and broke. During the arguments, as always, the Zaydeh sat at the head of the table wordless, breathing hard, in agonies of silence. The Bubba bent over the group wringing her hands, over and over almost keening while the shouting rose, "Oi! Oi! kinder, kinder!" None of the children heard the supplications of their mother: the noise was about money. The Girls worked hard. Why didn't the others contribute to the upkeep of the house? the Girls asked.

"Why should we? We got houses of our own to support. You should lend us money better. You make enough. What's bothering you girls? It doesn't cost for the old people."

"Look how big this place is," Bella said. "We got to feed four here; with food so high, and gas, and light; and the Zaydeh has to go to the doctor every week for treatments. Why don't you pay for X-rays and medicine? What about his cigarettes and candy that he needs, hah? Nobody gives but us."

"You make enough between the two of you. The Bubba cooks for you and cleans for you and washes your clothes. You got enough."

"Never," they said, "never enough money."

It would always come to the same pass: Tessie stood, screwing her face, plucking at her bodice for a handkerchief, about to weep, saying:

"Who told you to run out and marry the first man you laid eyes on, what was burning you? I have to save for my dowry. I'm still a young girl. I have to get married. Who will give me a dowry if I don't save it up myself? Not you cheapskates. You wouldn't give nothing, nothing at all to help anybody."

"Who gave us dowries?" they asked.

"So what? Who cares for you?" countered Bella. "We won't run out into the street like dogs first thing. We're going to be decent and have weddings for ourselves like people."

The eldest sister, who had come over first and sent passage money for the others, asked:

"Well, it's about time to have them, no?"

"You shut up," screamed Bella. "Who needs your advice?"

After which exchange the two stomped into their bedroom and slammed the door.

"Come on, where's the deck?" Hannah said when they were gone. "Come on, children, let's sit down and play a poker. Out with the money. Bring a dish for the kitty."

In ten minutes the weekly poker game was swinging. In an hour the Girls would be enticed out. They would march to the great table with a haughty indifference and brusquely say:

"Give us seats."

And Jacob would caution with a wink:

"You better have cash if you want a hand in this game."

So the quarrels ran on. Through the long depression they were forever accumulating their dowries, there was never enough for themselves and the Zaydeh and Bubba to live on. When the depression slackened shortly before the war, the family migrated to the Bronx, to a new apartment building at the edge of the Park. The Girls brought up every stick of their old furnishings. The decrepit kitchen linoleum was ripped from the floor, cut and patched to fit the new room; the bedroom and dining-room suites remained exactly in former patterns, sombering new walls to create the dreary former dispositions. Still they clung together, the Girls and their parents living on the third floor, and others disposed on various floors above and below in the same building. None wanted the trouble of the old folks staying with them, yet none could bear the accusation from the others of not aiding to support them; thus the old tribute was extorted by the Girls. And they would have more: they were living at a much higher rental; everything had gone up and they couldn't manage alone. The others let it ride and sent in their random subsidies for the sake of quiet.

During these years Tessie still claimed boyfriends. Discussion was unnecessary: no eyes were laid on any one of these heroes because she could never get herself engaged. When the war broke, however, things livened up for her at last; she had what the family conceded to be a boyfriend. Who knows? they said; maybe, maybe. There bloomed announcement of a dinner. Tessie's man was guest of honor. They awaited him about the table in the parlor, crowded, impatient; each in his best attire: black dresses and dark blue suits.

The spread was simple, indeed meager for an occasion of such rare importance: two bottles of sweet grape wine, an almost empty pint bottle of whiskey, two plates of heavy dark honeycake, a platter of sorry apples. The Zaydeh, informed that a boy was coming to see Tessie, occupied the head of the table; he turned anxiously to each of his children, annoyed by the grandchildren who clattered through the apartment, whooping, sliding over the floors. Tessie sat at the window, aloof; she watched the street while Bella in the kitchen assorted fugitive chinaware into settings clean and ready, scolding the Bubba for this and that ineptness when they blocked each other's way.

The buzzer rang up from the street entrance. Tessie started up and scurried to the bedroom for one more look into the mirror. Her sisters carefully arranged their dresses, patted hairdos into place. They waited for him, composed as stones.

At last he entered, was introduced to the Berawitzes: Private Aaron Goldin. Short, plump, he bulged in his khakis; his hair was blond, almost brown, and he wore a shaggy brown mustache. He was near forty; tired red eyes, pouched beneath, lusterless. Tessie seized his arm when he stepped inside the door and clamped herself to him till the moment they should sit for dinner.

The guest was placed opposite the Zaydeh, who, though greeted courteously, answered by a grunt only. After the offspring were herded to the kitchen for their dinner, Jacob, the firstborn, filled with a flourish the boyfriend's glass with the last of the whiskey and, rising with his own, which brimmed with the cheap red wine, toasted: To Mr. Aaron Goldberg . . .

He was interrupted by Tessie:

"Please, Goldin, Goldin."

". . . a long and prosperous good life to you," Jacob blandly went on. "Your health, and yours, my beautiful Tessie."

Tessie, mollified, grinned next to Aaron Goldin as the men reseated themselves. Bella, who had already gulped her second tumbler of wine, gushing, broke into a spate of chatter in an attempt to make conversation for everyone across the table.

"Tell me, Mr. Goldin, so you work hard in the army?"

"Yes and no," he said; "sometimes."

"Do they treat you very bad if you can't keep up with the younger boys?"

"I keep up," he said.

Tessie frowned disapproval at Bella, who went deliberately on, with a tone of ingenuousness.

"Is the food good? It's very greasy, isn't it? I hear they make you eat a lot of potatoes, and pig. Are they sending you to fight?"

While she questioned him she fastened greedy eyes upon him, and while she spoke she scratched her arms. Private Goldin drew patient breath to reply when the Bubba entered with plates of pale yellow chicken soup in which swam limp greens, and served them out in her usual order for the Sunday dinner: starting with the Zaydeh, then Jacob, and running down the sequence of her children; after Tessie she brought a plate at last for the guest of honor. Tessie bit her lip with chagrin. Bella caught this and smiled a thin sardonic smile. Tessie's man was well-mannered enough not to notice any oversight of the old woman's. It was to be expected that such a fellow, if he were truly near engagement to Tessie, would know what dinner with her family would be like beforehand. A mob of sisters casting glances avaricious, critical, hostile upon him; the men eating quietly and drinking, striving to make it good, and failing; and the gloomy bloody-eyed old old man couched opposite from him, snorting sometimes over his meat. Even if Private Goldin had guessed it all beforehand, he had his manners, he kept his thoughts to himself.

The group was quiet during soup. Next, the Bubba carried in the mainplate of a big boiled rooster, which squatted upon crushed carrots and radishes, enmeshed in feeble celery stalks. The bird was blueish-white with black pins studding its body and half its feathers sprouting from the maimed stumps of its wings. The Bubba herself had pulled it, and it was hard for her to get all the pins out. Stripping her own fowls for years, she couldn't conceive having it done for her for fifteen cents. The Girls were humiliated. Though they had given their mother more money to buy the food for this important meal, she was so accustomed to frugality she never gave scope to what they might possibly intend when they told her:

"Here's money; buy a big bird. Make enough food for everybody, you hear! Enough."

Tessie blushed when the monster was brought in, all dripping from the pot, but when her mother started to cut it, picking up the pieces with a corner of the dishtowel because they were too hot for her to lift with her fingers, she couldn't control herself. She rose and roughly shoved the Bubba aside, muttering:

"Get away, get away. Go, bring in the potato kugel."

The Bubba returned with a great golden-brown smoking potato kugel that might have set things right. But the damage was done. Bella sniggered as she ate and looked slyly to attract Aaron Goldin's attention to her joke: Imagine that, the bird's so tough and the carrots so soft, and they were boiled together in the same pot! Bella was amused, however, by more than this joke, it seemed, and by more than Tessie's discomfiture; perhaps her delight was amplified by the Malaga. Whatever its source, there was no remedy for the laughter swelling in her. The more Tessie glowered, darting curses at her, and the more the others tried to catch both Tessie's reprimands and Bella's humor over the progress of the feast, the less hope there was of quenching her. She was a victim of comedy.

As the empty dishes were being collected, distracting the company at the table, Bella looked gravely once more at her sister's man and asked him straight out,

"Aaron Goldin, have you got a friend for me maybe?"

Everyone somehow heard her. The room became silent.

"Well," he drawled, helplessly in this appallingly somber room . . . what should he say?

Bella continued without his answer:

"Then the next time you go out with Tessie tell him to go

along with you to meet her sister. Tell him she's got a beautiful sister. All right?"

"Bella!" her sisters hissed in despair.

Tessie flung out of her chair, plucking at her boyfriend's shoulder. Come! she commanded. The Berawitzes watched him with faces that said, If you stay we of course apologize for her: if you must get out, well then go. Tessie pulled at him again, her nails dug into his arm.

"Come!"

Aaron Goldin stood up as politely as he could and said as he raised his glass to them, "Nice to meet"—Tessie tore at him—"it's a real pleasure to have met you folks . . ."

As Tessie dragged her hapless boyfriend out of that room packed with grim Berawitzes, through the front door, Bella's jagged sniggering burst into shrieks of laughter that pealed along the hallways, and rocked them down the elevator shaft.

The family did not scoff, only it knew the way it must be with its Girls: their fellows never follow through. Whatever happens doesn't matter; along the line somewhere a rupture is inevitable. The family sense here was final; it snuffled out significance, judged and pronounced even before the fact was born. The family knew the proper end it wished for all things, and contrary movement was nonsense, and partly dangerous—not to the unshakable family, but to the mover, who by that must lose his destiny. Tessie's liaison with Aaron Goldin seemed set to drag for several years in the customary fashion, Tessie dating week in and out, Bella waiting up nights to be told not to wait, the whole family waiting too all that time, holding its breath, awaiting the collapse of this latest mirage, waiting for Tessie to go on again becoming an old maid: her boyfriends merely paltry excursions from the road to spinsterhood. However, it was made out serious this time. The man was shipped. There were letters. It was rumored possibly, maybe actually, there might come betrothal. Nothing said in words; rather, tighter breathlessness, expectancy in the family. The test had come: Tessie was determined to break the doom forecast by her sisters and brothers.

Then a long silence. The war ended. The soldiers returned. Tessie's too; but no wedding. Silence. Obviously matters had gone again as the family had foreknown, gone as Bella secretly must have wished if she were not to be stranded with her ageless parents, and gone as even the old Zaydeh and Bubba had long long given up speculating or thinking about. What had happened? It was learned in a general way that Aaron Goldin proposed marriage, that Tessie accepted, and that everything had crept with the tortuousness and mystification characteristic of the Girls toward proclamation of this fact. And then, when he asked for the money, her dowry money, to set himself up in business and establish their home, she balked. Tessie absolutely refused to give it to him—her resources were several thousands by then—until after the ceremony was over. So he picked himself up, as they said, and disappeared!

Twenty years those Girls had slaved for dowries. The family couldn't help recalling that they would never lend money on account of these dowries. Now the prince who had come to the place where she was marooned, the last man who could have justified those twenty miserly years, had gone away because he himself couldn't have the dowry. In defense it was said he had really cared only for the dowry, anyway.

Tessie never mentioned him. Bella, at last sure that things would be as they must, kept peace too, not gloating or teasing or triumphant toward her bedmate, but benign. She had not been very secure while Tessie fought on valiantly for a cause from which she'd retired. Perhaps she ought to have been out there still too; perhaps it wasn't that Tessie was too obstinate to know when she was licked, but saw something where Bella was blind;

or perhaps a twist of fortune might throw one slim chance her way. Bella knew these skinny perhapses less than worthless. She also knew they would not fade until Tessie was joined with her in retirement.

The loss to Tessie was amplified a thousand times by the forthcoming marriage of a cousin much older, who would herself have been called a "girl" if the Girls hadn't dubbed her years ago: "the Greenhorn, the Greener." And this Greener was marrying a hackie, a widower with two sons, a man whose short five feet weighed three hundred pounds. But she was marrying; and she had accomplished a complete family of her own with the same stroke! For the Girls the last straw: the Greener married! Only Tessie and Bella left, butt of jokes and false pity. The reaction of surprise backwashed into jeers and laughter—see what a husband the Greener got with her recklessness! Among the Berawitzes no achievement escaped breakdown to its components of absurdity. At the dinner party celebrating the Greener's wedding, Bella made herself drunk very quickly, threw her legs up on the table and scratched her thighs and laughed until she fell back unconscious on the couch.

The old man, the Zaydeh, died soon afterward, very ill and very unwillingly. One morning at seven he fell on a patch of ice before the synagogue and lay helpless in the cold for half an hour, hip broken. By the time he was brought to the hospital and his leg had been set he was very weak: pneumonia. He needed oxygen but fought off the mask, crying:

"They will kill me with this. I am afraid of them here. Take me home, children."

The children gathered by turns at bedside for the watches of two nights; they tried to cajole him into having the mask strapped to his head; they pleaded with him, but he refused, though strangling. They took turns holding the rubber contraption down against his face while he wept to be released, and begged for a cigarette.

"Take me home, children," he moaned as he declined. He bled; his nephritic kidneys could not bear the strain of the heavy sulfa doses. As they watched him die, the children about the bed heaved with bitter unvoiced reproaches against one another. They waited for him to cease this frantic clawing at the mask which they must press down on him themselves, while avoiding a father's curse from his bleary eyes: You are helping them kill me, ingrates. Why do you do this? At last they must step back and witness the invincible pale nurse bind it to him. The two nights passed; when the Zaydeh ceased to struggle against the mask on the morning of the third day it was no longer of any use to him. At noon he was dead. His children left him then.

For some days after the funeral the family convened in the parlor of the Girls' apartment to mourn. As is customary for this first week of bereavement, the rooms were kept dark, no shoes were worn in the house. The more distant relatives and friends came to console, bringing with them gifts of flowers and baskets of fruit, assorted sweetmeats and chocolates. The Bubba was quiet after the first day, for she had not loved the Zaydeh much. Toward the end of this week, the stream of visitors dwindled and the sisters were left together for the long days. They lounged in the stuffy room on orange crates and cardboard cartons, disheveled, tired, cranky. The chat turned itself toward recrimination— the fact of death was so heavy on them, heavier than the accustomed bulk of the living Zaydeh. Hannah, one of the middle sisters, asked Tessie where she'd been when the Zaydeh shuffled out that morning.

"It was so cold, why didn't someone keep him home? Or at least why couldn't you get up from bed to take him down to pray?"

Bella, the one most afflicted with tears at the Zaydeh's death, took her up balefully. She raved about their guilt, all sinners, all evil.

"You're a pack of goodfornothings. Nobody cares about us, about anyone else's troubles. Who ever came up to help us with him, to dress and undress him? Who ever took him to the synagogue? Where are you all the time? Do we have to sit here forever when we want to go away on a weekend? Who wants to take the Zaydeh and Bubba into his house for a week so we can enjoy ourselves? Nobody! You all should drop dead, not the poor Zaydeh."

Bella lost her head; she ran to the kitchen, started hauling china out of the cupboards, dashing it to the floor, stamping it to bits with stockinged heels. They watched the crockery-smash solemnly; then they seized her and put her to bed in a huddle. She remained hysterical for days. When she calmed they saw in her still waters running deep. She had been suffering many years. Though her grievances against them made her sullen, the family eulogized her as "reformed"; they said she had settled down, wasting grief had made her mellow. As if to corroborate their opinion, Bella's eczema subsided, vanished. She had recognized officially that the jig was up, seen the soldier's disappointing performance to be the last hope of marriage for either of them.

When routine re-established itself after the burial of the Zaydeh, the Girls became yet more clamorous in their demands on the family for contributions to support the Bubba, though she was less a burden now than when her husband lived. But, since the Bubba must remain with the Girls (were they not unmarried, was she not their mother?), since she was the only parent left to the whole tribe, she was dearer to them, and therefore her value as a hostage dearer. Spokesman for the Girls was Tessie. Tessie did the talking in the circle, the accusing, and collecting of money for jobs like maintaining the plot in the cemetery, and buying a stone for the grave: a big stone, a carved monument, indeed the

very greatest she might have short of a granite mausoleum. Her
attention turned to things other than beauty parlors, clothes, the
varied mancatching paraphernalia. In this respect she was still
some years behind Bella. Now it was Tessie in trouble who refused to admit it, while Bella had slipped away to a serene apathy,
neglecting even her shop. When she was laid off, Tessie collared
her:

"Out, if you're going to carry on. Out of this house! I won't
support you. Not one piece of bread for you, if you don't earn
it with your own hands, understand?"

Bella found another job and behaved herself. She went to
work, sat before the sewingmachine as of old, and brought money
into the house. But what good was it, if no one had any use for
the cash? That account was, if still considered the dowry, rotting
in the bank like an unused trousseau, mumbling while it rotted
it was dead. The conclusion they made was that it might be useful still. The next anyone knew they were taking driving lessons.

The Girls were going to buy a car, an Oldsmobile with automatic shift. They intended to drive it themselves, the two of them,
Tessie and Bella in a three-thousand-dollar automobile. This was
news as incredible as the announcement of an engagement might
have sounded in days of the boyfriends.

"What, is the game over already, no more men?" asked Jacob.

"Imagine, children," said another, "Tessie and Bella flying in
a new Oldsmobile sixty miles an hour for a weekend in Atlantic
City! And Tessie will tie her speckled bandanna around her
head!"

The family roared with merriment.

"Impossible," gurgled Hannah, "they wouldn't shoot that old
dowry gold into a car, couldn't be! And the upkeep!" she added.

"But everybody drives today," one observed.

"Yes," they chorused, "but the Girls?"

Yet it was true. A new world had opened. So, if they failed the driving test after five lessons each for fifteen dollars? They stuck with it until they had had thirty lessons. Another fifty bribed the inspector who gave them roadtests. In the end both received operator's permits in the mail.

Then, their car. Only Oldsmobile would do. Tessie did the buying hastily; a few hundred to the dealer "under the table" got them the car they wanted. Both had chipped in for it; but Bella came out owing what was given the dealer, so Tessie wouldn't let her drive till she'd paid her share. Talk was no use till Tessie should be reimbursed, though Bella's claim was she could just as well have waited.

"What was the rush?" she sneered. "What was burning you? You didn't have to run out and bribe the first man you laid eyes on for this car. As far as I'm concerned I own half. Just do me something!"

And as far as Bella was concerned she would drive it. She started sneaking out at night during the week, driving the Oldsmobile through the streets fast and half out of control. It was as if Bella, having confabulated with herself, resolved to know herself for dead; from now on she lived her life as befitted her own valuation of it. But she was not desperate, she had long finished with despair; she was done; nothing signified. In the space of a few months she became as addicted to her night driving as she could have been to no stimulant. After a day of work she was exhausted, but the car fed strength into her. Sleep never restored; sleep had been a waste of tossing, attrition only so much slower than the working day punctuated by the unbrakable staccato machines in the shops. Bent over her Singer all day as the cloth ran between her fingers, or bent over the wheel and steering the great car through the dark with terrific urgency, a road flowing between its wheels, beneath her legs—no difference to Bella, who steered nowhere in particular, up and down the highways and parkways that fed the city: it was all of a piece: the cloth ran and the roads ran.

For her part, Tessie wasn't done yet. She needed that Oldsmobile for trips over the highways to somewhere: to hotels: she was still the gypsy glamour girl, would queen it in her new car to the Catskills, and to Atlantic City for her dreary vacations, as if not to carry her dowry scrawled in a bankbook, but for once to let it carry *her* through the world. It was her last illusion. Whatever toil it cost for years to earn it, she was mothering a good one: a solid steel and chromium-garnished giant that served her as nothing ever had before.

There were the two of them with the one shining car which rolled through two worlds; utter strangers; visions in strife: Bella driving, driving fast to reach some end of the open road, Tessie struggling to keep from being dragged with her.

Spitefully Tessie rented a garage on the sly and tucked the Oldsmobile away. She was deaf, knew nothing of its whereabouts —unless she was paid what Bella owed her on it. Somehow Bella found out where the car was cached, tipped the garagemen to keep them mum, and resumed her drives.

Tessie woke one night starting up, and felt for her sister in bed. She was out. Again. Into their room gleamed a winter moon spreading cold sheen over the wrinkled place beside her where Bella had crouched and feigned sleep, waiting to find herself once more in the car, facing down the ghostgray roadtop streaming toward her. Rising, angry, Tessie went to the phone (they'd gotten a telephone too when the car came, for they no longer spared themselves the luxury). She was told by the garage that Bella had taken the car out some hours ago, just before midnight. She hung up. That thing found the car! She crawled back into bed rehearsing the scene there would be in the morning. She'd have no more of this monkeybusiness from her. Bella's using up my car; some way she's got to be stopped. In a few minutes, it seemed, the telephone rang, bringing her out of sleep. Hospital calling. Bella had run into the concrete wall of a dead-end street. The Oldsmobile was wrecked.

Tessie dressed and went out. It was past four. Half the winter stars to the west were still sparkling in the blueblack; in the east most were out and the electric blue from the sky where one or two morning stars hung pervaded the empty streets through which her taxi rattled, making enough noise to wake the sleepers, and the distant dead Zaydeh too. Except for this vague glimpse of the sleeping people who soon must work, she wasn't conscious; ringing in the cold were the shrill echoes of the phone that had summoned her from sleep on this errand. The rest of what there was for her to know struggled to clamber up in this halfsleep as if from an abysm in the mind, but she refused to look on it. She sat in one corner of the cab, frowning, as it lurched downtown.

When Tessie arrived at the hospital, a clear blank dawn-white light was hinted by the skies over the city. Bella was in surgery. Later, she lapsed into a comatose condition. Tessie watched all afternoon; most of the family was with her by then, a circle of people sitting tense on the edges of settees in the lobby of the hospital, gazing at one another, hoping for Bella to mount back to waking. They had been told she would be paralyzed: her spine was hurt. Tessie felt that Bella had driven her to the wall. She was finished; the car was gone, and her sister. In the old familiar plaint, protesting, asking, denying, she lamented to them while they waited to hear that Bella was out of danger of her life.

"I told her not to take it out at night. I took away the car from her. She had no right to use it. It wasn't hers. She owes me five hundred dollars. Every night she takes it out and goes everywhere. That Bella, she's crazy, crazy. All night long she drives, all night. My God! she can't keep her hands off that wheel. Look, she's a

cripple now. And what about me, hah? My Oldsmobile is gone.
Now what shall I do?"

Tessie saw the mortification of her sisters and brothers as it
loomed, she shared in it as it engulfed their features. She knew
what they were thinking because she thought as they did. A swell
of self-pity rolled over her. A short swell—the Berawitzes could
not much pity anything, not even themselves. The pity. Then
anger, fury grew in her as she read their faces: she saw that she
would have the old woman and an invalid sister to live with and
support: the three alone together.

# THE GREAT DROUGHT

There had been no rain for months and months now, and New York was moving into its July heat. It seemed to him the city, the country, the very world was drying up, that God was taking a preliminary survey of the wasteland. He had seen the posters blossom in the subways and on sides of buildings, begging all citizens not to waste the precious last few million dregs of gallons in the dwindling watersheds. Certainly the water that dribbled from the faucets tasted drier to him nowadays. What would happen if the drought continued, he wondered, what would happen to everything? It could not continue; it must not; but he realized that it would; he could visualize all.

The skies remained serenely blue. Every morning he rose and looked out the window eagerly for a wisp of cloud. Nothing. Nor would the radio promise a drop of rain to the city, or the whole eastern seaboard for that matter.

He talked to no one about the drought anymore. It had not rained in May and June, and now that it was approaching the middle of July the subject of drought was definitely no longer a topic for discussion: it was too serious. No one could tell him anything he didn't know or feel and perhaps much more acutely at that. And there just wasn't any sign of rain. Intrepid amateur pilots had dropped ice from scores of sports planes wherever a cloud took shape over Long Island, but that was past and forgotten weeks ago. There didn't seem to be a drop of moisture anywhere in the atmosphere. Would the New York, New Jersey, Connecticut, Pennsylvania, and Delaware watershed soon be dry? It seemed that way. All the great 12-, 16-, and 24-foot aqueducts had already opened their valves utterly to the great metropolis, and New York's millions and millions of sinks and toilets and baths had flushed their contributions down the drains out into the sinking harbor forever.

That harbor, New York's fine estuary, was nothing more than a slimy swamp cluttered with furious mounds of sunken wreckage and garbage: tin cans, steel scrap, immense heaps of ancient stone and concrete rubble from demolished buildings; old black barges, hulks of sailing ships, burst tugboats, foundered steamers; and the skeletons of vast numbers of seagulls, fish, cattle, murdered humans and suicides; and the rails of trains, dumped railroad cars, autos, airplanes, lost machinery and the scuttled goods of smugglers: the whole vast precipitate and sediment of three hundred years' commerce in the greatest port of the world. Down the middle of the bay ran the central channel of the once mighty Hudson River, now but a stinking stream, a rivulet maundering between the deserted docks of Manhattan and steep cliffs of the

Jersey Palisades, running over baked cracking mud flats, once
the entire bottom of the river. The brooklet, fed by the tributary
waters, black and filthladen, of the city's sewers, was daily de-
creasing so much in volume that it could not carry the sewage
loads along with it; so that the rill trickled its way through a
noisome quagmire, hewing out a little Grand Canyon from
mountains of black refuse which, hardening, assumed the pic-
turesque formations of its western prototype.

The air over this muck fairly shimmered with pestilence in the
July heat. He became aware of it, as must millions of others, in a
sensation of sour flavor tinging the dust that always floated in
the air now as haze.

What was becoming of the world's water? Where was it all
going? Certainly the situation was drastic. To be sure, great modi-
fications were changing everyone's way of life, but his own dis-
comforts interested him most. The very act of living, even alone,
was growing difficult, and strange. The private signs of desicca-
tion absorbed his attention: it needed every moment to observe
their increase. And it was the same for everyone else, he supposed.
So there was no time left to spend with people. Besides, there
were few to be seen on the once swarming streets of Manhattan.

Fears that the eastern seaboard states would turn to desert were
not unfounded. The dunes of Cape Cod, multiplying enormously,
lifted themselves up and began to migrate westward, northward,
southward. They came over the whole desolated coast like hordes
of barbarians landed from the seas, overrunning towns and
cities: unbelievable yellow hordes, invincible, ubiquitous, pouring
in from nowhere. A Sahara! Like herds of elephants they roamed
up and down the streets of New York, their drifts flooded the
steps of the Public Library and floated spectrally through the
silent subway tunnels and basements and shops of the city. Soon
cactus and joshua would be growing everywhere, he imagined,
if there were water enough even for that.

He retreated finally to his own apartment, stocked amply with every variety of canned food. He hoped to hold out until rain fell. Occasionally he wondered if it would be any good at all if it did. How much could it rain? And think how much was needed! Rain falls over the Sahara, perhaps torrentially at times, but it all evaporates before it reaches the ground. And suppose some oases formed in New York. How many of the millions could live off them? They would mob them and strip them bare and dry in a minute. Then they would all die like flies; no, not even flies, but in numbers like the grains of sand that lay drifted as far as he could see.

Starkly remained the immediate problem: what to drink? Perhaps there was food enough in his house, hoarded in closets and on pantry shelves, but what to drink? Water there was none. That was long since. The tub and sinks and toilet had dried up, leaving rusty streaks on the bathroom tiles from their last sputterings. He imagined what had befallen outside since his judicious retirement: there had been temporary gigantic flurries in various businesses as the civilized thirst of the world moved through different sources of supply. Milk went when the cows dried up for want of grass. Then candy and drugstore fountains sold, for some time, seas of soda over their counters. After that the bars witnessed the greatest binge imaginable in history; until all the beer was consumed, and then all the wines and whiskeys—Christ! the world woke with such a horrible racking thirst . . .

Meanwhile, as he hung grimly on in his apartment high above vacant streets, his own thirst grew daily more vehement. All his canned fruit juices went. Then he drank great quantities of sauerkraut juice. After that, nothing was left to drink. He had only cans of food: meats, vegetables; but his body lost more liquid in perspiration than it could retrieve from food unless he ate enormously; but when he ate so much his supply shrank at an astonishing rate. And his sealed apartment grew hotter and hotter during the blazing dry days of August. Then his bladder, that eternal spring of waters, began to dry up, and he ceased to urinate, save for the thick yellowish syrup which he expressed from himself to drink again, as he might drain dry the udder of a cow. He drank, rather constantly swallowed, his saliva, lest his panting breathing evaporate too much precious liquid from his mouth. Yet the steady loss of water from every pore of his body was inexorable.

By October the food was all gone. Everything in the world was surely lost now; yet the drought had not ended. The air in his rooms had been gradually replaced by dust which floated like waters in a doomed submarine closer and closer to the ceiling where he buoyed himself up, clinging desperately to his life.

With last flurries of strength he floundered to his bathroom, where, in his final moments, he remembered all the pure and glorious waters he had enjoyed in his life, long long ago before the world dried up: the sweet rocking waters of his mother's womb that enclosed him like the dust in which he was smothering now; the waters he had washed with, wallowed in here in the tub, or by the seaside; waters he had voided and dabbled in; waters he had drunk; waters that had run from taps, chrome taps and his own flesh tap, seemingly forever: the inexhaustible waters of birth, life, decay: waters gone forever from the whole wide world: waters . . .

# ABOUT THE AUTHOR

Born in New York City in 1929, Jascha Kessler received his B.A. from New York University and his Ph.D. from the University of Michigan. He has taught at various colleges and universities including the University of Michigan, NYU, Hunter College, Hamilton College, and is presently associate professor of English at UCLA. Mr. Kessler was a Fulbright Research Scholar in Italy and has won the Hopwood Award for poetry. His short stories and poetry have appeared in various magazines including *Accent, The Paris Review, Commentary, Midstream, Saturday Review,* and *Epoch.* Mr. Kessler has also written plays and the libretto for a full-length opera, *The Cave,* and he is presently at work on a novel. He is married and the father of three children.